REVENGE GAME

A Novel of Suspense

Lynn Campbell

Revenge Game: A Novel of Suspense
By Lynn Campbell

Published by Veronica L. Freeland

authorlynncampbell.com

Copyright © 2022 Lynn Campbell

All rights reserved

The characters and events portrayed in this book are fictitious. Any similarity to real persons living or dead, is coincidental and not intended by the author.

No part of this book may be reproduced or stored in a retrieval system or transmitted in any form or by any means, electronic, mechanical, photocopying, recording or otherwise without the express written permission of the publisher.

Cover by Electronic Ink

ISBN 978-1-966176-00-8

Printed in the United States of America

CONTENTS

CONTENT WARNING

Rape

Strong sexual content

Violence

CHAPTER ONE

March 1998

Springtime sun streamed in through the windows of the gymnasium at San Diego's East High School. The sound of bouncing basketballs and laughter filled the room as the team practiced. Three teenage girls sat on the bleachers and talked quietly while a preschool aged boy bounced a spare basketball near the team bench. A man in his early twenties, who appeared to be his father, looked on. A tall, red headed player made a longshot. The girls cheered him just before they were silenced by an explosion ripping through the gym and shattering the lighthearted Saturday morning practice.

*   *   *

Special Agent Rachel Keaney pulled up to the police barricade and flashed her FBI badge. The uniformed officer made room for her to drive into the parking lot. She scanned the scene as she parked. What was once a high school gym was now a heap of twisted metal and singed concrete blocks. The surrounding buildings had also sustained broken windows and other damage from flying debris. Rescue workers and dogs searched through the rubble. From the looks of the building, Rachel doubted there would be any survivors. When she got out of her car, she looked for special agents Charles Longview and Austin Davis. She spotted them immediately in front of an adjacent building. Charles' meticulously creased pants and starched white shirt stood out against such a chaotic scene. Austin's look was a little more thrown together like he was at the beach when he received his call. He often left the Field Office in the evenings wearing khaki shorts and a print shirt. She herself had been reading and sunning on her deck when she received the call from Special Agent in Charge, Mark Sergan. Upon hanging up the phone she threw a suit over her bikini, loosened her chestnut hair from its ponytail, and rushed out.

Rachel walked purposefully toward the two agents.

Charles turned and saw her just as she reached them. "Agent Keaney, thanks for coming so quickly. It'll be nice working this case with you."

Rachel shook his hand, then Austin's. "No problem. Mark called me to help because I guess you're shorthanded."

"Yeah, the flu has knocked out half of the Weapons of Mass Destruction Task Force," Austin interjected.

"Well, I'm considering a transfer to Weapons, so I'll help in any way I can."

She saw a look pass between Austin and Charles. A smirk began to take shape on Charles' face, but he quickly squelched it. She would give this case her best work, and they would come around.

"What have we got so far?" she asked, interrupting their unspoken communication.

"All we've got is a list of victims," replied Charles. "The basketball team was having a special practice this morning. There were three girlfriends who came to watch. One player brought his brother and nephew. Another kid on weekend work detail was also inside at the time. Including the coach. That puts the count at nineteen, and that is if we have everyone accounted for. A lot of these people we know about because of the frantic phone calls, but there could be more."

Austin Davis fished a notepad out of the back pocket of his slacks and wrote as Charles talked.

"Do we have a suspect or motive?" Rachel asked.

Austin looked up from his notes. "We don't have a suspect for who planted the bomb, but judging from the condition of the scene, this is a well-made, powerful explosive. Possibly Hargrove Technologies. We'll know more when we find the bomb."

"Isn't Hargrove Technologies a company in Paseo Del Oro?"

"That's the one," Charles answered. "Later on, we'll tell you all about their side business."

"I found the little one," a rescue worker called.

Rachel rushed over to help him just as a paramedic brought over a gurney.

She and the two men pushed aside the rubble, freeing the crushed and broken body of a four-year-old boy. Blonde curls framed a sweet, smudged face. The paramedic put his fingers on the side of the boy's neck, then placed a stethoscope on his chest. He shook his head.

Rachel's heart sank, and she had to fight back the tears that always threatened to come whenever young children were victims. She walked away from the group and took deep breaths to calm down.

Her attention was drawn to a uniformed officer walking toward her. He spoke, but for a second, a low flying helicopter drowned out his voice, so he had to repeat himself once he reached her.

"Ma'am, the head of the maintenance department says he may know something."

"Great. Let him through as far as the parking lot." Rachel ran to get Austin and Charles and within minutes, the trio met with the middle-aged maintenance man.

"I don't want to believe what I'm about to tell you, but I can't get it out of my mind. "He looked down at his tennis shoe clad feet, exposing the comb-over on the top of his head. "There's a kid at school I've befriended. His name's Tyler Olson. He's a nice kid but a loner. He hangs out with me while I do my work and tells me how other kids bully him. He was asking me what Larry Firth, the ringleader, would be doing for weekend work detail. I said he would be touching up the paint in the gym most likely. He got a big smile on his face. I hadn't seen him look that happy in a long time. I don't want to believe he had anything to do with it."

"It's a start anyway," Charles said, shaking the man's hand. "Let's get the principal to give us the kid's address."

In a half hour, the three agents were on their way to pick up Tyler Olson for questioning. It would be a long time before the scene was ready for a full investigation, but at least they had a suspect.

*   *   *

Rachel entered the interrogation room with Charles and Austin. Tyler and his mother sat in two chairs. A juvenile officer, who looked annoyed to be there on a Saturday, took a third. Feeling claustrophobic in the crowded room, Rachel stood in a corner and let Charles and Austin do the talking.

Tyler, a pale, skinny teenager with a mop of dark hair, stood up at their entrance. His mother, a woman in her mid-forties, sat in numb silence.

"It's okay son, sit down," Charles said, pulling out his own chair and taking a seat.

Austin leaned against the gray wall behind Charles.

"Listen, Tyler, we know you're not a bad kid, but we need to know if you planted that bomb," Charles said, softening the stern expression he usually wore.

The young teen said nothing, only looked at the floor.

"High school is such a tough time, especially if you're not part of the 'in' crowd," Charles continued softly.

"I remember being fourteen," Austin interjected. "I was small for my age, never wore the right clothes, and I wouldn't do what the cool kids were doing. I got picked on a lot, and I remember how much I wanted to get back at those kids."

"Whatever your reasons were, I'm sure you believed it was the only way," Charles said. Tyler broke down sobbing. The rickety table shook with the heaving of his shoulders.

After a while, he calmed down and turned swollen eyes up at the three federal agents.

"I didn't know there was going to be a basketball practice. I just knew Larry Firth was going to be in the gym for his work detail. In fact, I even knew the principal would be in his office because he never stays with the work detail kids." Fresh tears streamed down his face. "I didn't mean to hurt those other kids. I just wanted to stop Larry. I was afraid to go to school because of him. Oh man, what's going to happen to me now?"

"You'll be taken into the custody of the juvenile authorities, and we'll collaborate with them to decide what to do with you," Austin replied. "What we need right now is to know how you got the bomb. If you made it yourself, we need to know where you got the instructions. If you bought it, who did you buy it from? It would help you and us a lot if you'll tell us."

Rachel left the room for a moment to call an investigator on the scene. When she returned, Tyler had not revealed the source of his bomb, and the juvenile officer decided the interrogation was over. While Austin and Charles took Tyler for a bathroom break, Rachel bought two sodas and gave one to Ms. Olson. The older woman's hand shook as she sipped the soda. The two women stood in the hallway in silence until Rachel spoke.

"Ms. Olson, it looks like Tyler won't tell us where he got the bomb. What we need is the hard drive on his computer and any indication of where he got the money to pay for it. The call I made a while ago was to our investigators on the scene. They found enough of the bomb to know it was a professional, high-tech explosive."

"Do you have children, Agent Keaney?"

"No."

"Then you can't possibly understand what you're asking me to do. You have my son's confession, but I know enough about our legal system to know that the prosecution will still need evidence. You will use the evidence, then turn it over to the District Attorney. Then Tyler will be convicted." She wiped her tears on the Kleenex that Rachel handed her.

"The objective is to find out who put a bomb in Tyler's hands," Rachel said gently. "These people are not amateurs and are responsible for other explosions. They need to be stopped. Because of them, sixteen young people won't see graduation and another little boy will never make it to kindergarten. We can get a warrant for the hard drive, bank records, and anything else we need, but with your written consent, we can get it faster and stop them sooner."

Ms. Olson's dark, doe eyes stared into space for a moment. She then threw away her Kleenex. "What do I need to sign?"

Rachel pulled the appropriate document from her briefcase and handed it to Ms. Olson.

Austin, Charles, and Tyler emerged from the restroom just as she finished signing the Consent to Search form.

"Where's the juvenile officer?" Charles asked.

"He's down the hall filling out the paperwork," Rachel replied. "Let's give Tyler and his mom some time alone before the officer is ready to take him."

"Rachel, we'll send you to get a warrant for the Olson's residence," Charles said once Tyler and his mom were out of earshot.

"Not necessary, I have Ms. Olson's Consent to Search." She handed the document to Charles.

Another unspoken communication passed between the two men; this time, Austin raised an eyebrow.

Once Tyler was in the hands of the juvenile corrections officer, the three agents followed Ms. Olson to her home to collect evidence.

*   *   *

Alexander Hargrove switched off the big screen television leaving the room dim; the sun had almost set behind the desert mountains of Paseo Del Oro. The evening news had more details on the explosion at East High School. A few hours ago, the news anchor said two boys and one girl were found alive under the rubble.

The most recent report announced that the three kids had died at the hospital. What in the hell was Robert thinking?

After running a comb through his auburn hair, Alexander left his apartment on the third floor of the Hargrove Technologies building and took the elevator to the basement. Andre Giardello and Jason Morris, the two most trusted men in both his businesses, had picked Robert up at his apartment in town without incident.

When he exited the elevator, Alexander found Robert waiting between his two assistants. Alexander noticed the contrast between Andre and Jason every time he saw them side by side. Andre's broad frame stood out against Jason's wiry build. Andre had dark, graying hair while Jason was blonde and youthful looking.

Alexander looked down at Robert. His stocky frame and well-muscled arms together with his pockmarked face made him look intimidating, except to Alexander, who had reduced many such men to heaps on the floor.

"Hi, Alex. They said you wanted to see me right away," Robert motioned to Andre and Jason. "Do you need a delivery, or do we have a rush order you need help with?"

"There's another matter we need to discuss." Alexander took Robert by the arm, and Andre and Jason fell in behind them. They headed down a long white, hallway filled with storage rooms.

"Why are we going this way?" Robert asked, slowing down until Jason gave him a nudge to keep him moving.

"We need to talk," Alexander said in an icy tone.

By the time the four men reached the storage room that doubled as an interrogation room, Robert had beads of sweat on his forehead.

"Alex, if I did something wrong, we can work it out. Just tell me what I did, and I'll fix it."

Andre and Jason shoved Robert inside the room, quickly entering after him, followed by Alexander. Jason pulled a set of keys out of his pocket, locking the four of them inside the brightly lit room containing only a medical exam table with restraints.

"How long have you been with me, Robert?" Alexander narrowed his brown eyes.

"Four years," he replied.

"And how many deliveries have you done for me?"

"Ten, at least."

"What's my policy on who I'll sell to and who I won't?"

Robert's face went pale. "Oh shit. I heard a little about that high school bombing. That was ours?"

"It certainly was. Since the boy is only fourteen, he didn't think about giving you a false name, so it wasn't too hard to figure out. When you found out the buyer was a kid, why didn't you abort the exchange? You know I don't sell to kids."

"I was about to call it off, but he paid me some extra money to go through with it anyway."

"Oh, extra money. What did you do with your kick-back?... Never mind, I don't care." Alexander backed the man up to the medical table in the room. "The fact is, I hid you from the police and paid you well for your work. Now, you've taken a bribe from a kid and put my whole operation in jeopardy. Kids talk, and the Feds could be at our door any day. I'm afraid you're now a liability instead of an asset. I hate liabilities."

"He won't talk, I threatened him really good. Alex, please, it's not as bad as it all looks."

"Andre, help me strap him to the table."

Robert began to struggle, but the two other men overpowered him, and he screamed in terror as leather straps restrained his arms and legs.

*   *   *

Special Agent in Charge, Mark Sergan, pulled up in front of a row of three apartments walking distance from Ocean Beach. He got out of the car and straightened his jacket around his slight form, then walked to Scott Kraver's apartment and knocked at the door. At eleven o'clock on a Sunday night, a light still shone through the front window. Scott was still up. He wanted to get this meeting over with quickly. Something in the pit of his stomach said this was a bad idea, but Quantico had already approved everything. Despite his reservations, he walked up the path to the door and rang the bell. The man who answered was tall with unkempt blonde hair, an oversized T-shirt, shorts, and bare feet. The scent of cigarette smoke mingled with the ocean air.

"Scott Kraver?"

"Yes."

"My name's Mark Sergan. I know you know who I am because you've emailed me several times in the last six months."

"Yes, come in," Scott said, moving some newspapers off the couch. "Have a seat."

Mark sat down and hand-combed his silver hair, trying to fix what the wind had ruffled. A cat brushed against his leg while another darted down the short hall and disappeared into the only bedroom. He reached down to pet the friendly tabby before stating his business.

"You say you can help us get rid of Hargrove Technologies for good?"

"Yes, I've been researching his company for a year now, since that shopping mall in New Mexico blew up. As I said in my emails, I've managed to hack into most of his files, and I found out he has a self-destruct system. Every time he beefs up security, I find a way around it. However, I can't get through the firewall to get the code to activate the system. Even so, I created a chip that someone can use in conjunction with the code to set off the self-destruct system from another computer. If I had that code, I could get rid of Alexander Hargrove and his operation and do it from here on my computers. Problem is, if I do it, it's domestic terrorism. If you do it, it's government business."

"We got that code about a week ago, but I was reluctant to use your chip until now. The arrogant son of a bitch took out a whole team and a dedicated coach, not to mention other innocents. I got the okay from the top to buy your chip, but some loose ends need to be tied up before we can proceed."

"That's fine. It'll take time to get the chip from where I have it safely hidden," Scott said.

"You'll get half your money tonight, and the other half after the job is done." Mark paused before going on. "You need to understand that this will change your life. We will be watching you from now on to make sure you do not use this event for your own gain someday. If you do take this to the press, it could mean a lot of trouble for you."

"I don't plan to take this to the press. I have my own reasons for offering to help you. I do have one concern, though. Maybe I watch too much television, but these criminal organizations find things out. I want my iden-tity protected so I don't wind up in some landfill. I don't want you or any agents meeting me here anymore. I will deliver the chip in a public location where it looks like I'm just casually meeting someone. So, I don't want to meet some guy in a suit driving a big, blue car."

"You do watch too much TV, but all of that can be arranged. I'll be in touch soon."

Mark got back into his blue Mazda Miata to drive home. The gnawing feeling in his stomach was worse than when he arrived.

*   *   *

Rachel walked into the waiting area outside Mark Sergan's office. When she arrived at work that morning, she found a voicemail from Mark telling her to see him as soon as possible.

"Is Mark available?" Rachel asked Su Lee, his secretary.

"He's with someone, but I know he wants you to wait," Su Lee said as she turned red eyes up to look at Rachel.

Su Lee then coughed, covering her mouth with her hand.

"You don't have the flu too, do you? Most of the Weapons Task Force has it," Rachel said.

"I'm afraid I do too. I just didn't want to stay home. Mark has his hands full with this school bombing."

"I bet he does. I spent the whole weekend working on it. It's so sad."

Su Lee threw a tissue into an overflowing trash can. "Scary too. I'm afraid to send my kids to school. They're only in second and fourth grades, but still, you never know."

At that point, Mark and another agent walked out of his office.

"Rachel, I'll be ready for you in a minute."

When she entered his office a few minutes later, Mark stood, matching Rachel's 5'5" height. He gave her a half smile.

"Is everything okay?" Rachel asked with a concerned look.

He waited for her to sit down in one of the tan leather chairs before he began. "You didn't do anything wrong if that's what you're asking. However, this is a serious matter we're discussing. In fact, any records of this meeting will be destroyed once the assignment I'm offering is complete.

"What do you know about a company named Hargrove Technologies?" he asked.

Rachel set her briefcase on the floor. "Agents Davis and Longview told me a lot about them while we worked together over the weekend. They believe Hargrove Technologies supplied the bomb to the perpetrator of the school bombing. I know the company makes airbags and ejection seats and things of that nature, but it's also a front company for an organization that makes explosives. We've tried to stop their operation unsuccessfully many times."

Mark nodded. "I now know they supplied the bomb. We have been collaborating with the Bureau of Alcohol, Tobacco, and Firearms for years trying to shut them down. In fact, we've had an insider there for the past eight years trying to build a case."

"Eight years?"

"Yes, building a case has been difficult. Their building is in Paseo Del Oro, in the mountains west of El Centro. Their leader, Alexander Hargrove, is an insane genius. His bomb is the size of a VHS tape. One can bring down a ten-story building. He sells this bomb to any fringe group with no regard for where they're from or what they believe as long as they have the money. We have the chance to help destroy his whole organization. A few years ago, Mr. Hargrove set up a self-destruct system in case he needed it to avoid prosecution. Our undercover agent now has the system's code.

"What I need you to do is pick up a computer chip from a liaison. He's a computer hacker who has figured out how to make the code work from our computers."

Rachel's eyes widened. "We're going to blow up a building?"

"I have to tell you, Rachel, I don't like operating this way, but I don't see any other way to stop this guy. We've even had him audited and tried to get him for tax evasion just to get him behind bars. He and his book-keeper know the rules too well. They account for every penny, and his tax record is squeaky clean. Aside from us and the BATF, the military has also been after this guy. The CIA has confirmed that his explosives have caused trouble outside the U.S. They would like to see him stopped as well. Problem is, every agent, except our insider who got close to any evidence, has been found out and killed."

"Can't we arrest him for murder, then?"

"He covers his tracks too well. We know he's doing it, but there isn't enough evidence to convict him," Mark said, taking off his wire-rimmed glasses and rubbing his eyes.

She looked down for a moment.

"Rachel, if there was another way, we would do it. You know that," Mark said.

She nodded.

Mark continued. "I need to know first thing tomorrow morning if you'll do the pick-up."

Rachel left Mark's office with her head spinning. All she could think about was Tyler's tear-streaked face as he said he didn't mean to kill the other kids; he was after one person and killed nineteen. What if this went wrong too?

*   *   *

Rachel leaned against the railing of her deck, bundled in sweats against the cold. At nearly midnight, the Mission Bay waters reflected the full moon. The calm water and quiet of the bay stood out against the turmoil she felt inside. All night, she had been wrestling with the same question. Should she take the assignment or not? She couldn't get it out of her mind that a lot could go wrong. What if some factory workers working overtime or the night cleaning crew didn't get out of the building on time? What if the insider didn't? Could she live with that? Then again, this man and his company had to be stopped. His hand was suspected of being in several bombings and would be in several more if nothing was done. But if innocent people die, is the FBI any better than Alexander Hargrove? Images of dead teenagers and grief-stricken parents and siblings ran through her head like a slideshow.

Rachel sighed. She would go in and try to sleep. Maybe she would come to a decision in the morning.

*   *   *

The next morning, Rachel was back in Mark's waiting area. This time, Laura Galloway, a petite, short haired brunette, was at Su Lee's desk.

"I'm glad Su Lee decided to take the day off. She looked wrung out yesterday," Rachel said, stifling a yawn and sitting on the couch that butted up against a potted palm tree.

"No offense. but you look exhausted," Laura said.

"Didn't sleep well, but that comes with the territory."

The intercom buzzed, and Mark told Laura he was ready to see Rachel. She shut the door behind her, sat down, and took a minute to put her words together. "I've decided to take the pickup assignment. I don't agree with the methods, but all night, I kept dreaming of the four-year old. His small, lifeless body in that rubble was heartbreaking. Something has to be done. How many people will go down with the building?"

"At most two. Alexander Hargrove and a fugitive named Jason Morris. Everyone else involved in the business will be home, or at least away from the building at that time."

"I still don't like it, but I'm in."

Mark explained the details of the delivery that would take place the following night.

*　　*　　*

Laura Galloway was straightening Su Lee's desk when Mark walked out of his office and locked the door.

"If you're finished up, I'll walk out with you," he said.

"That's okay. I think I'll get things ready in case Su Lee comes back tomorrow."

"All right. Please leave a note telling her that there is an important file on my desk. She'll need to put it in the appropriate place when she comes in."

"Will do."

When Mark left, Laura slipped a key out of the zipper pocket in her purse and opened his office. Once inside, she nervously leafed through the papers in the file on his desk. She was part way through an important document when she heard someone coming toward the outer office.

"Forgot to look up an address before I left," Mark told Laura, now seated at Su Lee's desk.

"You want me to look it up for you?"

"No, I've got it. It will take me some time to find it," he answered, then disappeared into his office.

*   *   *

That evening, when Laura arrived home, she set her keys and purse on the hall table, then picked up the phone and dialed.

"Hargrove Technologies," a familiar male voice answered.

"Alexander, please."

"May I ask who's calling?"

"I have some business with him. Put him on."

When Alexander picked up the extension and she identified herself, she heard him excuse someone in his office.

"Laura, what is it?"

"I can't be sure because I got interrupted. There's going to be a delivery of some sort regarding Hargrove Technologies tomorrow night. I don't know if I have enough to do you any good."

"Read what you have, and I'll find out the rest on my own."

"You're not going after the agent, are you?"

His voice took on a calm but angry tone. "I pay you to give me information, not to advise me on how to manage my end of things. What do you have?"

CHAPTER TWO

Rachel parked her yellow Mustang GT at Pacific Beach and took a minute to put up the car's rag top. The evening was turning cool. Once this was done, she sat down on a low cement wall and scanned the beach. The boardwalk to the north stretched out into the ocean. From the boardwalk, shops, restaurants, and vacation rentals ran down the entire length of the beach.

No sign of Scott, the blonde man in the blue jogging suit she was to meet.

Aside from some joggers and people watching the sun set, the beach was deserted. The college kids on spring break that crowded the beach during the day were in their hotel rooms preparing for dinner and the nightclubs.

She hoped Scott would appear soon. She would say the correct words and pick up the chip. Mark made her promise to call him at home as soon as she had possession of it. Everything about this assignment was strange. She had no surveillance, and she was told to wear casual clothing and drive her car instead of a Bureau car. She felt for the reassurance of her 10mm Glock, and her badge carefully hidden under her sweater. The sooner this was over, the better.

While she waited, she mentally went over the dossier on Hargrove Technologies and its founder.

Alexander Hargrove was born in July 35 years ago. His flower child mother overdosed on heroin when he was two. His remarkable intelligence was discovered after his adoption by Frank and Justine Hargrove at the age of six. Despite all the efforts of his adoptive parents and the best schools, there was no reaching the angry child who would not bond with anyone. In his late teens, he disappeared from his parent's home and led a life where he was a suspect in various crimes but without enough evidence for a conviction.

The pounding of the surf mixing with the cool breeze made Rachel feel a little more relaxed just before she felt a presence behind her, and her world went black.

*   *   *

Rachel came to and realized she was in the trunk of a moving vehicle. The pain in her throat indicated a chokehold had been used to subdue her. When she began to stir, she could tell her wrists and ankles were duct taped. Was this meeting a set up? Maybe not. These men could be street thugs out looking for a woman to rape and abuse. If that was the case, then she would try to use her position as an FBI agent to convince them to release her. If her abduction was connected to her assignment, then she knew the night ahead would be rough.

The ride seemed to go on and on. They had to be well out of San Diego by now. Most rapists just drove to a nearby, secluded location. The further they drove, the more she believed she was set up. Chances were, that these men knew who they had picked up on Pacific Beach.

When Rachel felt the car stop and heard two doors open and close, she prepared herself for the confrontation that would follow. After a minute, she heard a key unlocking the trunk and fluorescent light streamed in blinding her for a moment.

"Well, hello there. You must be someone important," said a man who looked to be in his mid-forties.

Another man in his early thirties held up her badge and gun. "Obviously, she is. Come on. We have our orders." The older man proceeded to cut the duct tape from her ankles and helped her out of the trunk more gently than she expected.

She realized she was in an underground parking garage. She could see an Exit sign with an arrow, but the exit itself was not visible.

In a moment, the men each held an arm and led her through a metal door and down a hallway lined with closed storage rooms. Some were labeled, some were not. Some had small windows, and others had solid doors. When they reached the unlabeled door they wanted, the older man held her to the wall while the younger man pat-searched her. Rachel instinctively fought as they opened the door and pushed her inside. Once she realized she was alone, she raised her hands above her head and quickly brought them down with her elbows brushing her sides, instantly tearing the duct tape.

*   *   *

A half-hour later, Alexander Hargrove stood looking through the small window in the door of his interrogation room while he waited for Andre and Jason to arrive.

Slowly, he shook his head. He knew she could not see him because he kept the hallway dark.

So, this is the Rachel Keaney I've learned so much about, he thought.

Alexander took a minute to study Rachel. She was thirty-three but looked younger. Her blue eyes and delicate, heart-shaped face showed a strong mix of fear and determination. Her thick hair and graceful arms and legs made her look like she should be advertising expensive cars instead of fighting the criminal underworld.

A small smile played on Alexander's face. They had many tools at their disposal to get information from prisoners, but he didn't even consider the more traditional methods. He knew her reputation and that she would be a challenge. He liked a challenge.

*   *   *

Rachel stood in the nearly empty room, trying to avoid looking at the small window where she figured they were watching her. The only piece of furniture the room contained was a medical table with restraints. She had heard of rooms like this but had never seen one. She took a deep breath and fought to control the anger and fear that ran through her like tidal waves. Rachel knew the questioning techniques that these men would use would be brutal. She had received training in handling an interrogation, when the military offered it as optional training for the FBI agents, but this was a little too real. All the murder-victims she had seen, either in the flesh or photographed, flashed across her mind. What would her body look like when it was found? Would it be found with a bullet through the brain, or beaten beyond recognition? Would it be found whole, or would there be pieces missing? Would it be found at all? The question that weighed on her mind most was, would it hurt to die? How much pain would she have to suffer before it was over? A million related questions raced through her thoughts.

She knew she would lose it if she continued thinking that way. The most important thing was to stay in control. Information about her assignment was too valuable to reveal no matter what happened to her. If she died tonight, someone else would pick up the computer chip and destroy this place.

Her heart quickened once again as she heard muffled voices right outside the room, then a key in the door. Seconds later, three men dressed all in black were in the room.

Rachel recognized Alexander immediately. He had the athletic build of a runner or a swimmer. Medium length auburn hair fell in natural waves around a hard angular face with a stern jaw. She usually associated brown eyes with warmth, but his were cold and piercing. His presence and attitude were terrifying. He carried himself like a man who knew he had absolute power over his domain.

The man beside him was tall, larger boned with dark, slightly graying hair pulled into a ponytail. Cold fear settled into a knot in her stomach as Rachel studied his 6-foot, broad shouldered frame and unsmiling face.

The third man was thin and wiry looking with pale blue eyes and combed back blonde hair that reached his shoulders. The look in his eyes told her that he was a little too pleased to be part of the interrogation.

Looking at the three men in front of her, she knew her last hours on earth were going to be hell.

Alexander finally spoke. "Rachel Michelle Keaney, graduated top of your class in the Police Academy at the age of twenty-one, promoted to detective at 25 because of your natural talent, went to work for the FBI under Special Agent in Charge Mark Sergan at the age of twenty-eight. Graduated top of your class at the FBI Academy as well. Have I left anything out?"

Rachel just stared at him.

"I understand you were on an assignment that concerns me. Tell me what I need to know about the assignment, then you're free to go. With some stipulations, of course."

Rachel knew he wouldn't let her go free. He had allegedly killed too many people. She kept silent. The minutes felt like hours as they loomed threateningly over her, but she bit down on her tongue, determined not to speak.

"Well, I have to say it's an honor to have someone of your caliber here. Most of the people I interrogate are sniveling lowlifes. I don't know, guys. Getting her to talk could actually be fun," Alexander said, turning to the two other men. Then to no one in particular, he asked, "How should we go about this? We could beat the hell out of her until she talks." He waved his hand as if dismissing the thought. "I don't know, three of us beating up a woman seems so low class."

He circled her. The heels of his leather boots tapped out a staccato rhythm like a clock ticking away the last moments of her life.

"We could give her a shot to sedate her. Then maybe she will be more willing to tell us what she knows," Alexander said, again addressing the air. With another wave of his hand, he said, "No, that's too easy. There's no fun in that."

When he seemed tired of this verbal game, he approached her. As he came nearer, she stood still, refusing to run from him. She wouldn't give him the satisfaction of watching her try to get away when there was no chance of succeeding.

"You boys have to admit, she is beautiful."

Her heart pounded like it would break through her ribs as he stood right in front of her. In what seemed like one motion, he pulled off her sweater and tore off her bra. Sharp, shooting pain radiated through her breasts while he groped her bare upper body.

She summoned her strength and tried to push Alexander away, but the blonde man grabbed her arms and held them in an iron grip behind her.

Alexander looked, up and their eyes met. "Tell me what I need to know, and this can stop now. Keep silent, and we'll all fuck with you."

She remained silent.

Alexander looked over at the blonde man." Jason, help me strap her down."

They lifted her onto the table. Leather straps bit into her wrists as she lost the struggle with the two men. Alexander pulled off her pants and looked over her body, naked except for satin panties, while he undressed. In minutes, he removed her only barrier and forced his way into her. Cologne and deodorant mixed with a day's sweat wafted up into her nostrils. She closed her eyes to stop the room from spinning. The sounds of his pleasure echoed inside her head until he spoke.

"Open your eyes," he demanded.

More pain shot through her breasts. Alexander looked into her eyes until his violation of her was complete and he fell limp on top of her. Rachel fought hard against the despair that seemed to close in on all sides. She would not let them see her cry.

After a moment, he climbed off the table and motioned for his assistant who wore the ponytail.

"You're next."

"Put her on her knees." He said while unfastening his belt and unzipping his pants.

Alexander released Rachel from the table and forced her downward until her knees and shins slammed against the concrete floor.

Her heart seemed to sink into her stomach. She knew that further resistance would only make things worse, so she submitted to what he obviously wanted. When he was done, she thought she was going to be sick. Everything in her wanted to spit the fluid all over the man in front of her. She didn't.

The third man and Alexander jerked Rachel to her feet and pushed her toward the table. The cold metal dug into the soft flesh of her abdomen when they leaned her over the table and again restrained her wrists.

Pain shot through her. The room seemed to darken into a tunnel. Rachel forced herself to stay cognizant. She couldn't shut down now. If there was any hope of surviving, she would have to be clear headed. If she had to die tonight, it would be with the bravery expected of someone in her position.

She gritted her teeth against the pain, but there was no way to block out the obscenities and degrading remarks he whispered into her ear.

When all three men finished with her and unbound her wrists, she shakily stood, holding onto the table for support. From deep within herself, she found the courage to face her fully clothed assailants while covered only in sweat and semen.

Alexander threw something dark and blue at her; instinctively, she caught it and realized it was a factory worker's coverall. She hastily put it on and slipped her feet back into her tennis shoes.

"Andre, take this bitch down the hall so she can think about telling me what I need to know."

Without a word, the dark-haired man took her by the arm and led her down a hallway to another storage room. Once in the dark, dusty room, she collapsed on the bare mattress on the floor.

Her emotions were numb, but her body from the waist down ached.

CHAPTER THREE

When the sun rose the next morning, Mark Sergan had already been in his office for two hours. Papers were scattered across his normally organized desk: e-mail messages, his own notes, and a map of Paseo Del Oro and its surrounding area.

He hadn't slept a wink all night. He waited up until midnight for Rachel to call. When she didn't, he drove to her apartment in Mission Bay, then to Pacific Beach. By 2:00 a.m., he had contacted Scott, the liaison, and found out that he couldn't find her when he jogged up and down the beach. Scott had scoured the entire area and waited until well after dark in case she got the meeting time or place mixed up.

Mark knew where she was and said a silent prayer that he wouldn't find her in the same condition in which they found his other two agents. He was 55 years old and a little over a year from retirement. He couldn't lose another agent during his last year, especially not Rachel. How did this happen? There was no reason to think anything would go wrong.

Mark took more notes and went over the facts in his head. Her car was missing, which meant they had taken it or forced her to drive it to the building. The former was more accurate. If Rachel were driving, she would have thought of something to get out of the situation.

That morning, Mark had received a coded message on his home email from Leo Acratelli, the insider. When he decoded the message, he knew Rachel was alive and that she hadn't told anyone what she knew.

Why did he send her on that assignment alone? Because he had to involve as few people as possible in an assignment of this nature. Now that everything was a mess, more people had to get involved. He needed help to find the best way to get Rachel out of there and destroy Hargrove Technologies. Being smaller than average, he learned early on to use his mind and his words to accomplish goals. He would find a way. However, his years as head of the San Diego Field Office told him that making a decision like this on no sleep with raw emotions could prove fatal.

*   *   *

Leo walked toward Rachel's cell carrying a brown paper bag. Shalayah, an African American former drug dealer, sat outside the cell's door reading a romance novel. He knew Alexander assigned her the duty of guarding Rachel because of her gender and her loyalty to him. He would have to play his cards right. Alexander ordered her not to let anyone near Rachel unless he called ahead. She stood up when he approached, her hand on her cell phone ready to call Alexander if needed.

"Take this to the FBI agent in the cell," he said, giving her a bag with food and a bottle of water.

"Alex didn't order this." Shalayah cocked her head. "In fact, he said she wasn't supposed to have any food, only a little water. He said it would make it harder for her to hang on and keep quiet."

"Just do what I tell you." He said in an icy tone.

"No way! I'm not going against his orders. You want me to tell him that you are?" Leo looked her straight in the eye. "Take this food to her, then destroy any evidence of it, and keep quiet or he'll find out about the last time you disobeyed orders."

Her dark eyes widened.

"We understand each other, then?" he said, raising an eyebrow.

She snatched the bag from him and proceeded to unlock the cell door.

* * *

When Rachel heard the muffled conversation outside the door, she began to mentally prepare for another meeting with Alexander. She took deep breaths and tried to calm her racing heart. Being locked in a small, dusty room with nothing but a mattress and a bucket was horrible, but the thought of facing Alexander and his men was worse.

She was surprised to hear the man's footsteps retreat down the hall. At least for now, she wouldn't have to deal with Alexander. Maybe the FBI would come through and rescue her before he sent for her.

Shalayah, who had come in several hours ago and introduced herself, entered the room alone and offered her a paper bag containing food and water. Rachel had no appetite but was very thirsty and knew she had to eat to keep her strength up.

Shalayah plopped her stocky form down on the dirty floor. "If I were you, I wouldn't mention the food to anyone."

"I won't. Thank you," Rachel said.

"I don't know what you got on us, but it must be good for you to take what you took and still keep quiet."

"You know about that, huh?"

"Jason likes to brag, and I was the only one he could brag to. As if I wanted to hear all of that. Believe it or not, you're lucky because you didn't piss off Alex. It could have been a lot worse if you had. Only a few people know you're even here, and some of them would love to have a look at you, but he ordered them to stay away, and no one would dare cross Alex around here."

"I see. So he says jump, and everyone says how high?" Rachel murmured.

"He takes good care of us, and it can be bad if we step out of line."

Rachel looked at the floor for a moment. "I feel sorry for the women around here."

"I'm the only woman close enough, and I'm willing to give him what he wants. He knows how to light the coals for me," she said with a gleam in her eye.

"I'm sorry. That wasn't my experience," Rachel practically spat the words.

Shalayah continued, "I guess when all is said and done, I don't know how to pick the right men. If prince charming came in here right now, I'd probably tell him to go back to Never Never Land where he came from. I have no interest in good men. How 'bout you, girl? You got someone at home worrying about you right now?"

Rachel shook her head. "Only the people I work with."

*　　*　　*

Later that evening, Alexander sat on his large, third-floor balcony with Andre and Jason. The people who worked the legitimate business had all left an hour ago, and the night crew who worked the secondary business had not come in yet. On most nights between 6:00 and 7:00 p.m., he liked to unwind with the two men, who were not only business associates but also friends. Tonight, unwinding wouldn't be easy. He couldn't keep his mind off Rachel locked in the basement. What did her assignment mean to him? Jason's voice brought him back to the moment.

"Will you be dealing with our prisoner tonight?" he asked as he lit a cigarette.

"Yes," Alexander replied. "Tonight, I'll see if she's ready to talk after having 24 hours to think it over."

"I'd give her forty-eight. I'm sure she'll really be ready to talk after being locked in a dark room all that time with no food," Andre said, taking the last swig of his soda.

"I wish we had that luxury. I have to try and break her tonight."

"Well, I have to say, Alex, you never cease to surprise me," Andre said.

"Oh, how's that?"

"Well, I hadn't expected you to handle the interrogation quite the way you did. I mean you have so many ways of turning grown men into blithering idiots at your feet. Now we question this FBI piece of ass, and you decide to rape her?"

"The reason is simple." Alexander leaned back in his chair. "Women deal with pain much better than men do. Think about it. They have babies; not just one, but most go through that hell a couple of times. They stay in relationships where men beat the crap out of them. Women will take a lot of pain but will do anything not to be raped."

"That's true," Jason said with a sardonic smile. "All the women I messed with begged and pleaded with me not to fuck 'em."

"Well, if that's true, what do you make of the agent in the basement? We put her through hell, and she's still not talking." Andre brushed sandwich crumbs off the glass-topped steel table.

Alexander tossed the crust of his own sandwich into the wastebasket before responding. "If she talks, someone else goes down. I've even wondered if she's protecting one of our guys. However, it's probably some blue suit high up in the FBI. Either way, I intend to find out tonight. I'll tell you another thing: it's just too bad she's a Fed. I'd recruit her to work for me in a second if she wasn't."

"I don't see why that should stop you. Even law enforcement can be bought." Jason crushed out his cigarette. "You've got the local authorities ignoring us. I don't see why she's any different."

Alexander shook his head. "She's too principled. I can see that very clearly. Besides, this town was dying out before I came along to jump-start the economy. The kick back is only one reason they look the other way.

"Jason, why don't you go get the night shift started, and we'll be down in a minute."

"Right away," he said, walking through the back door and out of Alexander's apartment.

When Jason was gone, Alexander leaned over to Andre. "I don't know why the FBI hasn't already come looking for her because they have to at least suspect that she's here. If they or the police show up with a search warrant, I'm going to page you with this code."

Alexander wrote a series of numbers on a yellow sticky note and handed it to Andre along with a key. "If you get this code, take her to my private storeroom and stay there with her until I page you again. Under no circumstances is she to be left alone there."

The private storeroom was a combination storage room and office located in an obscure corner of the basement. Not many people even knew it existed. It was in this room that the delicate paperwork and bomb making supplies were kept. Alexander had never given anyone the key to that room.

*   *   *

Rachel stared at the ceiling in the darkness and wondered if anyone would be coming for her. Someone had to know she was here. Where the hell has the insider been all this time? Was he gone? Would Mark send someone else to pick up the chip and have the assignment carried out in her absence? If that were the case, she would die with her captors. A wave of sadness coursed through her at the thought. Then she calmed herself. Agents die for their country every year. When she joined the FBI, she knew she ran the risk of being one of them. It was crazy to think that way, though. If Mark knew she was there he wouldn't allow the building to blow.

She had to turn her thoughts away from her current situation and how miserable she felt. The dust threw her sinuses into turmoil, and the desert air was drying out her skin. She thought about the many times she had driven through Paseo Del Oro on her way to visit her cousin in Phoenix. She remembered seeing the place blossom. Hargrove Technologies breathed life into the community by providing jobs. Soon, developers built planned communities attracting other businesses and retail establishments.

A new sound interrupted her thoughts, two sets of footsteps and conversation between Shalayah and two men. In the next moment, Alexander's two assistants entered her cell.

She didn't know what would happen next, but whatever these bastards would do to her, keeping quiet was the only way to sentence them to the same fate that they condemned so many others.

"He wants to see you now to discuss your information," Jason said.

Andre locked her wrists behind her with leather handcuffs. She winced and drew in her breath when the cuffs tightened around her bruised wrists. When each man put a hand on either arm, she cringed under their touch. Her heart pounded at the thought of another "interrogation." They walked her past the original interrogation room and further down the white hallway lined with more closed storerooms to an elevator.

"I hope Alex will let us join in again," Jason said to Andre, then addressing Rachel, he added "Fucking you last night was incredible. You have a nice, tight ass." He grabbed her buttocks with his free hand. "If he won't let us join in, maybe he'll let us watch. Hell, Andre, watching her go down on you, I almost didn't make it to my turn."

"This isn't necessary," Andre snapped.

"What's the matter? You're not going soft, are you? You sure as hell weren't soft last night."

"Shut your mouth or I'll shut it for you," Andre said.

There must have been something to the threat because Jason didn't speak again.

Once in the elevator, Andre used a key to gain access to the third floor. Where they led her was more terrifying than an interrogation room. They took her right into Alexander's bedroom.

He got up from his bed dressed only in an emerald-green silk robe. Her eyes darted around the room instantly taking in the black lacquer dresser and nightstands, ivory leather chair, and abstract prints on the sea foam green walls.

"Leave us," he said.

When they were gone, he crossed the Berber carpeting and stood close to her. He moved some loose strands of hair away from her face and flicked his tongue teasingly up the side of her neck. The scent of his body once again assaulted her nostrils, bringing the previous night vividly into her memory.

She felt a shudder run through her. In spite of herself, tears spilled onto her cheeks. She knew she was moving closer and closer to the breaking point. The questions that echoed through her mind all day repeated themselves again. Would anyone be coming for her? Could she take much more? Where in the hell has the insider been all this time?!

Alexander spoke in a low voice. "Some of my men say I should give you one more chance to talk, then kill you if you don't. However, I know enough about you to know you would die with the knowledge and consider it an honor. I have a proposition for you instead. Tell me what you know, and I will release you back to the FBI. Refuse, and you become my unpaid whore."

He caressed her breast through her coverall. "Think about it. You would fulfill all my desires. Your body would be available to me whenever I wanted it, for whatever I wanted to do with it. I have quite an appetite, and it's not always easy to get my needs met out here. If you don't tell me anything, my needs will always be met. I have a plan in the works to make it look like you're dead so the FBI will stop looking for you."

More tears flowed down her cheeks. The mild sinus headache that had been with her all day now made her feel like her head would explode.

Alexander continued, "Besides, you have to know that any transactions have already been rescheduled." He caught a few tears on one of his long fingers. "I don't understand why you don't just tell me and end this. Who are you protecting, Rachel? Just give me a name."

She looked straight ahead. Her eyes fell on an alabaster silhouette sitting on the dresser. It was the image of a big cat ready to attack its prey.

He stood so close, she could feel his excitement building.

He unzipped the front of her coverall down to her stomach.

"I need more time to think it through," she said, trying to keep her composure.

"Tell me now or perform your first duty," he said sharply.

At this, Rachel felt her knees go weak, and she lost her balance. Alexander caught her and sat her down. She sank into the cushioned leather ottoman that matched the ivory chair.

After a minute of silence, he took off his robe and stood, naked and erect, in front of her. A second later, he seized the hair on the back of her head. It became clear to Rachel, as he took what he wanted, that he was holding back to make his pleasure and her humiliation last longer. By the time it was all over, her jaws ached.

When Alexander brought Rachel out of the bedroom, he once again ordered Andre to take her back to her cell because he had business to discuss with Jason.

"You've hidden her car far from here?" Alexander said when they were alone.

"Yes. Do you have a plan for it after you kill her?"

"We're not going to kill her. Soon, we'll use the car to make it look like she disappeared on her own and met with an accident. Then she's going to be serving me for a while. I have a gut feeling that keeping her alive is insurance right now. I guarantee that someone in the FBI knows she may be here, and they're not moving with their plan until they can confirm she's safe."

"I've already changed the times and places for our next three deliveries." Jason said.

"Good. It always pays to be cautious, but her information is not about our business transactions. There's some other reason she's not talking."

Jason listened carefully as Alexander explained the logistics of the bogus accident.

*   *   *

Leo stared at the door of Alexander's private office/ storeroom while he saved valuable information onto a disc. Even at that time of night, he was afraid of being found there. The high-speed computer was too slow for his comfort tonight.

It was an honor to be chosen for the assignment of infiltrating Hargrove Technologies. He had so carefully played the game of being Andre Giardello, Alexander's assistant, while providing valuable information to Special Agent Mark Sergan. He remembered the process that led him to his current, elevated position.

Leo had done a lot of undercover work in illegal guns. Most people on the street believed he could get guns for anyone who could not obtain them legally. Using this belief as a base, the FBI concocted an elaborate story about a deal gone bad complete with newspaper headlines, police bulletins, and witnesses. With his new status as a wanted man, he headed for Paseo Del Oro where he hoped to connect with Alexander's people. It wasn't long before a meeting was set up. The meeting was etched in Leo's mind.

A dust storm had kicked up outside as they sat down in a crowded sports bar on the outskirts of town. Leo, a.k.a. Andre, offered to buy Alexander a drink, but he turned it down explaining that he didn't like anything that dulled the mind.

"I'm in a lot of trouble. One of my gun deals went down all wrong and I shot a cop. I hear you have a place where people have gone to work for you and to hide," Leo/Andre said.

"If I do, why should I take you there?" Alexander asked. "I would think in your line of work, you'd have plenty of friends on the inside to help you. Besides, don't you have any Mafia connections in your family?" he said with a smirk.

"If I did, I wouldn't be coming to you for help, would I? You know as well as I do that cop killers don't fare well in prison. If I'm caught and convicted, those guards will find ways to deal with me. Besides, I have ways of working with people, and I'm an expert with computers." Leo looked around pretending to scan the crowd for police. "I can do you a lot of good."

Cheers erupted as a team on the television scored.

Alexander waited for the noise to subside, then lowered his voice. "If I decide to help you, there are a few things you need to understand. One, I will not trust you until you prove yourself. Two, I demand complete loyalty. Three, your life as you know it now is over; you'll be paid and treated like an employee in any company. But when it comes down to it, you belong to me."

"Agreed." Leo wiped the sweat from his palm before shaking on the deal.

Leo spent the next few months doing everything from filing papers to sweeping floors. Anything Leo was told to do, he did without question or complaint. His first lucky break came three months into his work. He caught a young man trying to contact the police and brought him immediately to Alexander. Because of this event, Alexander allowed Leo to use his superior computer and technical skills to make Hargrove Technologies as secure as any military operation. All phone calls and computer communication, as well as the comings and goings of the employees could be monitored at will. Leo purposefully left holes in the system known only to him so he could communicate with Special Agent Sergan.

His second break came a year later. It was one of those rare times when Alex met with a client in person. He and Alexander were in a deserted parking lot meeting with the leader of a radical white supremacist group. As they were about to exchange a bomb for cash, Leo noticed a man crawling out from under a car with an AR-15 pointed right at them. He shoved Alex to the ground, threw himself on top of him, then shot and killed the would-be assassin and the white supremacist leader. It was after this incident that he moved into an apartment on the top floor of the Hargrove Technologies building. Within two years, Leo had Alexander's trust and respect. It was after this two-year period that he helped set up the self-destruct system without knowing the code.

Very recently, Alexander revealed the code to him. It was going to be so simple. First Rachel would pick up the computer chip from the liaison, then Leo would be called away on emergency, and the building would be destroyed. Now, at the age of forty, he was ready to finish the assignment, but things had gone terribly wrong. He had done things he wasn't proud of in his role as an undercover agent, but he never thought he would sink this low. Everything in him wanted to help Rachel before anything happened, but one wrong move could have gotten them both killed.

He had to play the role at any cost. He deeply respected Rachel for not giving up what she knew. Coming face to face with Alexander caused the strongest men to break down and beg for their lives only to die painful deaths. If she had told Alexander about the chip and the code, she would have blown his cover and destroyed everything he had worked to accomplish.

Finally, he received his orders via coded e-mail: get Rachel and himself out of there and pick up the chip. He left the office and walked quickly to the security office where he fumbled with an old security tape and pushed the play button, so all appeared normal inside and outside the building.

He then put his graying hair into a ponytail and headed for Rachel's cell.

*   *   *

Shalayah sat outside Rachel's door with her head down on her chest. She had probably been asleep like that for a few hours.

He gently tapped her shoulder. "Alex says you can go home now. He wants Rachel for the rest of the night."

She seemed to snap out of her sleepy fog. "Why didn't he call me to say you were coming?"

"He's too preoccupied, so he just told me to get her and send you home. You can call him to check, but I wouldn't. He's agitated over the fact that he hasn't broken her down yet."

"In that case, I'll take your word for it." She then headed for the door leading to the parking garage.

Leo unlocked the door to the cell and quietly walked in. Seeing Rachel's crumpled form on the mattress broke his heart. His only comfort was knowing that in a few hours, the son of a bitch responsible for this and many other tragedies would be dead.

*   *   *

In a fitful sleep, Rachel did not hear the man enter her cell. When his hand covered her mouth, her eyes flew open, and she found herself looking into the face of Andre, Alexander's dark-haired assistant.

"It's not safe to talk, but we are getting out of here and picking up the chip."

In a minute, she understood what was happening and her mind began to whirl. This was the insider she had been protecting. Why didn't he rescue her until now? How could he have used her in such a way when he was on her side? She had heard enough stories of undercover work to know the answers to these questions, but her head was spinning so fast, she couldn't bring these thoughts to the forefront of her mind.

They walked out of the cell together and took the elevator to the main floor.

"Here," he whispered, pressing a pistol into her hand.

She recognized the familiar feel of her 10 mm Glock, and its weight told her it was loaded.

Using only the backup lighting, they made their way past several offices with interior windows. The dark windows and dim hallway would have looked eerie to anyone. To Rachel, they were comforting because they showed that no one burning the midnight oil would happen upon them and question their presence. Finally, they reached the open, glass-fronted reception lobby. After deactivating the alarm system, Andre unlocked the main door.

Once outside he took a flashlight from his pocket and clicked it on and off three times.

A dark blue car came out of hiding and met them at the edge of the parking lot. Rachel recognized the driver as Charles Longview, the Weapons Task Force agent she met at the high school bombing. Now that she was safe, she melted into the back seat.

Andre climbed into the passenger seat. "Leo Acratelli, undercover agent, Weapons of Mass Destruction Task Force. Let's get to our liaison and destroy this place," he said.

The car drove off down the hilly desert road.

"By the way, Rachel, these are yours too." Leo handed her the FBI credentials that the two men took when they abducted her.

She looked over her coverall and realized it had four pockets. She chose a pocket for her credentials and another where she would later conceal her gun. For now, she placed her firearm on the seat beside her and relaxed against the back rest.

*   *   *

When they had driven a short distance, Leo glanced into the back seat and saw that Rachel was sound asleep. Charles pulled his attention back to the business at hand.

"How's this code and chip going to destroy the place?" he asked.

"First, it's going to break down the security system, then some key bombs will be triggered by the computer.

Alex placed those bombs so that when they go off, every-thing crumbles, destroying everything related to Hargrove Technologies. I've got a valuable disk on me, so if he were to live through it, we could finally get a conviction. Of course, Alex believed that he would activate the code and get out in time so there is no way to stop the pro-cess. Couldn't happen to anyone more deserving if you ask me."

*   *   *

Once the agents reached downtown San Diego, Charles pulled off onto a patch of dirt where Logan and Crosby streets meet. From their location, the sil-ver backs of the suicide hot line signs could be seen at the foot of the Coronado Bay Bridge. A second car was already parked in the alley adjacent to the dirt patch. The three agents got out and shook hands with Scott, the man Rachel was supposed to meet the night she was abducted. The cool, moist air felt like a "welcome back" greeting to her.

"Are you sure this is going to work?" Leo asked.

"Positive. I want him stopped as much as you do. I lost my best friend when one of his explosives was discharged. I've spent the last year tracing where the bomb came from, then figuring out how to destroy his operation," Scott said.

"We have a lot riding on this too," Rachel said when she took the envelope containing the chip.

"What happens now?" Charles asked when Scott drove off.

"We get Rachel some food because she hasn't had a lot to eat recently, then we get her to a hospital to be checked out. From there, you take the chip to the Field Office," Leo replied.

*   *   *

When Charles went into a Denny's to get some sandwiches, Rachel saw Leo turn in his seat. She figured this would happen once they were alone and calmed herself to deal with whatever he had to say.

"Rachel, if it means anything at all, I didn't want to do what I did in there. Any of it."

She nodded.

"And if you decided to take this to the Office of Professional Responsibility, I'm not planning to deny what I did or fight any disciplinary measures they want to take."

"I don't know what I want to do about any of this yet. I do know that I don't want to go to a hospital, I just want to go home and have as few people as possible know about this."

"Rachel, you could be injured, and you're definitely at risk for infection. It's important to make sure you're okay."

She sighed and rested her head against the back seat. "I know. I'll go."

When they arrived at Scripps Mercy Hospital, Charles drove off in the Bureau car toward the Field Office.

"Can I call someone for you?" Leo asked.

"No, you've done enough. I'll take care of myself from here."

"Okay." He turned and walked out of the ER.

Once inside an exam room, the sympathetic nurse offered to call the police to take her statement. She refused, showing her gold shield and ID, and insisting that the events happened during an assignment and the FBI would interview her later.

*   *   *

Three and a half hours after Rachel and Leo's escape, Alexander awoke to Jason bursting into the room.

"I'm not sure what's happening, but our computers have crashed, and our security is breaking down."

"Something has gone wrong; the place will blow up. Where's Andre?" Alexander yanked a shirt off a hanger.

"I can't find him anywhere," Jason said, still out of breath from running.

"Whatever you do, make sure Rachel and Shalayah get out alive. Bring them to the Hummer at the East end of the building. Don't come without Rachel."

Jason hurried off. Alexander finished dressing and ran to a hidden wall safe where he kept emergency cash, a new set of identification, and important papers. Once he had taken what he needed, he headed for the stairs leading to the parking garage and ran to the Hummer, keys in hand. Rage began to overtake him. Andre was the only other person who knew the code to the self-destruct system, and he was missing. Alexander would find him, but it would have to be later.

He pulled the Hummer forward out of the path of destruction and waited impatiently for sight of Jason, Shalayah and Rachel. Time was short now. He expected the building would blow at any moment. Where in hell were they? He pressed the accelerator to the floor and drove off into the desert night.

Suddenly, a huge explosion ripped through the building, destroying everything Alexander built.

*   *   *

A little before sunrise, a cab pulled up on Mission Boulevard. Rachel got out and walked between two apartment buildings into the common alley and parking area leading to her apartment against the bay.

The light blue building with gray trim was a perfect location for Rachel. It sat on a quiet part of the bay, walking distance to the activity of Mission Beach and Mission Bay Park.

She climbed the stairs onto the large, slatted deck and walked past the chaise lounge and patio table to her front door.

When she had spare time, she liked to eat or read on this deck. Sometimes, when she needed time to think, she would just look out at the bay or watch the sun rise. This morning, she just wanted to get inside.

When the door closed behind her, she looked around at the familiar living room with its navy and hunter green furniture, as if to reassure herself that the apartment was the same as she had left it nearly two days ago. She walked down the hallway lined with family pictures to her bedroom.

It was here that her feminine side really shined through. She had adorned her bedroom with framed Monet posters accented by silk flower arrangements in crackle finished vases. The one LLADRO figurine she owned stood on her dresser.

Once in the safety of her bedroom, she realized, for the first time since her ordeal started, that she didn't have to be strong and put on a brave front. With this realization came all the overwhelming emotions she had held at bay during her imprisonment. In the middle of the soft cream, pink, and mauve bedspread she dissolved into tears as the sun's rays broke through her bedroom window.

CHAPTER FOUR

Leo walked into the conference room. Mark Sergan hadn't arrived, but two other men were already there. One of them was Charles Longview who Leo recognized from the night of his and Rachel's escape.

Leo was struck by the contrast between the two. Charles was fiftyish while Austin was twenty something. Charles' salt and pepper crew cut and spit-shined shoes revealed his military background. Austin's more casual look and blunt cut blonde hair made him look like he was more at home with a surfboard than a briefcase. Leo instantly dubbed them the soldier and the surfer.

Mark walked into the office to begin the meeting. "Leo, you remember Charles Longview from our Weapons of Mass Destruction Task Force." The man with the crew cut shook his hand.

"His partner is Austin Davis. Austin is a valuable asset to Weapons, but he's also great at finding missing persons, so his services will be doubly valuable."

The blonde man shook Leo's hand.

Right off, Leo could sense a coolness in their manner. Was he reading them correctly or did his own guilt about last week's events color his perception? He had a case to clear and couldn't afford to let his struggle with the turn of events get in the way. He would deal with that later.

Mark sat down. "Rachel Keaney won't be part of the team. I've granted her request to be taken off this case, so she will stay with Violent Crime for a while at least. Jason Morris, one of Alexander Hargrove's accomplices, was found dead in the building. Alexander himself is still missing. We started an immediate search for him that has yet to turn up anything except his torched Hummer in the desert across the border. We will continue the search.

"Now, Leo, why don't you start the meeting for our case code named HARTECH." Leo took some folders out of his briefcase and handed them to Charles and Austin. "These folders contain all the information I have about the five surviving people who worked the explosives business. Of course, they took off in all directions that night, not wanting to talk to authorities and be recognized. In addition to the Social Security numbers, I've included photos along with the names of significant people in their lives and possible places they may have gone."

"Thank you, Leo," Mark said. "The three of you will focus a lot of your attention on finding these five accomplices. Once they are found, Austin and Charles will interview them. They won't want to talk, so you can offer them immunity in exchange for their testimony. Leo, in addition to finding survivors, you need to compile reports on the documents you took from the building. You won't be interviewing because these people won't trust you since they thought you were one of them. Finding out that you were an undercover agent the whole time will make them clam up for sure. I cannot stress to you three how important this is. If the fact that we destroyed the legitimate business and blew up the building ever becomes public, then I want a complete report of our reasons for doing so. The words of these accomplices are a big part of that report."

The meeting was adjourned, and Austin and Charles put the folders in their briefcases. Leo approached them. "Looking forward to working with you gentlemen."

The two men nodded curtly and left the room.

*   *   *

Rachel put a Kenny G CD in her compact disc player and slid between the cool sheets of her bed.

Tomorrow would be her first day back to work from stress leave. A few months ago, she passed her five-year reinvestigation with flying colors. She hoped her assault wouldn't hinder her ability to do her job. There was no hoping about it. She wouldn't let it affect her performance.

She had spent her three-week leave taking in the beauty of Mission Bay. Sometimes, she walked or rode her bicycle around the sprawling green park or sailed on the Bay's peaceful waters. Other times, she walked along Mission Beach and talked with a wide variety of locals and visitors. She chose to live in Mission Bay because she thought it was one of the most beautiful areas in San Diego. Now, she was letting that beauty aid in her healing. The nights were the hardest part for her because every time her mind got quiet, vivid images of her assault returned. The sound of the melodic soprano saxophone helped her fall asleep. Going back to work would be good.

*   *   *

Mark called an update meeting on the HARTECH case hoping for good news. The look on the faces of Leo, Austin, and Charles told him the search had gone nowhere.

"Agent Longview, your update?"

"We've hit some dead ends, but we've come across some promising leads recently and we're optimistic," Charles replied.

"I know you're all doing the best you can. Keep after it and report to me as soon as you find any of the accomplices."

Su Lee rang his office. "Rachel's in the waiting area. Do you want me to have her come back another time?"

"No. Send her in. We're just about finished."

When she entered the room, Mark smiled brightly, not at all like the day he gave her the Hargrove assignment. "Rachel, welcome back," he said.

"Thank you. I was on this floor, so I wanted to let you know that Chantelle came to my apartment and took my statement. Will it be part of the file on this case?"

Mark noticed that when she talked, she avoided looking in Leo's direction. Leo looked uncomfortable.

"I'm afraid it needs to be," Mark answered. "Your testimony won't go beyond anyone in this room. Would you be more comfortable if only I read that portion of the file?"

"Yes, that would help a lot."

"You should also know that the chip worked. The building is completely destroyed."

"'Is he dead?"

"Missing. His vehicle was recovered in Mexico, so we're working with the Mexican authorities to find him. We have also alerted the authorities in Europe since he may have gone there from Mexico. They're all being very cooperative."

"Good," she said with a catch in her voice.

"You two can get started." Mark motioned to Austin and Charles. "Leo, could you wait in the anteroom for a few minutes?"

*   *   *

When he and Rachel were alone, Mark talked in his normal, soft voice. "Rachel, if you need more time off to recover, I'll approve it,"

"No, being here is the best thing for me right now. I can't believe he got away. I just wonder if he'll stay gone or if this whole mission will come back on us."

"I have every belief that he will be apprehended, provided he didn't become the victim of foul play in Mexico. If he tries to make trouble for us over this, we'll handle it. If he's as smart as he's supposed to be, he'll probably cut his losses and start over somewhere else with something else. Even though you're not on the case, I'll keep you posted on any new developments."

"Thank you," she said with a sigh of relief.

When she left the office, Mark called Leo back in. Mark studied the sadness on his agent's face.

"She was raped, wasn't she?"

Leo nodded.

"The son of a bitch. You couldn't do anything to help her, I know."

"I'm afraid it's worse than that, sir," he said before telling the whole story.

*   *   *

Later that day, Leo went down to the building's firing range to practice his target shooting. He practiced often to stay sharp. When he entered the shooting range, it was empty except for Rachel. Because of the ear protection and the sound of the gunfire, she didn't hear him enter the room and did not turn around. He took a minute to watch her.

She was an excellent marksman. He noticed the steadiness and confidence with which she fired every shot. His admiration for her increased, as did his sadness over the circumstances of their meeting. Had things been different, they might have become friends. He knew this was impossible. Still, he couldn't help but notice how beautiful she was. She clearly worked at keeping her medium frame in shape. He studied her outline and the way her hair cascaded down her back. Then he left the room unnoticed.

*   *   *

Days later, Leo sat in the cafeteria of the FBI building. It was late and there were only a few people scattered about the many tables.

Leo preferred it that way.

The hot beef sandwich might as well have been Styrofoam and cardboard. As he ate, he thought over his situation.

He wasn't sure how things got messed up the way they did, but the whole scene played over and over in his memory. The emergency phone call he had been expecting had not come, and it was getting later. Then Alexander paged him to wear all black and meet him in the basement saying it was urgent. He and Jason, also wearing all black, met at the elevator. They found Alexander outside the interrogation room wearing an expression that was difficult to read.

His eyes locked on Leo's, and his expression hardened. "This is no time for an attack of chivalry." Then addressing both of them. "Come on, follow my lead."

He always figured he would arrive at the FBI Field Office to a hero's welcome. The whole eight years of his assignment he dreamed of being known as the man who brought down Alexander Hargrove. Instead, his colleagues regarded him with a mixture of understanding and suspicion. He was sure Rachel hadn't talked to anyone about his part in the awful events that took place. But he was among detectives, and it seemed they figured out what happened to her and knew he did nothing to help her. When he read the faces of his coworkers, he could tell they viewed him as an accomplice to an assault on one of their own. For this reason, they worked with him but did not try to get to know him. It was just as well because once the HARTECH assignment was over, he would get a transfer. He didn't care where.

He also ate late lunches to avoid Rachel and help her avoid him. He really couldn't face her. It was hard enough seeing himself as a sex offender without having day to day contact with his victim. Every time he saw her, he felt the weight of his crime. The thought of forcing a woman in such a way had never entered his mind. The fact that he had to think quickly and do something did not ease his guilt.

Since Alexander survived the explosion, Leo now feared for his life and Rachel's. Mark was confident that Alex would never set foot in the United States again. Leo wasn't so sure. He had been there too many times when someone had crossed Alex and died painfully as a result.

*   *   *

Rachel had been working out of the building most of the day and wanted to spend a few hours at her desk before going home. She decided to grab a quick snack before she began her paperwork. After she bought a soda and a bag of chips from the vending machines, she noticed Leo at a table by himself. She took a minute to look at him because she knew he didn't see her.

His six-foot frame slumped a little in the chair as his chin rested on his hands. His dark hair flecked with gray was now cut short. She couldn't help but notice how sad and alone he looked. She tried hard not to be angry with him. He was put in an unbelievably bad spot. She knew that. However, not a day went by that she wasn't frustrated that he did not help her sooner. He couldn't have. She investigated the options she had for making him pay for what he did. Despite the pain that constantly tore around inside her, she couldn't bring herself to follow through with any of them. She learned a lot about people in her years in law enforcement and had become a good judge of character. In her heart, she knew he wasn't a predatory rapist.

When she approached his table, she saw the look in his eyes which confirmed what her heart was telling her.

"Do you have a minute?" she asked, even though it was clear he wasn't going anywhere.

"Sure, have a seat if you want."

"This is hard, but I need to say it anyway. I want to thank you for getting me out of there."

"I want to thank you for saving my life," he said. "I don't know how much you were told, but only Alexander and myself knew the self-destruct code. It would have been all over had you told him what you knew."

"I did know. That's one reason I hung on the way I did. I believed he was going to kill me, and I wasn't going to take you with me."

"Please don't take offense to this, but I honestly didn't think you were going to hold out. I've seen hardened criminals bigger than I am grovel at his feet. I've never seen anyone stand up to him the way you did."

"Then why didn't you get away while they were working on me?"

"I thought about it, but abandoning you just wasn't an option for me. If I had left you there to save my life, I wouldn't be able to look at myself in the mirror. I'm having a hard enough time as it is."

Rachel started to get up from the table.

"Rachel. . .Be careful."

She nodded knowingly and headed back to her squad room. Her anger had dissipated some in the last five minutes.

*   *   *

Charles Longview, along with his partner Austin Davis, used Leo's notes to search for Alexander Hargrove's five accomplices.

Austin was on the computer searching for information on Shalayah Michaels, a former employee at Hargrove Technologies.

"Okay." Austin leaned back in his chair. "Shalayah was hired recently by Rite Aid in Fallbrook, California. The Social Security database has her new address."

"Great, we'll drive out to Fallbrook this afternoon," Charles replied.

Meanwhile, Charles was scanning the same database on his computer. According to Leo, Alan Solano couldn't resist publicity and starting new businesses. The three years Alan hid out at Hargrove Technologies were frustrating for him since he had to live without a lot of luxuries he was used to and couldn't be his own boss.

"I found Alan Solano. His new advertising business is up and running in Phoenix, Arizona." Charles consulted his desk calendar. "I'll schedule a flight out for us to interview him next week."

*   *   *

Rachel entered the women's restroom and smiled at Laura Galloway, secretary to the assistant special agent in charge. Laura pressed the soap lever too hard, and pink gel went all over the faux marble counter.

"Oh no," Rachel said, grabbing some paper towels to help her clean up the mess.

"It's…it's okay, I've got it." Laura wiped up the mess, threw away the towels, and left the room in a hurry.

Rachel was struck by how nervous the secretary seemed. The petite brunette was always quiet and kept to herself. Very few people in the building knew much about her. She always seemed on guard like someone who had been through a lot. Rachel thought about it more. She realized that during the last three weeks, every time she and Laura crossed paths, Laura either looked away from her or left the room. She hadn't acted this way before.

*   *   *

That evening, Rachel jerked open the car door and threw her purse onto the passenger seat. Why was she going on such a small assignment? Mark told her to pick up some important papers from Scripps Mercy Hospital. He told her they would be waiting for her at the emergency room admit desk. Wasn't this the kind of job a secretary could do? There were many reasons she did not want to do this job. The main reason was the possibility of running into her ex-boyfriend, Police Detective Bradley Walsh of the Sex Crimes Unit. When Leo insisted she go to the hospital for her rape exam, she worried the whole time that Brad would be called in on a case and see her there.

She drove through the stop-and-go traffic thinking about their long relationship. They went on their first date shortly after she was promoted to the homicide unit. On their fourth date, he was paged to go to the ER to interview a thirteen-year-old sexual assault victim. Seeing him talk to the girl with such sensitivity and compassion won her heart. He made the poor girl realize that she could tell him anything. Because of this, she didn't leave anything out, and they were able to arrest and later convict the perpetrator. The relationship between the two detectives grew into one of love and mutual respect for each other's talents in their fields.

Things were great until he started wanting to settle down and have a family right about the time she wanted to pursue her dream of working for the

FBI. They broke up shortly before she left for the FBI Academy. Many of her female friends criticized her for giving up her man in favor of a job. The truth was, due to their conflicting goals, her man wasn't going to stay around, and she knew it. At that point, he was already showing interest in other women. They remained friends and talked frequently until he started seeing the ER nurse he later married and had a daughter with. She ran into him here and there, and occasionally worked cases with the San Diego Police, but she didn't want to see him now, after everything that happened to her.

When she walked into the emergency room, Brad was not in sight. She collected the files and turned around just in time to see him walk out of an examination room and put his pen and notepad in his pocket.

He was never hard to spot even in a large crowd because of his 6'4" height. Brad looked the same as the last time she saw him with his short, neatly combed blonde hair and Tommy Hilfiger shirt and tie. His nose was a little long for his face, but that only seemed to add to his handsome, chiseled features.

Maybe she still had time to leave before he noticed her, but just as she was about to go, the nurse who had assisted in her exam stopped her.

"How's everything going?" the nurse said gently.

"It's going. I have my good days and bad days."

"That's normal. Believe it or not the good days will eventually outnumber the bad."

"That's good to know," she said, just as Brad appeared beside her.

"Hi Rachel, can I walk you to your car?"

"Sure," she said, trying to sound like her normal self.

Thick, moist air hung about Rachel and Brad as they walked up the ramp to the second level. Neither one spoke. When they reached her car, his face became serious.

"I was looking on my computer a while ago for the file on one of my cases. I found your name in the list of new files the hospital had transferred over. Her last name was similar to yours, so I think it was transferred by mistake. I just want you to know, I'm sorry.

Hard as she tried to control them, tears began to flow.

"Come on, my car's right over here." He put an arm around her. She breathed in the familiar scent of Polo.

Once inside, he held her. When she finished crying, he looked into her eyes.

"I'd like a few minutes alone in an interrogation room with that guy," he said. "It was one guy, wasn't it?"

She shook her head and held up three fingers.

"Oh man," he said, running a hand over his face. "I didn't read the file. If you want to tell me what happened, I'm listening."

"Don't you have a new case to get to?"

"The case is a dunker. The son of a bitch is already at headquarters. Let him sweat."

She relayed the story and cried some more.

"Is the case being investigated?" he asked.

"Yes." She pulled her keys from her purse.

"I know, you can't tell me much more than that. Can you tell me who brought you to the hospital or did you go by yourself?"

"One of our undercover agents insisted that I go and brought me here even though I told him I didn't want to. We both knew I needed to be checked out."

"Sounds like this guy had your interests at heart."

She nodded. "I need to get going." She got out of his car. "Tell Brandi I said 'Hi,' okay?"

Rachel got into her car to take the files back to the field office, then drove home.

She felt better knowing she didn't have to worry about Brad finding out anymore. What he said about Leo having her interests at heart made a lot of sense. She just wished she could shake the feeling that Alexander could be around the next corner.

*   *   *

A few weeks later, Leo heard a knock on the door of his apartment. He was surprised to see Rachel on his doorstep. He ached to talk to her to explain and apologize for his actions. When he told Mark everything that took place during Rachel's imprisonment, Mark advised Leo not to try to see or talk to her. The heartbreak Mark felt was evident in his eyes.

When Leo invited her in, he pulled out a kitchen chair for himself and offered her the couch. Rachel asked him not to talk, only to listen. He nodded, complying with her request.

"I've read Special Agent Sergan's private files on you."

When Leo looked shocked, she shrugged and said, "I was given access. Don't question it."

Leo shook his head.

"I've had a tough time not hating you these past two months for your role in what happened. I knew I was doing the right thing by not talking, but I wasn't ready for the fact that the man I was protecting assaulted me then took me handcuffed into Alexander's bedroom so he could use me a second time. In reading about you, I found out about everything you did for us and our allies from the inside. Your work on the inside made a significant difference. I understand now that you didn't know what you were walking into until you were right in the middle of it. If you hadn't played your role like you did, we would both be dead." She looked into his sorrow-filled brown eyes. "I don't regret protecting you."

At this statement, Leo dropped his forehead into a hand and cried. The two agents talked and cried for hours that night.

CHAPTER FIVE

Evening fell hot and muggy in downtown Los Angeles. Cars crowded bumper to bumper, and tempers flared as tense motorists made the trek home. Alexander watched as a young man with dirty clothes hanging from his wasted frame stumbled into an alley. He was tall and would have had a strong build. His eyes had the dazed look, and his skin the bad complexion of most drug addicts. Between two trash cans, he threw up the contents of his stomach.

Alexander had been watching for three days as the young man did whatever was necessary to get his next fix, anything from panhandling to turning tricks to trafficking stolen property. He noticed how carefully the young addict stole something from a vehicle or store. He seemed to get away unnoticed most of the time. On the few occasions he was approached, he talked his way out of the situation. He had the talent Alexander was looking for.

The young man tripped as he stumbled out of the alley. Alexander extended a hand in front of him. When he was on his feet, Alexander took him to a coffee shop and bought him dinner.

"Man, I can't thank you enough. If there's anything you want in return, I mean, I do just about everything," he said, giving Alexander a knowing look.

"That's all right. Men aren't to my taste."

"Oh man, if you're one of those religious people, then I'm really sorry I said all that."

"Let's just say I'm in need of a friend right now. By the way, I'm Alexander."

"Kevin."

"Well Kevin, a few short months ago, a trusted friend and a woman, who was about to share her life with me, destroyed everything I worked for. Others, who I thought I could count on, abandoned me. I'll take you off these streets and off the drugs in exchange for your friendship and a little help settling the score."

After dinner, they drove to Alexander's secluded house in an agricultural area north of San Diego.

When his company was destroyed, Alexander had driven his Hummer across the border and set it on fire. That same night, while the authorities were still concentrating on the explosion, he obtained a car with American plates and crossed the border again with his new identification. He then accessed money in Asian and European banks and kept a low profile.

Through news accounts, he learned that Jason had died in the explosion. He knew Andre was nowhere near the building when it went up. No news stories mentioned Rachel, but a few calls to the trauma centers near Paseo and in San Diego confirmed that she came into the Scripps Mercy emergency room about an hour before the explosion. Obviously, Andre's disappearance, Rachel's escape, and the explosion were connected. He would have to find out how connected.

*   *   *

The mood in the auditorium at the FBI headquarters was somber as the agents and support staff filed in and took their seats. Officially a room for large meetings and training, the dark woods and gray theater style chairs made the room drab and solemn. The event being held there today fit the decor.

Rachel took an aisle seat at the back of the room. Attending the Agents' Memorial Service every year around Memorial Day was hard but this year, the service took on a whole new meaning for her. She sat in silent reverence as the names were read and photos shown of agents killed in the line of duty that year. After this part of the service, an agent placed a rose for each fallen agent in a large ceramic vase. Rachel approached the vase and glanced at the photo of Special Agent Brenda Callahan. Brenda, who was nine years Rachel's senior, died in a raid back in January. When she studied the woman's photo, Rachel felt her chest tighten up, making it harder to breathe. She placed her rose in the vase and hurried out of the auditorium.

*   *   *

The wall of the bathroom stall felt cool as Rachel leaned her forehead against it. She slowly inhaled and exhaled until her breathing became normal again. Minutes later, she heard the gentle voice of Su Lee outside the stall door.

"Rachel, are you okay?"

"Yeah, the service just got to me, that's all."

When Rachel opened the door, the beautiful, Chinese American woman dampened a couple of paper towels with cold water and gave them to her.

"Thank you," she said, letting their cool dampness seep into the pores of her face.

"Agent Acratelli saw you in the auditorium and sent me to see if you were all right."

"I think I'll be fine now. It just hit me really hard when I realized that it could have been my picture and my name this year."

Su Lee gave her a sympathetic look. "If you ever want to talk about it, you have my home number."

"I appreciate that. For now, I'd better get going before traffic gets really bad."

When she exited the restroom, she found Leo standing just outside the door.

"Hey," he said with a concerned look.

"Hey," she said, trying to smile.

"Tough service for both of us."

Rachel nodded.

"I don't know about you, but I don't feel like being alone right now. I'm not sure where I want to go, but I know my apartment isn't it," Leo said.

"When I have days like this, I like to go to one of the beaches. Are you interested?"

"Yeah, let's go."

*   *   *

The beach in front of the Hotel Del Coronado was alive with tourists on the Friday evening of a long week-end. The historic, red and white hotel drew many visitors each year. Rachel loved to come here to people watch. She and Leo sat on some boulders at the edge of the beach and looked out at the ocean in silence for several minutes.

"I've always wondered, what was the original plan for getting you out of your assignment before everything went wrong?" Rachel said.

She took off her shoes and dug her feet in the glittering sand, realizing she was ruining a good pair of hose.

"I was supposed to get a phone call that my mother was critically ill and I would have to get to Phoenix, where I told Alex I was from. When the call never came and instead, I got a page out of nowhere for your interrogation, I knew something was very wrong."

"That must have been frustrating, considering how long your assignment lasted."

"Yeah, Mark offered me a way out of the assignment a few times, but I always said no. From the moment I met Alex, I knew I wanted to be the one to stop him, so I continued. I gained his trust and knew it was a matter of time before we'd bring him down."

Rachel continued sifting sand with her feet. "How did you do it all those years? I've done undercover for short periods, but you did it for eight years."

"It has to do with a way of thinking. I have the ability to think like a criminal. Whenever I was around anyone in that place, I was Andre Giardello, former gun runner. When I was alone, I became myself again and thought about everything and everyone I love and enjoy. I suppose it helps that I look like a criminal."

It was true. With his mustache-goatee, sunglasses, and Armani suit, he looked the part of a man involved in the criminal underworld.

"I'm glad you stayed with the assignment," she said after several minutes.

"Really? Why?"

"Yes. Because I think a lesser man would have run and saved his own skin rather than take the risks you did."

Leo said nothing, but gingerly squeezed her hand and let it go.

"Will you ever do undercover again?" She asked.

"No, I've paid too high a price for doing the assignment I did."

A group of bronze-skinned, sun-bleached teens walked by with waffle cones full of rich ice cream. Rachel and Leo watched them in silence.

"How are you doing with everything? Are you getting counseling to work through it all? If that's none of my business, just say so," Leo said.

"It's okay. I'm seeing a terrific counselor. I started seeing her right away."

She looked up at the sky which was becoming cloudy in the early evening. "Years ago, I lost my father to a lingering illness. When he was gone, it hurt like hell, but with the hurt, there was peace and acceptance. Peace because he was no longer sick, and acceptance because we all expect to lose our parents eventually. The pain I'm going through right now is so much harder to deal with because there is no peace or acceptance. This was never supposed to happen." She looked down at the sand, then up at Leo. "I decided, when you got me out of that hell hole in the desert, that I'm going to overcome this thing. Everything that happened brought me down further than I ever imagined I could go, but I'm not going to stay here. I just wish I knew for sure where he was. Sometimes, I feel like he's hiding in the shadows."

"Me too."

"Mark says he could have met with foul play in the desert. Do you believe that's a possibility?"

He shook his head. "Alex did business in Mexico all the time. He speaks fluent Spanish and knows his way around the underworld there. I would be surprised if he were killed and buried out there."

Rachel nodded and looked out at the ocean.

*   *   *

On a jutty of rocks near the water, Alexander sat with a pair of binoculars. He had never been a stalker before but following and spying on people seemed to come naturally to him. He could blend into just about any crowd. The only thing that made him stand out was his hair that shone like a copper penny this time of year. Dying it wasn't something he was willing to do, but he could easily cover it with a hat.

What a pair Andre and Rachel made. Of course, he now knew Andre was not his real name. He'd have to find out who he really was. Today, both agents looked somber, more so than usual. They seemed to listen intently to each other, but the awkwardness and tension between them was visible.

He focused his binoculars on Rachel. Why did she have to be so beautiful? Why did she have to be so strong? If she weren't, he would have escaped into Mexico with her way ahead of time. He would have gone somewhere, started a new business, and had her too.

"What are you studying so intently with those?" a heavy set, blonde woman interrupted his thoughts.

"I'm working security for an important guest at the hotel. This is my post, and I really can't be bothered."

"Sor-ry," she huffed and continued on her way.

When the woman was out of sight, Alexander got up, put his binoculars away, and headed to his car.

He couldn't leave Kevin alone for too long at this stage of kicking his heroin habit. He paused with his hand on the car door. Did Rachel know who Andre was when they were interrogating her? He would find out someday.

*   *   *

Rachel sat in the glider rocker and looked out the window of the fifth-floor office at San Diego Bay in the distance. The gentle voice of Chantelle, the FBI's psychologist specializing in sex crimes, interrupted her thoughts.

"Rachel, you've talked a lot about the aftermath of your kidnapping and sexual assault, but you've never told me how you felt during the attack. I think it would be good for you if you did."

Rachel turned and looked at the beautiful woman with coffee colored skin, deep brown eyes, and wild, curly black hair held back by a headband. Tears blurred her vision as she described how she felt.

"I thought my life was over. I've never felt more helpless. When he had me down on that table and ordered me to look at him . . . I knew he could do anything he wanted with me and there wasn't a damn thing I could do about it. When all three of them finished with me, I felt like there wasn't anything left for them to use. The next night, when Alexander told me he would keep me there for himself if I didn't talk, a part of me was sure I was never going to leave there alive."

"But you did leave there alive."

"Yeah, Leo got me out of there."

"Do you think that's why you've been able to forgive him?"

"I think so. I know he was forced into it too. I've worked with male sexual abuse victims, and I know about arousal non- concordance."

"Yes, men are a lot more physical than we are. For them, a sexual response can be separate from their emotions."

"Right, so I know why he was able to do what he did. I've gotten to know him a little, and he just isn't the type to willingly do that sort of thing."

"You never told Alexander about the computer chip even though he told you that you could stop what was happening. Why is that?" Chantelle rested her hands on her six-month pregnant stomach.

"Because I knew he was going to do what he wanted whether I told him anything or not. Also, I was protecting the insider."

"You also told me a few weeks back that you spoke very little during your imprisonment. Do you know why?"

"A verbal confrontation would have given him more power over me than he already had. I was afraid if I said anything he would know how scared I really was."

"Do you see what I'm seeing here Rachel?"

Rachel shook her head.

"At a time when you felt the most powerless, you were still making choices. He may have forced you into sexual acts, but he couldn't make you give up your principles by revealing your knowledge. You chose to protect Leo, you chose not to let go emotionally, and the way I see it, you chose to live because he may have killed you had you said or done the wrong thing. Do you regret any of these choices?"

"Not for a second." Rachel dabbed her eyes with a tissue.

"Then he didn't have all of the power, did he?"

"No, he didn't," she said straightening in her chair.

*   *   *

The phone rang at 2:30 in the morning. Against her own better judgment, Laura answered it.

"Laura, it's Alexander."

She was silent.

"I know it's been a while. I'm sure the search for me has quieted down some.

"Yeah, it's still going on, though."

"While you worked for me did you ever leave out any information?" he asked calmly.

"No, I swear, never." Her voice rose in pitch.

"Then why didn't I find out that an FBI agent was inside my organization, you miserable bitch!"

"He never kept anything on Leo in his office. No one ever talked about him. I don't think anyone but Mark knew about him," she said.

"Well, I hope you're right. So, his name is Leo, then?"

"Yes, Leo Acratelli."

"Listen, I still need you to work for me. Only this time, I need you to be a little more aggressive in seeking out the information. I'm going to give you a number where you can reach me no matter where I am. This is also the last time I will call you on your home phone. All other calls will be cell phone to cell phone. I will continue to send you the money via FedEx like before. Relay every bit of information you have on my case in real time. I also want regular updates on Leo and Rachel."

Within a week, Laura contacted Alexander to tell him everything to date on the HARTECH case including the fact that the FBI had Shalayah and Alan's statements on file.

CHAPTER SIX

While Rachel entered information into her computer, she waited to hear from Mark. When she came in that morning, she requested to talk to him as soon as possible. Ever since her return to work, her squad supervisor had been giving her light duty detective assignments while all around her, the rest of Violent Crime buzzed with activity. When she questioned him, he explained that he was following Mark's orders. Mark himself hadn't given her any delivery or pick up assignments. In the middle of her menial task, Leo entered the squad room and asked to see her in the hall.

"I went to the Fish Market last night after work. They had a great deal on mussels."

"Really? I love mussels."

"Well, I have a great recipe for them, so I went nuts and bought a lot of them. I wondered if you would like to come over and share them with me this evening."

Before she could answer, Mark turned the corner.

"Rachel. . . oh Leo, I wasn't expecting you to be here."

"Hi Mark," Leo said.

The look in Mark's eyes made it clear that he thought Leo should not be near Rachel.

"Su Lee said you wanted to talk to me, and I was on this floor, so I thought I'd come by," Mark said.

"Yes, I did want to talk to you. Leo, sounds great, could you excuse us?"

"Sure, I'll see you."

As Leo left, Mark stared after him, then turned to Rachel. "I told him not to make any contact with you. If he bothers you, I want you to tell me. I know he's sorry, but he shouldn't be causing you problems because he wants to make amends."

"It's okay. I went to his apartment a few weeks ago of my own free will, and we talked. We worked it out, so he doesn't have to stay away."

Mark looked surprised.

"What did you want to see me about?"

"What's the deal with these assignments I've been given lately? I need to do the important stuff I did before."

"I just thought you might want a break, so I gave you a lighter workload. You went through a lot."

"I went through hell, but one of the hardest things for me is being treated differently by everyone who knows," she said, her eyes tearing up.

Mark suggested they take a walk in the courtyard. They took the elevator and crossed the lobby in heavy silence.

Finally, Mark spoke. "Rachel, I'm so sorry. I will start giving you the work you're used to. I just feel that what happened to you was my fault. I never should have sent you on that assignment. I think if I can keep you out of harm's way, then I can make it up to you somehow. I've never told you, or anyone else here this before, but you are the same age that my daughter would have been had she lived. You remind me so much of her. Your eyes, your logical mind, the way you see the strengths in others. Every time I deal with you, it's like I get to see how she might have been. I've often thought that if she had lived and followed in my footsteps, you two would have been the best of friends. Or the toughest competitors, I'm not sure which. When I found out what happened to you, I felt the same as if it had happened to her."

Rachel took a second to process what she was hearing. She knew Mark had a daughter who was killed in an accident on the way to a school function at the age of sixteen. Since he didn't talk much about it, she never knew the connection in his mind. Mark was the kind of boss who was warm and caring toward everyone who worked under him, so his treatment of her didn't seem unusual. She saw that the man everyone turned to now needed someone. Seeing the guilt pressing down on him, she tried to reassure him that the turn of events was not his fault as they talked for over an hour.

*   *   *

Kevin stumbled down the hallway toward the scent of toast. For the first time in what seemed like years, he could appreciate the beauty of the morning. When he woke up, he could feel that the drugs were finally clear of his system, and he saw the world with new eyes.

"Sit down," Alexander said, placing a plate of wheat toast, fruit salad, and yogurt in front of him.

"This is really good," he said, savoring the butter on the toast and sweet coldness of the cantaloupe.

"Food's better when you're not too high to taste it, huh?"

"Yeah. Oh man, I hope I didn't ruin those two blankets."

"Don't worry about it. I have a powerful washing machine. Came with the place."

Kevin looked around the house from his place at the dining room table. The small dining room gave way to a large, sunken living room with light blue overstuffed chairs and a matching L-shaped sectional. The walls were adorned with seascape watercolors and small, wooden shelves that stood bare. A picture window revealed hilly terrain scattered with tan boulders, dark green trees, scrub bushes, and patches of yellow and green grass. The kitchen to the other side of the dining room was a bachelor's kitchen, spotless except for the few dishes and utensils used to make the fruit salad. The solid oak cabinets hid any other dishes or cookware. The Formica countertops were bare except for a toaster, microwave, and coffee maker.

"Nice place. Have you lived here long?"

"Moved in a few months ago. A couple getting a divorce was trying to unload it through a realtor. I made them an offer they couldn't refuse for the place and everything in it."

Kevin took both of their plates to the sink, then the two men walked outside and stood on the front deck. To the west of the house, Kevin could see a tangerine orchard obviously left to its own devices. The view was fantastic from the home's location high on a hill. Neighborhoods, farm fields, and orchards dotted the countryside.

"This place is a dream," Alexander said, motioning toward the roads. "Highway 76, Highway 15, and Old Highway 395 meet down there. I can get anywhere I need to go but still live away from the crowded city. I also love the view of the West Lilac Bridge." He directed Kevin to look at the cement, single arched bridge in the distance.

Kevin smiled then closed his eyes and savored the warm breeze like he had his breakfast.

"I've been wondering, how did you wind up on the streets like that, anyway?" Alexander asked.

"Where to start. . . My mom raised me by herself until I was about twelve. She married a guy, and he became her world. Unfortunately, he had a temper and would blow up for no reason. I kept telling her to get rid of him. She told me that if I didn't act up so much, these things wouldn't happen." He wiped away tears with the back of his hand. "Once, when I was sixteen, he went after her instead of me. By then, I was big enough to do something, so I grabbed him, hit him, and knocked out three of his teeth. My mom yelled at me and said she would call the police. I got out of there and never went back. I had been getting by on my own for the past four years. I was doing really well until someone introduced me to H at a party. Everything was really going down from there until you found me."

Alexander shook his head. "I can't believe your mom and stepdad. I have no patience for grown men who hurt children. People sometimes came to me for help with situations. One guy years ago begged me to hide him from the authorities. I told him I would think about it and meet him the next night. Well, I did some checking on him and found out he produced kiddie porn."

Kevin made a disgusted face.

Alexander continued, "I met the son of a bitch, just like I said I would, only instead of hiding him, I beat the crap out of him and called the Feds with an anonymous tip about where to find him."

The two men walked back inside.

"What happens now?" Kevin said.

"Now, we get you stronger, and I continue looking for some people."

*   *   *

When Rachel walked into Leo's apartment later that evening, she sniffed the air that was heavy with tomato sauce. The place looked different than when Rachel first saw it. An entertainment center now held the television instead of a filing cabinet. A CD player was turned on low and instrumental jazz emitted from the speakers. The black leather couch was now accompanied by a matching chair. There were even pictures on the wall.

Leo led her to the kitchen where he finished preparing dinner.

"I have one of these rooms in my apartment. I wasn't sure what to do with it," she said.

"Oh, what did you do with it?"

"I store my refrigerator and microwave in it," she said, smiling.

Leo laughed. "My mother made sure all her sons knew basic cooking and sewing. Through her, I found out that I love to cook. In fact, this meal is my grandmother's recipe."

He gave her a taste of the sauce.

"Wow. That reminds me," Rachel said as they sat down to mussels in tomato sauce over angel hair pasta. "I don't know anything about your life before your undercover work on the Weapons Task Force. Are you from California or what?"

"I grew up in Walnut Creek outside of San Francisco. My parents still live there along with two of my three brothers. My other brother and two sisters live out of state with their families. While I was with the San Francisco Police Department, I became interested in guns and learned a lot about them. Mark soon recruited me to do undercover work in San Diego where there was a lot of illegal trafficking across the border. It was a collaborative effort with the BATF and the Border Patrol. I was really close to accepting a position with the S.W.A.T. Team when Mark convinced me to work for him. After a few years, he offered me my long-term undercover assignment."

"Were you ever married?"

"You're not afraid to ask anything, are you?"

"It's my job to ask questions."

"I was married, very briefly. It was one of those things; we were young. I was twenty-one and she was barely eighteen. She married me to get out of the house. I was going to save her from her family situation. It wasn't long before fantasy and reality clashed. I failed to live up to her expectations and she took off for L.A. The divorce was final a year and a half after the wedding. How about you, brothers and sisters, ex-husbands?"

"My parents didn't think they could have children until I came along when my mom was in her late 30s, so I'm it. I've had a couple of long-term relationships, but I've never been married."

"After my divorce, I threw myself into my work and dated casually. When I infiltrated Hargrove, I didn't want to involve a woman in my life. It was too dangerous."

At the mention of Hargrove, Rachel looked at the floor for a second.

"I'm sorry, Rachel, I need to remember not to talk about anything related to Alexander around you."

"No, I can't expect you to not talk about eight years of your life. You had to pretend to be someone you weren't for so long."

Leo nodded.

"I think we both need to be free to talk about our time there and help each other put it in the past as best we can," Rachel said. "In fact, I have to ask you something that maybe you would know. I have to be tested every six months to make sure I didn't catch anything because of what happened. You knew their lifestyle; I just wonder how much at risk I am."

"Other than sleeping with Shalayah when the mood struck, Alex would have a few one-nighters here and there. Jason frequented the bars in El Centro, Paseo Del Oro, and across the border on his days off. I know he picked up women on a regular basis"

The tears that came too easy spilled out of Rachel's eyes.

"I'm sorry," she said, wiping away the tears.

"No need to apologize," Leo said, taking her hand.

"I've interviewed rape survivors before. I made a point of being gentle with them because of what they had gone through. Until it happened to me, I never had any real idea of how awful it was for them. I mean, here are two men that I would never choose to be with, sexually or otherwise, and yet I know what they smell like, and how they sound when they're getting off. Things I never wanted to know about either one of them."

She could read the question in Leo's face.

"You're wondering why I didn't mention you in any of what I just said."

"Yeah, I am."

"Because I don't see you as my second assailant. Logically, I know what happened, but it's like Andre died in the explosion and you rose from his ashes. At least it's that way most of the time."

Leo squeezed her hand.

*   *   *

Rachel thought through her upcoming assignment as she drove to a building on a seedy street in Las

Cruces, New Mexico. Mark had been true to his word and gave her the assignment two days after their conversation. The building she parked in front of looked like any other on the street. It was an office supply warehouse, but in the back, a very different business was at work. Here, they produced false documents needed for illegal immigration.

She couldn't arrange to meet with her INS contact outside of his working area, so she would have to get in to see him and pick up the microfilm they needed. She looked her part: tight jeans, a purple tank top, and double the makeup she usually wore. She left her hair loose and ran her hand through it as she approached a burly Hispanic man. It was clear that he liked what he saw because he looked her up and down with a sparkle in his eyes. His height and bulk made him appear impassive. Suddenly, she felt very vulnerable in her barfly clothes. What if something went wrong? What would he do to her if he found out who she was? Her skin crawled and her heart raced, but she concentrated on the task at hand.

"I need to see Manuel Ortiz, please," she said.

"Do you have an appointment with him?"

"No, but I need to see him."

"Well, maybe I can give him a message for you, then," he leaned causally against a palate of computer paper and continued appraising her.

"Look, he picked me up in a bar a while back which leaves several possibilities of what I need to tell him. Is that the type of message you want to deliver?"

His eyes widened and his head jerked back slightly. "Wait right here, and I'll go get him." When Manuel came out of a back office, he looked at her as if trying to place where he knew her.

"Yes, you know me. We spent the night together a little over a month ago. Is there a place we can talk?"

The two agents went to a corner, away from the beeping of forklifts and idling diesel engines and pretended to argue, emphatically waving their hands.

Finally, Manuel raised his voice. "All right! If you say it's mine, I'll sign the papers, just don't come back here."

Rachel handed him the documents. He signed the papers terminating his phony parental rights to a nonexistent child and attached a small film cartridge to the second sheet of paper.

Rachel carefully slid the papers containing the film into the envelope she brought and sealed it.

When she walked out, she heard Manuel say to the other man, "If she comes around here again, throw her out."

She flipped off both men and left with the wonderful feeling of a successful mission. Her ability to get information from point A to point B was very much intact, and she was glad to be back to her normal work.

*   *   *

Laura called in sick and spent the day cleaning her small, attractively decorated house. She recently bought the two-bedroom, two-story house in Escondido and decorated it with a woodland theme. The house was something she could afford on her secretary's salary, but her insider money paid for the best in home furnishings and decor. For the past ten years, she invested and saved the money she got from Alexander and finally felt like it was safe to live a little.

At first, she liked slipping confidential information to Hargrove Technologies. It made her feel like she was living the life of the agents. The extra money was a big motivator. She didn't really know the agents who were killed because of her, and for years, she denied her part in their deaths.

Recently, however, the denial was getting harder. She had more contact with Rachel because of her work with the special agent in charge and Laura's boss, the assistant special agent in charge. Passing Rachel in the hallways or seeing her in the lunchroom filled her with remorse. Laura didn't want to think about what Alexander may have done to her, but she thought about it often. She knew Rachel wasn't the same person she was before she tangled with him. She was still friendly and focused on her work, but the shadow over her was quite visible.

Laura wanted nothing more than to cut all ties with Alexander and forget that part of her life ever happened, but she knew that this was not possible. If she quit relaying information to him, the FBI would receive an anonymous tip with evidence of her actions, and she would spend the rest of her life in prison. She couldn't call in an anonymous tip to help set a trap for him because Alexander never gave her enough information on his plans or whereabouts. Not only that, if he were caught, she knew he wouldn't hesitate to reveal her activities as part of a plea bargain. How did her life become this complicated? She knew the answer.

15 years ago, she was a bright, attractive scholarship student at UC Berkeley. She was studying to be a criminalist. The classes were hard, but she was making excellent grades. It was during one of her studying lunches in the student union that a good-looking, well-built redhead approached her and shut her book.

"Hey!" she exclaimed.

"Every time I see you, you've got your nose in a book. Do you even know what this room looks like?" he asked.

Alexander introduced himself and told her he was majoring in business administration. They talked for two hours that day. Soon, they began dating, and her life hit a high point. He taught her more efficient ways to study even though she rarely saw him do any homework. More than a year into their relationship, she began to see his dark side. She began to learn who he really was. The smart, witty, romantic man she fell in love with began verbally and sometimes physically abusing her. Around the same time, the mental games started. Her grades and motivation dropped dramatically. The relationship went on for two more years like that until he disappeared one day. Soon after, she lost her scholarship and headed to San Diego to put her life back together. She got her job with the FBI but resented the fact that she was filing their papers instead of helping them clear cases.

She didn't realize the hold Alexander still had over her until a year into her job when he called her unexpectedly. He told her about the illegal business he had just started and wanted her help in alerting him should the FBI be onto him or any of his deals. He said he would make it worth her while, which he had. What bothered her most was that even though she did it for the money and the excitement, she also did it out of devotion to and fear of him.

CHAPTER SEVEN

The mid-August night was clear, and many stars could be seen from the front deck of Alexander's ranch style, 1,500 square foot house. As with most summer evenings in the area, the air was alive with the sound of crickets and other nocturnal insects. Kevin sat in a lounge chair while Alexander sat on the railing of the deck looking up at the sky. Kevin felt better than he had in a long time. Kicking heroin was extremely difficult, but Alexander was there the whole time. He was never repulsed by the many bodily reactions to the detoxification process, just caring and supportive. Once Kevin was clean, Alexander got him working out and on a healthy diet. When he gained weight and began to fill in his 6'4" frame, Alexander ordered clothes for him over the Internet. Clothes that not only fit great but were of a higher quality than any he had ever worn.

In the middle of his thoughts, Kevin spoke up. "I've been doing some thinking, Alex. I'm feeling strong now, maybe I should look for a job in Fallbrook. That way, I can save up for an apartment in that town so we would still live close to each other, but you would have your place to yourself, and I wouldn't be leeching off of you."

Alexander sat in silence sipping Perrier for several minutes.

"It's not considered leaching if you're my friend, is it?"

"No, I guess not."

"I may like living in secluded areas, but that doesn't mean I like living in them alone. Eventually, you should get a job and move out, but not yet."

Alexander swirled the ice in his glass and looked pensive. "I turned thirty-six at the beginning of last month. Not long ago, I thought I had it all. A booming business, loyal employees and friends, and the type of woman you don't find every day. Then, in a moment, it was gone. When my building went up in flames, I felt like my heart had been torn out. Who knows, my best friend and girlfriend were probably plotting together for a long time to destroy what I built. Some employees that I thought were loyal didn't even see that I got out of the building alive. I went out of my way to help them out of bad situations, and they covered their own asses and left me behind.

"I found two of them, and we're going to see them and settle a few things. The amazing thing is, one of them lives in Fallbrook. I don't go into that town often, but I'm surprised I haven't seen her there. Don't get a job and move out yet. I need your help."

Alexander got up and went indoors, leaving Kevin alone to digest this new information. He couldn't imagine those people being so uncaring. How could his girlfriend and best friend have backstabbed him like that? A man like him didn't deserve all that. Whatever Alexander had planned for them, they had it coming. He never questioned Alexander's plans or where his money came from even though he seemed to have a lot for someone who lost everything. He trusted the man who plucked him from the gutter and turned his life around. He had no thoughts of betraying his new friend.

*   *   *

Rachel pulled her purse and tan leather briefcase from her desk drawer, then jerked the keys from the center pocket of the purse. The rest of her squad had gone home, and she stayed behind to get some work done without all the phones ringing and conversation all around her. She had spent the day in and out of the building. It seemed that every time she would settle in to do paperwork, someone paged her to help with a case. This was a day she would have preferred not to see anyone. Instead, she had to deal with other agents, the police, and witnesses all day. Controlling her emotions had been difficult.

She was almost to the door when Leo opened it and stuck his head in.

"Hey," Leo said.

"Hey," she said with a sigh.

"Everything okay?"

"It's just one of my bad days."

"I came to see if you wanted to have dinner tonight. If you want, I could cook dinner and listen to you."

"I don't know if that's such a good idea," she said as her voice broke and a few tears began to flow.

"I think it would help if you talked about it."

"You don't understand! I've been angry at you all day." Now she could no longer stop herself.

"A lot of the time, I'm okay with your part. Like I said, I usually don't see you and Andre as the same person. But sometimes, I'm still so angry. I just wish my emotions would stay one way or another!"

Now, she was crying freely and for the first time, Leo put an arm around her and led her to the couch in the corner of the room.

"Your feelings don't stay the same because you feel both emotions. It's going to take you some time to work it out. I'll give you all the time you need."

While she cried, she clutched Leo's free arm, grabbing his forearm tightly. The harder she cried, the harder she gripped. Leo didn't move, he just held her and let her cry.

When she finished crying, it was late. The two agents grabbed dinner at Rubio's and talked for a few more hours on Rachel's deck.

*   *   *

Alexander sat at the large mahogany desk with pieces of paper fanned out in front of him; notes taken on his Palm Pilot then printed out.

Leo and Rachel seemed to have job-centered lives. Leo was settling in nicely from what Alexander could tell. However, he kept to himself just like he did at Hargrove Technologies. Most times when he and Jason would go out, they would invite Leo only to be turned down. Now, he realized Leo must have done some of his best snooping during their absence. These days, he spent time fixing up the used BMW he bought or taking his guns to the FBI range.

Rachel had a few friends to go sailing or to the beach with, but mostly, she worked. He wasn't sure of her relationship with the man she was with in the hospital parking garage. When he followed the man, he found out that he was a cop with a wife and family. Alexander hadn't seen Rachel with him since that night back in May, so she obviously wasn't fucking him, but their body language suggested they were more than casual acquaintances. He wasn't sure if this man was anybody worth messing with.

In following Rachel, he could tell he hurt her as he had meant to, but not as much as he thought he had. By the time he settled in and began following her, she was back at work. Shortly thereafter, she and Leo began spending time together. This was a complete surprise to Alexander. He marveled at her strength, and his anger grew. The temptation to kill them both right away was almost too strong, but he would wait. He had other business to attend to in the meantime. Still, he could just taste the day they would see each other again. He would be the only one left standing when they did. He was sure of it.

Alexander broke a pencil with his right hand.

*   *   *

The next morning, Rachel was walking through the parking garage when Leo caught up with her.

"I just came from Einstein Bros. I got more bagels than I really need. Want one?"

"Sure,"

Instead of going into the building, the two of them walked into the tiled courtyard. When they took a seat on one of the benches' Rachel gave him a smile. "I've noticed a pattern you have of buying too much food and offering me some."

"I guess you found me out," he said, then looked sheepish. "The truth is, I really enjoy your company, and I wanted to see how you were doing after last night."

"Last night was good for me. I really needed to talk and vent those feelings. I just hope hearing some of what I said wasn't too hard on you."

"Are you kidding? I feel fortunate that you can even be in the same room with me, let alone talk to me."

"It's amazingly easy to talk to you. I guess because you were there, and you're the only one who really knows what happened in that room. You've seen me stripped of all the dignity I ever had. Both literally and figuratively. After that, what is there to hide from you?"

Leo looked deep in thought as he took two bites of his sesame seed bagel. "I suppose that's why I feel so open with you. You know the worst thing I've ever done. I mean, what are you going to do, reject me if I tell you that I tried a joint once in high school?"

Rachel laughed. "Considering that I did too, probably not."

The sound of Leo's pager cut their conversation short.

"Damn, I'm wanted in a meeting," he said, stuffing a napkin in the bag that held the bagels as he got up to leave.

"Thank you for the bagels. Just know you don't have to bring food. You can talk to me any time," Rachel called after him.

*   *   *

Later that afternoon, Leo was in the men's room preparing to wash his hands after he finished lunch. When he unbuttoned the cuffs of his shirt and pushed his sleeves up, Austin Davis, the surfer half of the soldier/surfer duo, emerged from a stall behind him and began to wash his hands.

He raised an eyebrow at the fresh, hand-grab bruise on Leo's arm. "Nice bruise."

"Yeah." Leo turned his attention back to washing his hands.

Austin glared, then walked out of the bathroom.

CHAPTER EIGHT

Shalayah Michaels woke up to a knock at the door of her small house. When she opened the door and saw Alexander and Kevin on her doorstep, her jaw dropped.

"Alex!" she exclaimed as she threw her arms around him. "They said you were long gone."

"I never went too far away."

She invited them in, and Alexander introduced Kevin. In a nook off the kitchen, they talked over sandwiches and soda.

"So, Kev, where did you meet this fine man?" She asked motioning to Alexander.

"He found me on the streets of L.A. and got me cleaned up."

"Sounds like me and many others, I came to him when my meth lab in Venice Beach burned down. I was high on Crystal when I met him. He said he would help me, but he had no patience for drugs and alcohol. So how long have you been clean, baby?"

"About three months."

"That's great! All I can say is don't start using again, cause if you do, Alex will kick your ass from here to Phoenix. By the way, Alex, are you just paying a social call, or did you need something? I'll help you in any way I can."

"Mainly a social call. I wanted to find out if the FBI had come to talk to you."

"Yes, they did, but I didn't tell them anything," she said. "I still don't know what exactly went down that night."

"The most trusted man in my organization stabbed me in the back."

"You mean Andre!"

"His name isn't Andre. It's Leo Acratelli, and he works for the FBI. Same as Rachel, the woman you were watching over."

"You don't say! That explains how they knew who we were, because I know any records must have been destroyed with the building."

"Not all. Before he escaped with Rachel, he took some important files, including the list of everyone who worked for me. However, I'm not here to talk about that. Let's just say I miss some things you used to do for me." He winked at her.

She smiled seductively. "I thought you might be coming around for that. Will your friend be joining us?"

"I thought I would keep this between us. Remember the game we played with handcuffs?" He held up a pair for her to see.

"You got it! Kevin, you can watch the TV. If I were you, I'd turn it up real loud," she said as the two disappeared into her bedroom.

*   *   *

Once inside the bedroom, Alexander took off his shirt baring his thin but muscular arms and chest. He grabbed Shalayah, and a hungry open-mouthed kiss found her lips. Her heart raced at the reality of being with him again.

"Take off that night gown, you sexy bitch," he whispered.

She felt her whole body tingle at these words and couldn't drop her gown fast enough. Her breathing quickened as he ran his hands and lips down her body. A trail of fire seemed to follow his touch. His breathing quickened as she gently caressed his downy haired chest and buried her face in his neck. She savored the scent of Drakkar mixed with sweat and the taste of salt on his skin.

He stopped her. The look in his eyes was one she couldn't quite read.

He tightened a side of the handcuff around one wrist, then led her to the bed where he cuffed her other wrist.

She barely heard the click of the handcuffs over her pounding heart. Wondering what he was going to do next was too much.

When she was secured around the bars of the headboard, he turned off the light. He straddled her and took off his belt with a snap. She flinched as the belt landed with a crack on the mattress beside her.

She was helpless, unable to move as the belt missed her by inches. A wild mix of fear and excitement coursed through her whole body.

Shalayah closed her eyes and drank in the ticklish sensation of the belt traveling slowly down her neck, between her breasts, over her navel and settled on the curly thatch that covered her mound. Her breath caught when he lightly struck her across her belly, once, then again.

He paused.

Would he stop now, or would the blows come harder and harder?

As if answering her question, he threw the belt aside and eased his jeans and underwear over the bulge in his groin. She wished he had left the lights on so she could more clearly take in his naked form.

His hands kneaded her full breasts until her breathing came in short gasps. Pleasure mixed with pain when he pinched and lightly twisted her nipples. Her arms jerked forward, and the handcuffs reminded her that she could do nothing about it. She was completely at the mercy of his will. A moan from deep down escaped her lips as his hands slowly moved toward the sensitive bud between her thighs. He was rough, just the way she liked it.

On the edge of her climax, he stopped again.

He couldn't stop now; she was too close. The tearing of a wrapper and the smell of latex surprised her. Before she had time to question him, he took her in one thrust. His erection inside of her was all she needed. Her body tensed as a powerful orgasm took hold of her.

*   *   *

Shalayah and Alexander lay in the darkness of her bedroom, neither speaking.

Shalayah broke the silence. "Let me tell you something. You really know how to light my fire. Far as I'm concerned, you can come over for this any time you want. I still don't understand why you used a rubber when you didn't before."

Alexander remained silent.

"Say, you better take off these cuffs so we can go check on your friend."

"Not just yet."

Alexander got up from the bed, wrapped himself in a towel, and retrieved the briefcase he told Kevin to leave by the door.

"I have a question. You say that the FBI came by and questioned you, but you didn't tell them anything."

She began to strain against the handcuffs. "That's right, why would I help them?"

"Oh, I don't know. Maybe immunity for your drug charges and everything you did while you worked for me."

When she heard this revelation of the truth and saw the instruments in his briefcase, she panicked and pleaded for her life until his open hand came down hard across her face.

"I happen to have a source who told me a lot about your testimony. It could cause problems for me, and it's causing problems for you right now. It's too bad this is all I have to work with." He shook his head. "I had so much more at my building."

A few hours later, Alexander left the bedroom and shut the door behind him.

"Take the glasses, plates, and soda cans we used and put them in this bag. We'll get rid of them later." He handed Kevin a plastic bag.

*   *   *

Kevin looked out the window at the dark, passing scenery. He couldn't get the sound of Shalayah scream-ing out of his mind. After the screaming came the quiet moaning, then the silence. All three rang through his mind until he thought he would go insane.

They were headed for Arizona to see an "old friend" as Alex called him. Kevin hadn't said anything for the last hour since leaving Shalayah's small, secluded house. From what he could figure, no one had seen them arrive or leave. Alexander seemed to know how to cover his bases when they went to visit her. When he came out of the bedroom and announced they were leaving, Kevin got in the car without question. He had no idea if Alexander left any evidence in the bedroom. Finally, he couldn't stand being quiet any longer.

"I didn't know you were going to kill her."

"I told you I had some scores to settle, and I would need your help. They're not all going to be as easy as she was, so I'll be needing more of your help with the others."

"There are other ways of getting revenge. I don't want any part of this! I don't want to help you kill people. Just let me out right here, and I'll disappear."

Alexander jerked the car over to the side of the road, almost causing it to spin.

"Shut up and listen to me right now! First, if it weren't for me, you would probably be dead by now either from an overdose, starvation, or a bad john. Second, you're in this with me, like it or not. The people we're going after betrayed me. I helped them, and they turned their backs on me. If you're planning to do the same, you will end up just like them. You see me as a murderer? What about the FBI? They tried to kill me, and they succeeded with one of my people when they destroyed my building. Not to mention all the jobs they took from innocent people. They're trying to justify what they did by going to my assistants and dropping their charges in exchange for information so they can do a report that makes them look good. There is no difference between myself and them except that what they do will somehow be protected under the law, and I have to hide. Understand?"

Kevin nodded, and they were back on the road.

A long time later, Kevin spoke again. "Tell me the real story of the friend and the woman and about the FBI. I think I at least deserve to know."

"The friend, I really considered my best friend. He saved my life; he ran both of my businesses expertly. I trusted him more than I ever trusted anyone. As I told Shalayah, he was an FBI agent, out to destroy me the whole time. The woman was an agent who was picking up a computer chip to use with my self-destruct code to blow up my building. My men captured her before she could obtain the chip. Seeing her in my interrogation room trying so hard to be strong and seeing the fear in her eyes, I knew right away what I wanted to do. I strapped her to a table and fucked her. All three of us had sex with her in one form or another. You have no idea what it's like taking a federal agent, a symbol of the law, and reducing her to the level of a common street whore." He smiled at the memory. "I enjoyed it so much, I was planning to let her live and keep her for myself. A mistake I will remedy."

Alexander glanced at Kevin. "Don't look at me like that. She couldn't have hated it that bad! Leo had me force her to her knees and made her give him head, and the two are together a lot these days. Through them, the Feds destroyed both my legal business and my explosives manufacturing business."

Kevin felt sick. He was in too deep, and he knew it. He didn't speak again the rest of the night. He figured out early on that Alexander had been involved in something illegal which didn't bother him given his own background, but what he knew now was too much.

*   *   *

They drove on through the dark desert; Alexander focused on the road ahead. He often dreamt of life with

Rachel. She would have done anything he asked, anything from simply putting out, to fulfilling his darker fantasies. She would have either submitted or been forced, it didn't matter to him. He had desires most partners wouldn't accommodate. With her, willingness would not have been an issue.

He pressed the accelerator to the floor.

*   *   *

At 5:00 a.m. Rachel awoke to answer her phone.

"Rachel, it's Mark. I'm offering you a case, but if you don't want it, I understand."

"What's the case?"

"One of Alexander Hargrove's accomplices was attacked some hours ago. Her name is Shalayah Michaels. Longview and Davis took her statement a few months ago. She's alive and in surgery at Palomar Hospital. Her brother Larnell called us after his daughter Carla found her. Apparently, he knew Shalayah talked to us, and that's why he called. It may be a police matter, but I want you to see what you can find out."

"I'll get right on it."

Rachel was already trying to think through the case as she hastily dressed. Shalayah was attacked. She gave her statement to Charles and Austin. Her brother knew she had talked to the FBI. Who else knew? Was her attack even related to HARTECH? She would do what she could to answer those questions.

*   *   *

Rachel made her way to Palomar Hospital's surgical floor where she found Shalayah's brother and his wife sitting with a Fallbrook Police officer who had driven out with them. On another couch sat their daughter, Carla, a dull-eyed teen-age girl wearing a spandex halter-top and a matching mini skirt.

Rachel introduced herself to Larnell and Bonnie Michaels, then walked over and sat down next to the girl. "I understand you found your aunt after she was attacked. Can you tell me from the beginning what happened?"

"Well, I was out partying, and it got late, so I knew Mom and Dad would have me locked out. They don't like me to be out drinking, especially on school nights, but I was going to ditch anyway. Auntie Shalayah lets me sleep on her couch when I'm locked out. I have a key, so I let myself in and told her I was there." Her eyes filled with tears, and she took a minute to put the rest of the story together. "She didn't answer me. She always says something. I went to her door and opened it a crack. . .She was all cut up."

"That's when she called 9-1-1, then us," Larnell broke in.

"You did the right thing, Carla. What time did you find your aunt?"

"It was about three o'clock." The girl wiped her eyes with the back of her hand.

"Any idea who might have done this to her?" Rachel turned to Larnell.

He sighed. "My sister never hung out with good people. Her friends were always from the dregs of society. Typical story, I guess. We grew up in the ghettos of L.A. She turned to selling drugs. Anyone could have done this."

Alexander's hard face and piercing eyes floated in front of her mind's eye. She would need more proof before allowing herself to focus on him as a suspect. After all, her brother said she had low life friends who could have attacked her.

The doctor came over to them. Larnell, Bonnie, and Carla rushed over to hear what he had to say.

Rachel stood to the side to give them space.

"Is she going to be all right?" Larnell asked.

"She's in a coma. We don't know at this point if she will wake up. If she wakes up, we don't know what condition she'll be in."

Carla began to cry at the news.

"Carla, look at me," her father said. "Shalayah wound up like this because of the choices she made and the friends she chose. Is this the road you want to go down?"

"No."

"Do you understand why I don't want you running around all night partying? Whoever did this is out there. What if they had gotten to you instead? Do you understand why we have the rules for you that we do?"

"Yes, Daddy." She fell sobbing into her parents' arms.

*　　*　　*

After ducking under the yellow tape and unlocking the door, Rachel looked around the living room of Shalayah's house.

It was clear that she kept her place neat and orderly. The furniture was simple, and the pictures on the wall were inexpensive, but she clearly took pride in her home.

Shalayah must have invited her attacker in; there was no sign of forced entry or struggle. Chances are, she knew him. She thought of the would-be killer as "him" because in her years as a detective, she rarely saw women perpetrate attacks such as what was described to her by Carla and the police sergeant. As she made her way to the kitchen, she saw a glass with a soda can beside it and a plate with the last part of a sandwich on it. There were crumbs at two other places at the table, but no plate, glass, or Coke can.

With her gloved hand, she opened the cupboards and saw what she already knew: two plates were missing from the set.

It was hard to tell if two glasses were missing since one could buy glasses in sets of varying numbers. However, the missing plates probably meant two missing glasses. There were two people involved. Officers dusted the whole place for latent fingerprints, but none were found except the victim's. Detectives vacuumed the scene and did not recover anything of any use.

Rachel stepped into the bedroom.

The mattress was bare and stained; the blood-soaked bedding had been removed as evidence. The sight of the bare mattress caused Rachel to shake off a memory that tried to creep into her thoughts. There was a case to clear, so there wasn't time to deal with ghosts from the recent past. When she looked closer at the headboard, she saw the obvious signs of a struggle. She found nicks and scratches on the headboard indicating handcuffs.

But how did she get into the handcuffs? One man could have held her at gunpoint while the other cuffed her. Both men could have overpowered her, then put the cuffs on. Maybe she was willing to be handcuffed to the bed as part of a game only to find out too late that the men weren't playing. One, maybe both, had sex with her because traces of a condom lubricant were found during the medical exam. The memory of Alexander in his green, silk robe came vividly back to her.

Rachel spent another two hours at the little house piecing together what happened but still finding no evidence to identify the attackers. All she had was her suspicion.

*   *   *

Rachel waited for her lunch at the Garden Center Café later that day. She reviewed her notes and thought about the investigation so far. She had to talk to someone. First, she tried Leo and got his voicemail. She was planning to call him later at home anyway, so she decided to wait. Mark was in a meeting and wouldn't be available for hours. Then she called Charles and caught him in the office.

"It's Rachel, do you have a minute?"

"Sure, what's up?"

"I feel like I'm getting nowhere with this case, and I just want to bounce it off someone."

"What do you have so far?"

Rachel flipped her notebook back to the first few pages she wrote that morning.

"I questioned several locals. No one saw anything unusual that evening. The few tourists who visit the Farmer's markets and antique shops during the week were gone around 7:00 p.m. The police interviewed and released the guests at the local hotels early this morning. No one checked in or out late last night at any of the hotels. I'm going to double check the backgrounds of the hotel guests because whoever did this is clearly experienced, so he must have a record. Shalayah was last seen driving home from her job at Rite Aid at 7:30 p.m. Her niece found her barely alive at three o'clock in the morning. No one heard any screams that night, but her house is on the edge of an avocado grove, so I'm not surprised."

"Sounds like you're doing everything you can," Charles said. "You know that many attacks like this go unsolved."

"I know; I just hate it when they're my cases. My next step is to go to Fallbrook Hospital where she was transferred about an hour ago, then Palomar Hospital where she was originally taken and talk to the doctors again."

"Keep after it. You'll figure it out," Charles said.

"Thanks," she said, then disconnected the call.

*   *   *

As Rachel looked over the comatose woman, she got an idea of what Shalayah went through. If she lived, her body would recover but would be left scarred. Who knew what shape her mind would be in if she awoke? According to Larnell, Shalayah was a fighter, which made Rachel optimistic. Hopefully, she would wake up and have the capacity to reveal the identities of the men she had entertained that night. Rachel had seen many victims in her career both living and dead. Her professional detachment was well developed but seeing Shalayah in that condition filled her with an overwhelming sadness.

She drew the blinds just before the tears came.

She hated the ease with which she cried these days. Chantelle told her that when a crying jag came on, it was best not to fight it but to go someplace where she felt safe to let it out. She wondered if she would ever be able to do her job the way she did before. While she cried, her time in the basement storage room came back to her.

Shalayah had kept Rachel from cracking under the pressure of her situation. She turned on a light during the day and turned it off at night, giving her a sense of time she would not have had otherwise. She also came into the cell at times during the day to talk to her. The conversation helped her gain an understanding of her adversary and stay focused.

Now she lay here, victimized worse than Rachel had been, possibly by the same man.

*   *   *

After dinner, Rachel returned home and dialed Leo's number. She told him of the emotions and memories she was struggling with during the investigation.

"I don't know, Leo. I haven't found anything pointing to the attackers. Everything checks out on all hotel guests. I had the evidence we have so far and the case file shipped to our crime lab. I hope they catch something I missed."

Rachel then told him of Shalayah's help during the worst time in her life. "I understand she wasn't the most upstanding citizen and she deserved to serve time, but she didn't deserve what was done to her. I haven't felt so personally involved in a case since I was a rookie."

"Why do you think that is?" asked Leo.

"The only reason I can see is that I know what it is to be a victim, to have things done to you and be unable to do anything about it. I have a real sense of what it must have been like for her."

"Now that you've been there, you may never be able to detach yourself from a case the same way again," Leo said. "Maybe you can use your new outlook to help you do your job better than before."

"Maybe."

CHAPTER NINE

Kevin turned over onto his back and stared at the ceiling of the hotel room. The drawn curtains billowed in the noisy air conditioning, letting light into the dim room. Sleep had been hard to come by since they left Shalayah's house last week. The fact that it was 2 o'clock in the afternoon only added to the problem. He had never been a day sleeper.

The night Alex picked him up, he told him that he wanted nothing more than friendship and a little help settling a score. This is what he meant. Kevin had a lot of time to think during the trip from California to Arizona. Somewhere east of Gila Bend, the magnitude of his situation hit him full force. Alex had no value for human life and in fact enjoyed taking lives when he perceived there was a reason. He had a hit list of seven people: one down, six to go. Now, Kevin was expected to return the favor Alex had done for him and help him kill.

He wished the room with its gaudy, southwestern decor would cave in on them both. He racked his brain for days trying to find a way out. He couldn't just walk to the nearest police station; Alex kept a constant eye on him since their argument leaving Shalayah's house. Running wasn't an option. Even if he ran to the other side of the world, it wouldn't be far enough. The rest of his life would be spent looking over his shoulder and jumping at every sound until the day Alex found him.

Kevin turned to look at Alexander's sleeping form, his chest rising and falling with his even breathing. He knew that on the floor on the other side of Alex's bed was his pistol. He also knew that it was locked up in a travel safe, and he couldn't get to it. Alex always had it locked up unless he was carrying it. Killing Alex had crossed his mind a few times, but he knew this was a fantasy. He didn't have the guts to kill anyone, even Alex. Damn it, he didn't even have the courage to end his own life to get out of his predicament. His only hope was to go along and hope that he would be free when Alex finished his killing spree. Right now, there were six more people on the list.

He turned his face into a pillow and cried.

*   *   *

"How is everything going?" Chantelle asked as Rachel sat down for her weekly appointment.

"Not so great." She leaned her head against the velour back of the couch. "One of Alexander's accomplices lies in a coma, and I can't find anything to identify her attacker. All I have is a gut feeling that it's him. This case has me more on edge than I was before because I at least thought that he was out of the country until Shalayah's attack. I had another nightmare and woke up convinced he was in my apartment. I even got up with my gun and flashlight and searched the place. The truth is, I feel like searching the place every time I come home."

"With all that going on, I'm not surprised," Chantelle said. "Finding her attacker can accomplish one of two things for you. Either you'll find out it was Alexander, then find him and bring him to justice, or you'll find out it was someone else and you can go back to believing that Alexander is still out of the country."

"You're right. I'm just going to keep after it. By the way, last Wednesday night, I realized it had been exactly six months since I was abducted. Leo listened to me nearly all night."

Chantelle's eyes widened. "You talk to him about your feelings surrounding the assault?"

"Yeah, he encourages me to talk about it even when I occasionally get angry at him," Rachel said.

"Considering you are both survivors of the same very evil man, I'm not surprised. Do you get mad at Leo a lot for his part in your attack?"

She shook her head. "Mostly, I'm angry at myself."

"Yourself? That's normal, but why?"

Tears came again to Rachel's eyes. "Why did I go against my better judgment? I knew I didn't want to take that assignment, but I did anyway. Why wasn't I paying attention? I had my gun on me. I've been to some dangerous places and yet this time, on a particularly important assignment, I wasn't aware of all my surroundings. Why didn't I hear the man coming up behind me? This happened because I wasn't on my guard. Because of me, Leo was thrown into a situation where he had to make a quick decision. Now Shalayah's probably fallen victim to Alexander too."

Chantelle let her cry until she got it all out of her system.

"You need to understand that everything that happened is only the fault of two people. Alexander, and secondly, his accomplice Jason. You've dealt very well with letting go of Leo's part, but now you need to concentrate on forgiving yourself and placing blame where it really belongs."

*   *   *

Charles Longview stood in the main lobby with Austin Davis ready to leave for the day. They began discussing the upcoming community outreach project the FBI puts on every year. Jr. FBI Day was a day when kids between the ages of 12 and 17 could tour the building, attend classes taught by the agents and forensics specialists, and participate in various activities. Charles and Austin always gave a class on weapons and explosives.

Out of the corner of his eye, he saw Leo cross the lobby's shiny, sand-colored tile toward them.

"I was considering giving a talk on undercover work that day," Leo said, joining their conversation.

"I don't know if you should do that, Leo," Charles said. "I mean people will have their children there, and I personally wouldn't want you near my daughter or my wife for that matter."

"What's that supposed to mean?"

"It means that while interviewing Shalayah Michaels, we found out what you did to Rachel," Austin said.

Just as the conversation was going to turn ugly, the three men heard a voice behind them.

"Would anyone care to hear from the victim in this deal?"

They turned around and saw Rachel coming toward them.

"As much as I hate referring to myself that way, it's the truth. A while back, a bad situation occurred.

Surviving it took everything I had. Getting out of Hargrove Technologies alive required Leo and me to think on our feet. Because we did, we survived. Leo will never do what he did in there to me or anyone else again. And if I can let go and trust him, then I think you two should be able to as well." Rachel took Leo's hand and held it as she talked.

Charles and Austin looked at each other.

Austin spoke first. "She's right."

The three men shook hands.

"In my military and FBI careers, I've been in some pretty tough situations where I had to think quickly myself. I guess I should have thought about that. Rachel, I'm sorry we had to find out, even though you didn't want us to," Charles said.

"It's all right. I'm coming to a place where I don't feel the need to keep it a secret."

Charles nodded, then he and Austin headed for the parking garage.

*   *   *

When Charles and Austin left, Rachel turned to Leo. "I'm sorry I had to do that. I know some men are uncomfortable with a woman coming to their defense," she said.

"It's okay. I think you made working with those guys a lot better. Since they interviewed Shalayah several months ago, they've been barely polite."

Leo and Rachel walked out to the tiled courtyard and sat down on one of the planters that held an immature tree. Behind them, Horton Plaza was starting to crowd with after work shoppers. Leo looked up at the high-rise hotels and bank buildings that surrounded them.

"Rachel, I don't know how you can defend me after what I did to you. I appreciate it, believe me, but I don't understand it."

"Let me ask you some questions. Had you ever forced your way sexually with a woman before our encounter?"

"No, definitely not."

"Were you so turned on by the experience of assaulting me that you've repeated it with someone else since then?"

"No. I've never had the desire to be with someone who didn't want to be with me. Even the couple of times in my life that I picked up a woman in a bar, I at least knew she wanted me for the evening and would enjoy herself too."

"I used to date one of the best sex crimes detectives in San Diego. Through him, and through the Bureau, I've learned what a rapist is. A rapist is someone who gets off on his power over his victims. Someone who is turned on because he gets what he wants despite his victim's unwillingness. I meant every word I said to Austin and Charles. You'll never do it again. Your body may have been able to perform, but you didn't enjoy it. You're not a rapist, Leo and I suggest you stop seeing yourself as one. Those guys are treating you the way they are because you're letting them. In your mind, you deserve it, and I'm telling you, you don't. You were assaulted too."

*   *   *

Parked between streetlights, Alexander looked up at the second-floor apartment in the upscale complex near Arrowhead Mall in Glendale, Arizona. He had been watching the place for a week now. The area, with its man-made lakes and golf courses, looked about right for Alan Solano. The smooth talking, former contact person in his business always liked to appear wealthy. He often acquired things he could barely afford. Alan and his girlfriend entertained almost every night even into the late hours. On this Friday morning, the apartment was quiet with only the living room light on. At this early hour, no one was out walking around. A light midnight breeze welcomed the two men when they exited the stuffy car.

Alexander turned to Kevin. "Let's go. Just follow my lead and do what I tell you."

Kevin said nothing, only nodded.

The two men climbed the stairs and rang the doorbell.

*　　*　　*

Rachel sat bolt upright in bed. The clock on her night table read 4:00 a.m. In a few hours, she would be getting up for Jr. FBI Day. She rested her head on her knees and breathed deeply, trying to calm herself. Her nightshirt was soaked in sweat. Another nightmare. In this one, she was in a large building alone. When she reached the main exit, Alexander was there to block the door. She drew her pistol only to realize there were no bullets loaded. She ran, but every time she reached an exit, he was always there blocking it. Over what seemed to be an intercom system, the words of Jason as he violated her rang through the room.

"I own your ass, bitch. We're not stopping 'till we're good and finished with you. You're a whore, aren't you, Rachel? You like being done this way."

Remembering those words made Rachel want to tear a phonebook in half. Alexander always appeared larger in her dreams than he was in real life. He was an average sized man standing about 5' 10", but in the dream, he was big enough to block the whole door.

Rachel got up and applied a cold washcloth to her forehead and neck. Trickles of water ran down her face, chest, and back, cooling her, and calming the effects of the dream. After sponging herself off, she changed her nightshirt.

It was interesting to her that Leo never seemed to be in any of her nightmares. Chantelle said that it was the result of her forgiving him. Rachel would miss her counseling appointments now that Chantelle was on maternity leave with her newborn son. She was working hard at her own healing and knew she could hang on until her counselor returned. Leo was always available when she really needed to talk.

Rachel crawled back in bed and switched off the light.

*   *   *

The FBI building was alive with excited kids and parents on the Saturday morning of Junior FBI Day. Rachel's class on the pickup and delivery of information was a success. Every year, she ended up giving the class at least three times due to the number of kids who wanted to attend. She stepped out into the long hallway for a break before her third class began. Once outside the room she saw Leo walking down the hall.

She called out to him. "How is your class going?"

"I don't know. I'm not sure I know how to talk to kids."

Just when he said that two teen age boys walked by. "Agent Acratelli! I want your job someday!" one of them said.

"Sounds like you really bombed."

While they talked, a blonde-haired, brown-eyed girl ran toward them. "Rachel!"

"Pamela! It's great to see you." She returned the girl's hug.

"I'm taking your class today, right now."

"Oh? Didn't you take it last year?"

"Yeah, but I like the way you talk to us kids and the way you explain your job, so I want to take it again."

Pamela noticed Leo and motioned that she wanted Rachel to lean down so she could whisper something to her.

Then in a whisper loud enough for him to hear, she said, "Is that your boyfriend?"

Leo looked a little uncomfortable.

"He's my friend." Rachel introduced Leo to the girl.

In another loud whisper, she said, "He's cute. You should go out with him."

Pamela went into the room and took her seat, still giggling. Rachel said goodbye to Leo and turned to go into the classroom.

She wasn't sure if she saw embarrassment or hopefulness in Leo's eyes when Pamela commented on the two of them.

*   *   *

When the Jr. FBI festivities were over, Rachel went to her squad room to do some follow up work on Shalayah's case. By the time she left the building, it was nearly dark. As she drove from downtown toward Mission Bay, she noticed a red, midsize car that always seemed to be either directly behind her or a few cars back. When she got on the San Diego Freeway, the red car did the same. Rachel took a deep breath.

She knew nobody would tail in a red car. There could have been a million places he or she could be going.

Instead of exiting the San Diego Freeway onto Highway 8, she exited at Garnet Avenue. The red car followed, but when she turned left on Ingram Street, the other car turned right on Foothill Blvd. toward La Jolla.

Rachel pulled up behind her apartment and let herself calm down before she got out of her car. She hated how scared she got these days. Sometimes, the slightest thing made her wonder if someone could hurt her again. In her line of work, there was always the chance of someone she helped put away coming back to stalk her. So far it hadn't happened, and she always knew she would handle it if it did. Now, she wasn't so sure. It would take time for her to regain her confidence.

There was a time when she was so self-assured, she almost believed she could handle anyone. She rested her head on the steering wheel and thought back to one such time. Three years ago, she was leaving a wedding reception in downtown San Diego. When she was halfway into the parking lot, her peripheral vision picked up a man deliberately trying to match her pace. To test this, she varied her steps. He would speed up and slow down according to the speed she walked.

Instead of panicking, she stopped, faced him, and flashed her badge. "Do you want to mess with a federal agent?" she asked looking him right in the eye.

"Shit!" He ran off.

She hurried to her car and tailed him while calling her ex-boyfriend at work.

"Brad, it's Rachel."

"Yeah, Rachel, what's up?"

"Some guy just tried to mess with me in the parking lot of the Hyatt on Harbor Drive. I'm following him now and thought I'd call in his description in case you're looking for him."

"Fire away," he said. "I've got a pen and notepad."

"Okay, he's a Caucasian male, mid to late 20s, approximately six feet tall and 200 to 225 pounds, dark brown hair, brown eyes, wearing a white San Diego Padres jersey."

"Did you say a white Padres jersey?"

"Yeah."

"Must be his lucky shirt. Two women in the last two months were raped by a man fitting that description wearing a white Padres jersey. Where is he now?"

"He's heading East on G street. Right now, he's in front of Horton Plaza heading for fifth Ave."

"My partner's alerting dispatch. Thanks, Rachel."

"No problem."

She followed the man until a uniformed officer arrested him.

During that encounter, she had no fear. The thought that he might succeed in assaulting her never entered her mind.

She got out of her car and slammed the driver's side door. Alexander Hargrove had changed a lot of things for her, and she hated him for it.

CHAPTER TEN

Sunday morning dawned cloudy and calm, but by the afternoon, the sun was out, and a gentle ocean breeze had kicked up. After such a busy weekend, Rachel decided to spend the afternoon sailing Mission Bay. When she arrived at the Seaforth Boat Rental counter to see what was available, she noticed Leo at the dock talking to a young employee. When she approached, she realized they were trying to find a life vest to fit Leo's large frame.

"Hi, Rachel," the buxom strawberry blonde said, smiling.

"Hi, Charlene. Leo, I see you took my suggestion to rent here."

"Yeah, this is a good place to rent from. You were right. I've got that baby ready to go. Would you like to join me?" he asked pointing to an 18-foot Capri with blue, yellow, and white sails.

"Sure." She fastened her own life vest over her red, one-piece bathing suit and black spandex shorts.

They started out toward the Hyatt that stood at the mouth of the docking inlet. Rachel worked the jib lines while Leo steered and worked the main sail.

She loved the activity of the bay on a Sunday afternoon.

As they passed Vacation Island, they listened to the music coming from the club and waved at people lounging outside their vacation condominiums. Once they passed the sprawling homes near the Riviera section of the bay, they switched places.

Rachel marveled at how well they sailed together. They ran the little boat like a well-oiled machine. She had sailed with other experienced sailors and became frustrated at how they wouldn't communicate with her. Usually, ropes would become tangled, or the timing would be off causing the sails not to work together properly.

They utilized the wind that kicked up and took the boat to its top speed. Every time they ran into oncoming waves, cold ocean spray washed over the bow, splashing them both.

They were laughing and smiling when they returned to the dock after two hours. When the boat bumped the dock, Rachel lost her balance and fell against Leo. He put his hands on her shoulders to steady her, then helped her up onto the dock.

They were both chilled from the wet clothes and the cool early evening. Leo suggested they walk across the street to the Red Hen restaurant and get some coffee. They were seated near a window overlooking flower beds planted with every color imaginable.

"So how long have you been sailing?" Leo asked.

"Since I was a kid. My father taught me."

"You're quite good at it."

"Thanks, you are too."

"Sounds like you and your father had a great relationship."

She smiled at her memory of him. "We did. He was so proud of me the day I graduated from the Police Academy. Sometimes, I would call him and vent about how hard it was dealing with some of the male officers. Instead of telling me to quit like my mom always did, he would tell me to get out there and just prove how good I was no matter what they said."

"I don't envy you being a former female cop. I've seen how rough it can be for women."

"It can. I remember when my father was ill. I was working homicide and trying to keep my clearance rate up while spending every day off helping my mom take care of him. Needless to say, I was stressed out. While catching up on paperwork, I spilled coffee all over a report. A few colorful words came out of my mouth just as a rookie with an attitude walked by. His comment was 'Whoa, break out the Kotex!'"

Leo's jaw dropped. "What did you do?"

"First off, the guys I worked with knew what I was going through, so they turned icy toward him. That helped. As far as what I did, you know how detectives are always getting uniforms to dumpster dive for them?"

"Yes, I had to dig through trash for evidence plenty of times," he said. Then realization washed over his face, "No, you didn't do that, did you?"

"Every time I needed it for the next six months, he was the guy I chose."

"Well, he had it coming." Leo laughed.

*   *   *

When Rachel returned to her apartment, she turned on the TV and flipped channels to find something to quiet her emotions. It made sense why she and Leo had become friends. The other emotions surrounding him didn't. Every time she looked into his oval face and warm brown eyes, she felt like part of her would melt. When he had touched her to help her keep her balance, she tingled. She stirred up inside when she studied his strong hands or his broad shoulders and chest. Feelings she thought were long asleep seemed to have resurfaced. She hadn't felt this way since she started dating Brad so many years ago.

*   *   *

Mark was working late in his office. Su Lee offered to stay, but he knew she wanted to go home to her family, so he told her he would be fine. His phone rang. He considered not answering it and continuing with his work, but he thought it might be his wife, so he picked it up.

"FBI, Special Agent in Charge."

"Yes, my name is Sam Colson of the Glendale P.D. in Arizona. I'm investigating a double homicide, and one of the victims is connected to one of your cases. According to our records, you gave him immunity for his testimony about a case."

After hearing the name Alan Solano, Mark knew he was one of the Hargrove Technologies employees.

"Tell me everything you have."

"That's the problem. We don't have much. No one saw anything. A few neighbors heard some yelling, but apparently, that wasn't too unusual. The killer gagged the male victim before torturing him to death. Forensics found traces of a leather gag in his mouth and throat. The female victim was shot, but no one heard gunfire, so the perpetrator must have used a sound suppressor."

"You retain jurisdiction for now. I'll be sending one of our agents out in a few days to look at the evidence. It may be related to our case, and if it is, we will take over."

After Mark hung up the phone, an uncomfortable thought came creeping over him. He continued reading reports but couldn't focus long enough to understand what he read. He had to talk to Leo.

He dialed the phone. "Leo, it's Mark. Alan Solano was found brutally murdered last night. Do you have any input about who may have done this?"

"Not really. Many people were out to get him."

"The details of the murder match Alexander's modus operandi, just like the attack on Shalayah. Alan was tortured whereas his girlfriend was shot. So, Alan was the real target and Tracy Sawhill was just in the way."

"What's your plan?"

"Rachel took Shalayah's case. I'm thinking of offering her this one too. This murder and Shalayah's attack will be part of the HARTECH case file."

"That makes sense. I think Rachel will be glad that you see her as strong enough to take Alan's case."

"I do see her as strong enough." Mark disconnected the call.

*   *   *

Rachel threw away the remains of a turkey sandwich and took a few deep breaths.

This was the night she decided to call and tell her mother about the horrific events that took place six months ago. At first Rachel decided never to tell her, knowing she would be more insistent about her quitting her job. Ever since Rachel's parents learned that she was serious about law enforcement, there were conflicts between mother and daughter. Every time a police officer was killed in the line of duty, Rachel found the newspaper article clipped out and placed on her chair at the table. She would then make sarcastic comments about how she could die in other professions.

"You know mom, if I became a teacher, a kid could run with a pair of scissors, trip, and throw the scissors exactly right so they stab me in the heart. It could happen."

Over the years, the two women ironed out their differences. Rachel's mother learned to accept her daughter's career, and Rachel learned to accept her mother's worry as a maternal right. Since then, she and her mother had a good relationship, and she was not used to keeping things from her. For this reason, Rachel decided to tell her when she was ready, and tonight she was.

She dialed the phone.

"Keaney residence, Elaine speaking."

She never knew why her mother still answered the phone that way now that she lived alone.

"Hi, Mom it's me."

"Hi, honey. You sound upset. What's wrong?"

"There's something I have to tell you, and if you could please not fall apart, that would be helpful."

"You're scaring me, Rachel, please tell me."

"A little over six months ago, I was raped." Tears streamed down her face.

"No," was all Elaine Keaney could say before she broke down.

Mother and daughter cried together.

When the two women regained their composure, they talked again.

"When?" her mother asked.

"In March, while I was on an assignment."

"Have there been any arrests made?"

"It's still being worked out. Unfortunately, that's all I can tell you. The Bureau's been very good to me through this whole thing."

There was a moment of silence on the line. "I'm glad you didn't quit the FBI over this."

"You are?"

"Yes. You're not letting the man who hurt you destroy everything you worked for. The truth is women are raped every day. Had you been a secretary or a nurse, or anything else this still could have happened."

"That's true enough. I'm so glad you feel that way. I was worried you'd try again to convince me to quit."

"I've been thinking about that recently. I've been letting my worry blind me to the fact that you're doing what you love. You just keep doing what you're doing and enjoying it."

Rachel smiled at the words she'd been dying to hear since her teen years.

Her mother continued, "If you had told me about this when it happened, I would have flown out to be with you."

"I know you would have, but I wasn't ready to tell anyone when it first happened."

"Why? You didn't do anything wrong."

"I understand that. Just know that my reasons for not telling you had nothing to do with you. It was a normal stage that I had to go through."

They talked for a few more minutes, and when Rachel hung up, she felt a sense of peace and a deeper connection to her mother.

*   *   *

Rachel arrived at her squad room the next morning to find an urgent message from Mark on her voicemail. She was to see him in his office as soon as she got the message. When she went to his office, she could see the concern in his blue eyes.

"I need you to investigate two murders. You're going to be in Glendale, Arizona for probably two days."

While Mark gave her the flight times and hotel information, he shuffled papers on his desk.

"Mark, what is it? You're not usually this agitated when you give me an assignment."

"One victim's name is Alan Solano; he's connected to Hargrove Technologies. The other victim is his girlfriend, Tracy Sawhill. It looks like the same person who attacked Shalayah may have killed Alan and Tracy, I'm not sending Davis or Longview on this case because I need them full time searching for the other three accomplices. Quite frankly, I'm worried for their safety. I even have my suspicions that one of them could be the killer. If anyone can put this case down quickly, it's you. The sooner we figure out what's going on the better."

*   *   *

Rachel and Leo stood on the deck of Rachel's apartment watching some families play in the water. The sun was going down behind her apartment on a rapidly cooling Tuesday evening.

For the last several months, the two agents had spent a lot of time together. They found reasons to see each other on some evenings and most weekends.

"How is HARTECH coming?" Rachel asked.

"It's moving along. I understand you're leaving for Arizona tomorrow to look into Alan's murder."

"Yeah, I hope I can clear it quickly."

"I know you'll do your best," he said looking into her eyes.

She smiled up at him. He held her gaze, then looked out at the families. He had not looked away quickly enough because she saw a look he seemed to be trying to hide from her.

"Leo, it seems that you want to say something, and it's driving me crazy because you won't say it."

"To be honest, I'm afraid to."

Now he was looking directly into her eyes. "When I got your forgiveness, I felt like the luckiest man alive. When I got your friendship, I couldn't believe it. Now I'm supposed to push my luck and tell you that what I feel for you is stronger than friendship? When you walk into a room, and I haven't even seen you, I know you're there because I can feel it. When you're around, I feel like a crazy teenager again. To expect you to return those feelings would be asking way too much."

"I'll be the judge of whether it's asking too much." She reached up and placed her lips softly on his.

Leo pulled her close and returned her kiss as if a dam holding back his emotions had burst. Rachel felt her body melt and her heart soar just as the sun slipped below the horizon.

*   *   *

Later that evening, Laura Galloway sat in her living room with a strong drink in one hand and a cordless phone in the other. The lights were dim, obscuring the prints of forest scenes that adorned her walls. The hunter-green throw rugs were dark patches on the tan carpet. Even in the dim light, she could clearly see the new emerald tennis bracelet that adorned her wrist. The jewelry store had one just like it with sapphires, and a slightly different one with rubies. She remembered taking an hour to decide which one to buy.

Her eyes traveled from the bracelet to the phone. Earlier that evening she dialed Mark's home number but hung up before the call went through. How many other times had she been in this same position, sitting on the couch ready to call Mark and tell him everything?

When she first started working for Alexander, it was simple. She would call him and tell him when his company was going to be searched. The agents always came back empty handed. When his illegal business grew, a few agents stumbled upon bits and pieces of evidence, but nothing that amounted to a conviction.

Laura never looked at the plaques that lined the hallways on the first and second floors. Each plaque had the name of an agent killed in the line of duty. Some of the names tore at her heart. Two agents posing as buyers were killed because she tipped off Alexander. Rachel was another matter altogether. She wasn't a memorial on the wall but living, breathing evidence of her guilt.

Rumors circulated about what happened to Rachel during her disappearance. Laura ignored them until she sifted through the HARTECH files and stumbled upon Rachel's testimony.

As hard as she tried to look past that report, the temptation became too great, and she read it from beginning to end. The testimony explained a lot: the dark cloud over Rachel, the tension between Rachel and Leo. She was very different after she returned to work in April. Why did Su Lee have to be sick that day?

If Su Lee had been at work that day, Laura would never have known about the assignment regarding Hargrove Technologies. She looked at the phone in her hand and moved her thumb to the redial button when suddenly, she threw the phone to the other end of the couch.

There was no way she was going to wake Mark up and confess to what she had been doing and lose everything. Rachel, as well as the other agents, knew there were dangers involved in the job. Rachel had to realize that she ran certain risks being a beautiful woman and going to some of the places she went. She was just lucky she lived through it as Alexander was not known for leaving those who crossed him alive. Besides, Rachel was dealing with everything very well. The dark cloud seemed less prominent, and any tension between her and Leo was gone. They seemed to be very much at ease in each other's presence.

The turn of events was not Laura's fault, and she was not going to betray Alexander. She knew if she did, he would seek revenge on her. Even if she went to prison, he would find a way to get to her.

She finished her drink and went upstairs to get ready for bed. She eyed her new bracelet again before taking it off and putting it in the wall safe. This weekend, she would go buy the sapphire and ruby bracelets.

CHAPTER ELEVEN

Rachel flew to Phoenix Sky Harbor Airport where Sam Colson picked her up and took her to the scene of the double homicide.

Being used to San Diego's temperate climate, she found the late September heat stifling.

While she walked the scene that was days old, her jaw began to tighten. Again, there were no fingerprints or any other physical evidence. There was no sign of forced entry, but no sign of entertaining either. The killers must have gotten right down to business this time. "I'm not finding anything here. I need to talk to the M. E. and look at the evidence in the crime lab," Rachel said to Sam.

*　　*　　*

The conversation with the Medical Examiner was more encouraging than the walk through.

"It seems to me the female victim, Tracy Sawhill, tried to defend her boyfriend," the Medical Examiner said. "There were traces of skin under her fingernails. She pulled some hair too. It seems when the killer got her off him, she ran to the kitchen to call the police or get a weapon. That's probably when he shot her, judging from the position of the body when we found it. The killer or killers, as you suspect, may have tried to get rid of the hair, but they didn't get it all."

As Rachel examined the photos, she recognized Alan as the younger of the two men who abducted her.

"Let's hope there's some with a root attached so we have some DNA evidence. I wish there was a fingerprint. The hair and skin samples only do us some good if there is a match on file. We're more likely to have prints on file," said Rachel.

"The killers were wearing gloves. Traces of the latex powder were found on Alan Solano's body," the coroner said.

"Were his wounds inflicted ante mortem or postmortem?" Rachel asked looking over the autopsy photos.

"Judging from the tissue reaction, I would say ante mortem. He was probably conscious for a lot of it," replied the coroner.

The file, hair, and skin samples were sent to the FBI crime lab where Rachel hoped the DNA specialists would find a match.

*   *   *

At about 5:30 p.m., Alexander's cell phone rang. He sat up in bed, rubbed his eyes, and answered it. "Yeah?"

"It's Laura. Did I wake you?"

He yawned. "I usually get up around this time. My current work requires me to sleep days and work nights."

"You may or may not know this, but two of your former people wound up dead, or I should say one is nearly dead. She's in a coma, and we don't know if she will recover. I don't want to know if you're involved," Laura said.

"What do the Feds know?"

"Nothing right now, but I thought you might like to know who's heading the investigation...Rachel Keaney."

There was a pause on the line. "Isn't that an interesting twist of fate," Alexander said.

"Have they found any of my other people yet?"

"No, they're still looking."

"That makes two of us. Thanks for the tip."

When Alexander hung up the phone, he spent a few more minutes lying on his pillow topped bed.

He knew two things for sure: he had to find the three remaining accomplices before The FBI could get to them, and he would have to be especially careful about covering his tracks. Through Laura, he knew that Rachel had a tendency to find things others missed.

*   *   *

On a Friday afternoon, Rachel flew back to San Diego where she briefed Leo, Austin, and Charles on her findings, or rather, lack thereof.

"From the looks of Shalayah and Alan's bodies, it appears as if the same person perpetrated both attacks," Rachel said. "Evidence suggests that there were two people involved."

After looking at the photos, Leo said, "This looks a lot like Alexander's work. Which leads me to two theories. One of our three missing persons is the killer and is imitating his work, or Alexander's back in the country. That makes the most sense."

"I have a question," Rachel said while pouring a cup of coffee. "Leo, you said you and Jason were the only witnesses when he did his killings. How would another accomplice know what to do to imitate him?"

"Jason was a big talker," Leo replied. "He enjoyed watching the killings as much as Alexander enjoyed doing them. I wouldn't put it past him to describe Alexander's method to someone."

"Leo, is there anyone you know of who would kill to avenge Alexander?" Austin asked.

"It's hard to say. People were loyal to him for a mixture of reasons. They were grateful to him for helping them hide from authorities or enemies. Once they were in with him, they were afraid of what he might do if they crossed him. He also took very good care of those who were loyal. Since the explosion, those factors no longer come into play, so I don't see why any of the accomplices would seek revenge for him. Jason is the only one I could see killing for Alexander. Jason came to him to avoid rape charges in Detroit. He had some weird admiration of Alex; he lived to please him."

"But none of this helps us now because it's been confirmed that Jason died in the explosion," Charles said.

"I'll keep poring over the evidence and interviews while you search for the three missing persons. Let's hope we find them before anyone else gets killed," Rachel said.

When the meeting was over Leo waited until he and Rachel were alone. She smiled at him thinking he was there to steal a kiss, but then she saw the serious look on his face.

"What is it?" she asked putting the case file in her briefcase.

"I don't want to think this way, but if Alex is behind these attacks, then we're on his list of intended victims." Leo replied.

"I've been thinking the same way. If you were the only one aside from him who knew the code, then he'd have to know you betrayed him. He probably researched the explosion and knows that I escaped, which means he'd want to finish me off too."

"I wanted to believe that he fled the country and would never come back. Now that we have two victims with his signature on them, I can't even try to believe that."

"We still have three accomplices who could be killing to cover their tracks. They could be using Alexander's method to throw us off." Rachel squeezed his hand.

"Maybe, but I don't think so," Leo said, giving her a quick peck before going to his squad room.

CHAPTER TWELVE

After forty-five minutes of taking in the wonderful scent of cooked seafood at Anthony's Fish Grotto, Rachel and Leo got a table overlooking the ocean. The lights of various ships showed in the distance on the peaceful waters. That night at dinner, they talked of anything but the cases they were on. The last several days had been stressful for her, and it was nice to just relax.

"How's your family?" Rachel asked between bites of sourdough bread.

"Great. In fact, I talked to my brother on the phone last night just to catch up." "Which one?"

"Michael. He's two years older than I am. I consider him my best friend. He's a hairdresser in San Francisco. I know you're probably thinking, 'hairdresser in San Francisco?'" Leo let his wrist go limp.

"Actually, I wasn't thinking that," Rachel said, smiling.

"You'd be the first, then. He's married with four kids. He and his wife own the shop."

"Sounds nice. I talked to my mom this afternoon. She's been sending me articles and books to help me recover. I'm so glad she's no longer trying to convince me to quit my job. That battle's been going on for years." She rolled her eyes.

"I have this feeling that few outside forces change your mind once it's made up." Leo made room for their dinner plates as they arrived.

"I got it from my father. He's the one who encouraged me to be a detective. He could see that I had a problem-solving mind and encouraged it any way he could. He would send me on these crazy treasure hunts all over the neighborhood, then later all over town, complete with clues and codes I had to figure out. Of course, neither of my parents knew how serious I was until they were called into a meeting with my school principal because I got into the school files and collected information on the teachers."

"What were you going to do with the information?"

"Nothing, I just wanted to see if I could get it. I nearly got away with it except that I left the notebook I was using in my desk, and my teacher found it."

While she talked, Rachel noticed that Leo was looking at her with a sparkle in his eye.

"What?" she asked.

"I was just thinking that you must have looked dynamite in a blue uniform."

She smiled and looked down for a minute.

*　　*　　*

After dinner the two detectives decided to walk the Gas Lamp Quarter, which was packed with partiers dressed to the nines, just like every Friday night. As they passed the bars and clubs that dotted the historic section of downtown, Rachel became pensive. Leo must have noticed because he suggested that they go to his apartment where it was quieter.

Rachel had been in Leo's apartment many times, yet tonight, it felt different. There was an electricity in the room that hadn't been there before. She didn't know if she wanted to say a quick good night or stay and drink in the energy that circulated in the air.

Her thoughts were interrupted by Leo's strong arms encircling her and pulling her to him so her back rested against his chest. He began to caress her arm from the hand to the shoulder.

"Why don't we go relax on the couch?" he whispered.

Without a word, she allowed him to lead her to his black leather sofa where he kissed her and continued stroking her arms and back.

"Wait a minute," she said, pulling away a little.

"Is everything all right? If I did something or you're struggling again, I would like to hear about it."

Rachel gave him a small smile. "You didn't do any-thing wrong, but there is something we haven't talked about yet."

"Whatever it is, I'm listening."

"About five years ago, my long-term relationship ended. We broke it off together because it wasn't going to work. After that, I decided not to fully have sex again until I was married. I began to realize that it's not smart to make such a strong emotional investment without a lifetime commitment. The problem is I'm scared that I won't like being touched after everything that's hap-pened. Part of me wants to have sex to find out, but the rest of me knows it's a bad idea to do it for that reason."

"I agree that you shouldn't change your decision based on what happened. Considering what we have been through together, we both need to take the physical side of our relationship slowly. We've only been officially dating for about week, so I certainly wasn't expecting anything this soon. No matter where our dating goes, I'll be the last guy to pressure you sexually. It's been a rough week for you. Why don't you lie down on the couch, and I'll give you a back rub?"

She lay down on the couch and let him run his hands over her back. She knew for a lot of men, the offer of a back rub was the perfect lead into more intimacy. She also knew this was not the case with Leo. He would stop at her signal. He started squeezing her shoulders, but this made her tense up more.

"Are you okay?"

"Yes, but I think you squeezing my shoulders is reminding me of being grabbed."

"I'll move to your back again," he whispered.

He began with his fingertips, then his whole hand in smooth, massaging motions.

She couldn't remember feeling so cared about by a man in her life.

As his large hands moved to her feet, she felt the tension leave her body. Sometime between his stroking the backs of her legs and her arms, she fell asleep. About 20 minutes later' she awoke and found Leo in a chair reading a *Guns and Ammo* magazine.

"I must have fallen asleep, I'm sorry."

"You don't need to apologize," he said, then kissed her. "Do you have any idea how honored I feel knowing that you can relax enough under my touch to fall asleep?"

She smiled shyly then reached out her hand.

Leo rose from his chair and took his place beside her.

They spent the rest of the evening talking and holding each other.

Rachel drove to her apartment feeling very relieved that one of her questions had been answered. When she was raped, she felt like she would never want a man near her again. Her falling asleep under Leo's caresses made her realize that positive physical closeness after a vicious assault was possible. She shut her apartment door feeling very much at peace.

*   *   *

The following Monday evening, Rachel was about to exit the FBI building for the day. Thoughts of the wonderful weekend drifted around in her mind.

Sandy, the main receptionist, caught up with her and interrupted her daydream. "Can I walk with you to your car?"

"Sure."

"Maybe it's none of my business, but did you and Laura have some sort of falling out?" The willowy blonde looked around and lowered her voice. "Maybe I shouldn't be telling you this, but Laura and I went to Horton Plaza yesterday and we saw you there. I told her we should go say 'hi' to you, but she said we didn't have time and we needed to get going. I said that it would only take a minute, then she got mad and said she didn't want to talk to you and insisted that we leave."

"Really?" Rachel pulled her keys from her purse and waved at Austin who drove by with a kayak strapped to the top of his car.

"I-I don't want to cause trouble, it just seemed strange. She wouldn't tell me anything so, I thought maybe you knew what was wrong."

"I don't know any more than you do."

"If you say anything to her, please don't say that I talked to you."

"I won't, I appreciate the information."

*   *   *

A week later, Rachel scanned the crowded lunch-room looking for a table by one of the large windows. Everywhere she looked, she could see jack-o'-lanterns, scarecrows, and skeletons. The rest of the building always looked the same no matter what time of year it was, but the cafeteria always displayed holiday spirit. While she took in the decorations, she spotted Laura at a table by herself and decided to get to the bottom of her strange behavior.

"Can I sit down?" She asked.

"Sure, I was just leaving. I've got so much work to do that I think I'll eat at my desk today."

"Please, I need to talk to you."

Laura's expression turned to that of a trapped animal.

"I can't help but notice that you're uncomfortable around me. If I did something to offend you, I'd like to talk it out." Rachel spoke gently in hopes of getting the other woman to open up.

Laura fingered a beautiful pearl and diamond slider on her necklace. "Ever since you were missing months ago, there have been rumors of what happened to you. I guess I just don't know what to say or how to act around you. That's all."

"I can tell you that the rumors are true. I was raped when I was abducted. I'll always wish it never hap-pened, but I am learning to deal with it. I have three wonderful people helping me through it. My counselor, my boyfriend, and my mother. Telling my mother was so hard because she always worries about me on the job. I told her that I had something to tell her, and I didn't want her to get all upset. Of course. I got one sentence out, and we both broke down. I paid a long-distance phone bill so we could cry together. We're closer now than we've ever been. I suppose the point of all of this is, I'm getting stronger because of working through this mess. The best thing you can do is treat me the way you did before."

Laura's pager went off.

"Oh man, I really do have to go now. Thank you," she said, dumping her tray, including the silverware that should have gone in the cleaning chute, and running out of the room.

Rachel shook her head and sighed. She noticed the subtle hand movement that Laura made causing her own pager to sound. If Laura wasn't willing to tell her the real reason she avoided her, there wasn't much Rachel could do about it.

CHAPTER THIRTEEN

Alexander walked into his home office and tore off yesterday's page from his calendar. Things were not going as he planned. He thought for sure his work here would be done by now and he would be in Canada making new plans for his life. Finding and silencing his former employees was taking longer than he anticipated. Leo had a birthday in November and Rachel turned thirty-four last week on January 8th. They weren't supposed to make it to their birthdays. Maybe having to wait this long would make the event even sweeter.

The good news was, the FBI wasn't having any better luck finding his accomplices. Somehow, Randy Klausen, Zack Williams and Harry Matteson were living their lives and were able to avoid using their Social Security numbers. He had a thought about finding Randy.

Alexander called information to get the number he needed then dialed the phone again. "Playboy customer service, my name is Callie how can I help you?" a girl with a high, squeaky voice answered.

"Yes, my name is Randy Klausen, and I haven't received my January issue. I moved recently, so I'm wondering which address you show for me?"

"How do you spell your last name sir?"

"K-l-a-u-s-e-n."

Callie gave Randy's Durango, Colorado address and promised to have another magazine sent out right away.

Alexander grabbed a map and calculated the distance and time it would take to reach Durango. Why didn't he think of calling Playboy before? He should have figured Randy wouldn't want to miss a single month of "the country's most beautiful women", as he called them.

Then he called to Kevin. "Get packed, we're leaving tonight for Colorado."

*   *   *

A week later, Kevin sat in silence looking down on the neighborhood of shabby, one-story apartments. From their perch at the top of a hill, they could see the comings and goings of the whole area. Alexander studied the neighborhood through his binoculars and took notes on his Palm Pilot. In just a few days of watching, Kevin and Alexander had a good idea of Randy Klausen's schedule and the activities of his neighbors. Things were quiet in the working-class neighborhood at night, so Kevin knew they would strike sometime within the next few nights. He knew he couldn't help Randy, but he had a plan to put a stop to this insanity. If his plan worked, Randy could be their last.

*   *   *

Austin Davis approached the receptionist at the Papago Acres nursing home in Albuquerque, New Mexico.

He showed his FBI credentials. "I understand there is a patient here named Marilynn Klausen. I wondered if I could talk to her."

"Mrs. Klausen had a stroke and is unable to speak. Can I ask about the nature of your visit?"

"She has a son named Randy Klausen, and it is urgent that we find him. Do you have an address for him by any chance?"

"Yes, he came to visit a few months back and left a new address. Luckily, he came by before she had her stroke. I understand they haven't seen each other in a while."

After copying down the address, he dialed Charles' phone number.

"Meet me in Durango as soon as possible. I'm on my way now. The lead to Randy Klausen checked out."

*   *   *

Alexander pulled his coat tighter around him as he and Kevin waited at the paint-chipped door for Randy to answer. The porch light came on and a minute later, Randy, rumpled from sleep, answered. He looked wary when he saw Alexander and his new partner on his doorstep.

"Randy, I know it's late, but I'm passing through and wondered if you had a few minutes for an old friend."

"Sure come in. Would you like anything to drink?"

"No, we can't stay that long." Alexander said as they sat down. "What have you been doing with yourself?"

"Doing what I can to get by, odd jobs for cash and stuff like that. I make enough to stay in this place." He motioned around the small room containing garage sale furniture and an old television. "It's not fancy, but it's warm. I've been keeping my nose clean lately."

"I admire you for that. I don't remember ever being a law-abiding citizen. I'm not sure I would know what to do."

After some small talk and catching up, Alexander stood up. "Well, I think it's time we moved on, Kevin. It's late, and this man has to work in the morning. Randy, maybe someday I'll find what you found and live life on the straight and narrow."

"I hope so," Randy said as he got up to see them out.

They had almost reached the front door when Alexander's fist came up under Randy's jaw like a sledgehammer, knocking him to the ground.

*   *   *

Kevin sat in the tiny, darkened bathroom listening to the dripping faucet until he heard Alexander call him. He always went to another room when the killings took place. At least Alex gagged the last two victims, so he didn't have to hear them.

Kevin emerged from the bathroom to find Alex packing his instruments.

He took off the latex gloves. "Take these and get rid of them later when we're far away. Check and see if I left anything behind. I'm sure I didn't. I'll get the car."

Kevin took a good look around; there were no traces of evidence he could see. Alexander was thorough as usual. Kevin hated being near the bodies after they were dead, but he had to check to see if anything was amiss.

He walked out of the warm apartment into the biting, wintry night. Just before shutting the back door carefully to avoid fingerprints, he dropped one of the latex gloves.

"You have those gloves?" Alexander said when he got into the car.

"Right here," he said, holding up a closed fist to conceal the fact that there was only one glove.

One thing was clear to Kevin: Alexander had to be stopped. But the only time he didn't keep an eye on him was when he went to the car, leaving Kevin to double check for evidence. He remembered the moment the idea occurred to him.

After Alan Solano was dead, Alexander was packing up his instruments. "I think Alan's whore got some of our hair. Check her hands and around her body to make sure you get it all if there is any."

Without a word, Kevin obeyed but left a few hairs behind.

He wasn't sure if the conveniently forgotten evidence would help, he just hoped it would. During the three nights they watched Randy's apartment and waited for the perfect moment to make their move, he thought of other kinds of evidence he could leave behind that might be more substantial. Of course, he knew if Alexander were caught, he would be arrested as an accomplice. That didn't really matter. Many of his friends on the street talked down their sentences by helping the authorities catch a bigger fish. If the FBI was willing to blow up a building just to stop Alexander, they would be willing to deal in exchange for his testimony. Prison wasn't the greatest place to go, but at least he would be alive and safe from Alexander.

*   *   *

The phone rang at 5:30 a.m. Rachel fumbled with the receiver, before answering it.

"Rachel, it's Mark. I need you to get to Lindbergh Field immediately. Davis and Longview found Randy Klausen who worked for Hargrove and went to interview him this morning. They found him dead in his apartment. We're flying you and Leo to Durango by Leer Jet."

"Leo's going to work this with me?"

"Yes. He knew Hargrove's people better than any of us, and he may pick up on something even you might miss."

Rachel changed into a wool pant suit with a cream-colored sweater. She knew winter would be in full swing in Colorado, and she would have to take her navy-blue FBI jacket as well.

After she dressed and put on a little make up, she headed for Lindbergh Field.

*   *   *

Once in Durango, Charles Longview picked up Rachel and Leo and took them to the scene. Randy lived at the end of a row of one story, weather-beaten apartments. Small backyards led to an alley, then to the yards of another row of apartments.

When they arrived, the scene had already been photographed, sketched, and the evidence documented. It was now safe to walk into the house and begin close-up photography and collecting the evidence.

Rachel saw the victim and immediately recognized him as the abductor who helped her out of the trunk in the parking garage.

Leo went with the Medical Examiner to the body and the two men began looking it over.

Rachel stood in the middle of the room and scanned the area. Local authorities were dusting for latent fingerprints, which would probably all belong to the victim, just like the last two scenes.

"Has that glove been documented?' Rachel asked pointing at a crumpled piece of latex hidden between the back door and a small trash can.

"I'll document it and have it photographed," said a uniformed officer helping on the scene. The officer put the crumpled glove in a plastic bag, labeled it, and handed it to Rachel.

"Leo, looks like our killer was careless." She held up the bag with the glove in it. "Let's get this to our lab and have some Sudan Black chemical applied to it."

"Great, we may have something concrete."

Leo led Rachel to a corner of the room. "This may not be Alexander's work. The body looks like something he would do, but he wouldn't be careless enough to leave that kind of evidence behind. So, this still leaves Zack Williams and Harry Matteson as our suspects."

"Well, whoever is doing this is not acting alone so it could be the accomplice making the mistakes," Rachel replied.

Leo nodded.

The body was taken to the local morgue, and arrangements were made for the Medical Examiner's report to be sent to San Diego upon completion. Austin and Charles stayed behind to finish up at the victim's home while Rachel and Leo followed the body to the morgue.

"Most likely, the cause of death is from deep cuts to the throat severing the jugular vein," the Medical Examiner said after photographing and performing an external examination of the body. "From the looks of things, several minor cuts and puncture wounds were made all over the body with different sharp instruments. The killer probably made these wounds before cutting the victim's throat. It seems to me the killer knew where to cut and stab to cause pain and bleeding, but not death, initially. Of course, I'll know more after I've done a complete exam."

"Did you pick up anything from the oral swab?" Rachel asked.

"Yes, traces of material that were probably used as a gag. The lab will have to confirm it, but it looks like leather."

"Just like Alan. So far, Shalayah is the only one who wasn't gagged and who didn't have her throat cut." Rachel took out a notepad.

"Has the time of death been determined?" Leo asked.

"Due to the amount of blood loss, postmortem lividity couldn't be determined. However, judging from the Rigor Mortis that is now in the entire body, I would say he's been dead eight to twelve hours. Any time between one and four a.m."

Rachel began to write as she compared the three deaths and the attempted murder. All the deaths and Shalayah's attack happened late at night into early morning. There was never any sign of forced entry. All but the shooting victim had cuts and puncture wounds. A time of death was easier to determine in Tracy Sawhill's murder. Tracy had been shot in the back of the head and fell face down, so her postmortem lividity, the coagulating and settling of blood to the lowest points on the body, was visible. Her and Alan's bodies were found around six in the morning, and their times of death were around one and three in the morning, respectively. The killers worked at night, like most of them do.

"We're going to embalm and hold the body to see if any signs of a beating before death show up," the examiner continued.

"You'll probably find that he was beaten only enough to subdue him. Just like Alan Solano." Rachel put her pen back in her purse.

"We've got to find those other two guys," was all Leo could say after leaving the medical examiner's office.

He said nothing more the rest of the way back to San Diego.

Rachel knew he was searching his memory for any bit of information that would lead to the remaining survivors. She understood the need of a detective to think without interruption. So instead of trying to engage him in conversation, she looked out of a window and turned her thoughts to what she would do if Alexander tried to get to her.

*   *   *

The next afternoon, just before lunch, Larry Rhyme from the crime lab rang Rachel's office. "Agent Keaney, can you meet me in the lab? We found two sets of prints like you said, and we have matches. I'll call Agent Acratelli."

When she and Leo were in the fingerprint examiner's office, he sat down across from them.

He pushed his glasses up on his nose before he began. "The prints on the outside of the glove belong to Kevin McCray. He's been arrested in Los Angeles over the last two years for petty theft, possession of drugs, and prostitution. Nothing of a violent nature like the crimes you describe. I called the L.A.P.D. He hasn't been arrested or even seen since May. The person who matches the prints inside the glove has been missing since March."

Rachel paled and took hold of Leo's hand. "Who?"

"They belong to an Alexander Hargrove. According to our records, Weapons has been trying to convict him on and off for years."

Rachel didn't hear the last part of his statement over her rapidly beating heart.

"Make sure all of this gets to Special Agent Sergan," Leo said. "Rachel and I are taking the rest of the day off."

*   *   *

Rachel sat on a folding chair on the beach in front of the towering Coronado Shores residential building, watching Leo's newly purchased kite sail high in the air. The two agents had driven to Seaport Village and ate what little they could for lunch. Leo then bought a large orange and yellow kite from Kite Flite. From there, they drove across the bridge to Coronado Island.

"I never knew you liked to fly kites," she said brushing strands of hair out of her face.

"It helps me think."

Then like a tidal wave, words came pouring out of him. "Eight years I worked trying to bring down that bastard and for what? I helped stop some of his deals and eventually destroyed his explosives business. For all I know, he's got another business up and running. Not only that, three people are dead, and one life hangs in the balance because he's on a revenge killing spree. All I wanted to do was put away an extremely dangerous man and now, he's more dangerous than ever. Like I said before, he's gearing up to come after us."

"I know."

"Whoever leaked the information that got you kidnapped is leaking information about us and these cases. I guarantee it. Now that we've confirmed that Alexander is behind these killings, I want you off this case. In fact, I want you to fly to Milwaukee to visit your mother until we catch him."

"No, I want to see him behind bars as much as you do. I will not run and hide from him. I've been doing some thinking about the possibility of coming face to face with him again. If I see him again, I won't be locked in a basement room in the middle of the desert."

Leo hooked his kite to his chair and knelt in front of Rachel, looking directly into her eyes. The fear in his eyes was something she didn't often see.

"We both have had long careers in law enforcement, and we've seen a lot. But the scariest damn thing I've ever seen was Alexander's killing ritual. I remember the first time I witnessed it. A man who bought four bombs insisted he would pay when some of his deals went down the next night. No money ever showed. Alexander's guys finally caught him and took him to the same interrogation room you were in. I had been with Alexander for four years, and he said it was time I knew how he handled people like that. The murder from start to finish took three hours. His pleasure at the man's pain and terror was obvious. Once, during the murder, he turned to look at me, and when I saw the look in his eyes, I just went cold inside. It was like all my vital organs had been replaced with ice. For the next two days, I didn't leave my apartment. I told him I had the stomach flu, but I'm sure he knew. Somehow, I learned to deal with it because Jason and I were in attendance during more killings. You had to be in close with him to see that part of the business. I'm not asking you; I'm begging you to go into hiding. I love you, and I can't let him hurt you again. This time you won't live through it."

Rachel could feel her jaw tighten. "I refuse to let that son of a bitch disrupt any more of my life than he already has. Instead of wasting my energy running, I'm going to use it to help catch him."

Leo knew by the look in her eyes and the tone of her voice that there was no changing her mind. He silently promised himself and Rachel that if Alexander ever came near her again, he would kill him, whether it fit FBI protocol or not.

CHAPTER FOURTEEN

The next day, Rachel and Leo were in Mark's office discussing the turn of events.

Mark's eyes held an intensity that was rarely seen. "The fact that Alexander Hargrove is in the country and behind these murders puts both of you in immediate danger. I want you two in a safe house. We can set it up today."

"I agree that Rachel should go into hiding, but I think I could be valuable in helping you find him. I want to stay on the case," Leo said.

"I do too," Rachel protested. "I think helping find and put him away will help me heal further."

Mark sighed. "As your superior, I could order you both into hiding. But I'll respect your wishes and hope to hell I don't regret it. My question to you, Rachel, is: when we arrest him, do you want to press charges against him for what he did to you?"

"If I can avoid it, I'd rather not. I'm not afraid to face him in court, but the defense would have a field day with Leo and cause the jury to question why I'm pressing charges against Alexander and not him."

"I'm not worried about an attorney grilling me on the stand. If you wanted to press charges, I'd do what I could to help you," said Leo.

"I appreciate that, but if we can put him away for murder and the charges related to his former business, I'll be satisfied with that."

"Which leads me to my next point," Mark said. "Rachel, I'm removing you as head of the murder Investigations. You're still on the case, but we need to avoid having you present evidence. Longview is now head of the whole HARTECH case."

"I'm fine with that," Rachel said.

"First, I'm going to make sure Shalayah has someone to guard her room in case Hargrove tries to finish her off. By the end of the week, I'm sending Davis and Longview to question his parents. We need to get Charles to change his weekend plans and cancel his day off."

"I could go with Agent Davis so Charles can keep his requested day off. I'm good at interviewing upset parents," Rachel said.

"Are you sure about interviewing his parents?" Leo put a hand on her arm.

"Yeah, I am," she said, looking at Mark for approval.

"You're excellent at dealing with parents of criminals and victims alike. If you're up to it, you can go. However, I'm sending you on a delivery for another case tomorrow morning. It's important. When you return, you and Davis will go to San Luis Obispo to interview Alexander's parents," Mark said, then he gave her the specifics of the assignment.

*   *   *

Rachel drove into the rundown apartment complex in Reno, Nevada. This was not the part of Reno shown on travel brochures but a low-income pocket just off the strip. The ragged children playing in the small yards and on the pavement seemed to fit right in. A few dogs roamed about; whether or not they had owners was anyone's guess. Several apartments had boards where windows used to be. She wondered how many complaints were filed against the owner of the place.

This was a side trip because she had successfully made her delivery an hour ago. If anything came out of this deviation from duty, she knew Mark would be pleased. Before getting out of the car, Rachel studied her file on Zack Williams. The skinny, prematurely balding man had done deliveries for Alexander. She was sure he would not be living at his old address, but when he went to work for Alexander, he left his wife behind. Records indicated that she still lived there. Austin and Charles had tried to get a hold of this woman many times and had never succeeded. Rachel remembered that Leo had told her how Zack had threatened her into silence. On a hunch, she decided to pay a visit to Kaye Williams hoping she would talk to another woman.

Rachel exited the car and walked up cracking cement stairs. When she knocked on the door she was rewarded with an answer. The tiny Philippine woman gave her a curious look.

"I'm agent Keaney of the FBI. Your husband is in danger, and I need your help to warn him."

Kaye stood aside, allowing Rachel into her apartment.

The apartment was kept clean as much as a broom and soap and water could keep it, but the few furnishings were old and broken down. The small kitchen contained cupboards with doors drooping on their hinges. The dish drainer contained mismatched plates and cups. From where she stood, Rachel could see into the bedroom which housed a single mattress on a frame and a paint-chipped dresser.

Kaye offered Rachel the only chair in the room and sat down on a wooden crate to listen.

"A man your husband used to work for is killing former employees," Rachel began. "We need to find him before this guy does. Do you know where he is?"

The woman looked at the floor. "I not tell. If I do, he come back for me."

Seeing the thin and scared woman in front of her, Rachel's heart melted. She made a point of not getting involved when there was business at hand. In her position, she couldn't afford to let the people get to her.

Even so, she began asking Kaye questions about her relationship with her husband in the past and present. Because she talked with the gentleness she used when interviewing victims of violent crime, Kaye trusted Rachel and began to pour out a tale of alcoholism, gambling, and violence until her husband left four years ago. Now, he sent her money every month that paid the rent, but little else. He sent her clothes every year, but for food, she relied on food boxes from charities.

"If you're afraid of him coming back, I can fix it so he can't find you. I know people who could teach you how to make a living on your own, and you won't have to be afraid anymore."

"You really do that for me?"

"Yes."

At that point, Kaye told Rachel what she knew of her husband's whereabouts, then Rachel made some phone calls.

*   *   *

Leo sat on a jutty of rocks near Dana Landing in Mission Bay. The sun was just setting, and people were either returning from a day's sailing or departing for a sunset cruise.

Leo liked to come here to think and watch the people and the boats. The breeze and scent of the ocean were refreshing after being inside all day.

Two young boys were unloading fishing gear across the boat ramp. Across the bay, he could make out the sprawling green of Mission Bay Park where he and Rachel spent a lot of their free time. He wished she were with him now, but she had left for a delivery assignment that morning and would come back late that evening only to leave again the following morning.

So many thoughts flooded his mind. He couldn't wait to bring Alexander to justice. When they finally put Alex away, he and Rachel could rest. Knowing he was at large caused them both to watch their backs constantly. Another of his recurring thoughts was of starting his own private detective company after retirement. Working for himself was an attractive option after years of doing Alexander's bidding while answering to the FBI. Thinking about the future always brought him to thoughts of marrying Rachel. There was no doubt in his mind that he wanted to spend the rest of his life with her. When his first marriage failed, he believed he was better off alone. His relationship with Rachel, which started from a friendship, challenged that belief. They had been through and overcome so much together that he knew they could take on anything life would hand them. He was even open to the possibility of children if Rachel wanted them. He had never thought much about being a father, but a child with Rachel was something he could envision.

Rachel was right. Alexander at large or behind bars shouldn't disrupt their lives. They needed to live their lives regardless of him. It was too soon to ask, but his mind was made up. If she would have him, he was going to marry her.

*   *   *

The quiet, middle-class neighborhood in San Luis Obispo was active on a cool Friday evening. People sat on front porches or visited with neighbors in their neatly groomed yards.

Frank and Justine Hargrove had lived in this beautiful neighborhood for 45 years.

Rachel walked up to the tan, brown-trimmed house. A chill ran through her when she realized that Alexander had spent most of his youth here.

"You okay with being here? I can do the interview and you can pick me up later," Austin said.

"I'll be fine." They rang the doorbell, and a woman about the age of Rachel's mother answered. She invited them in and called her husband from his painting studio in the garage.

Throughout the living room were family pictures. Alexander at various ages stared out from the photos. The same unsmiling, angular face was present in all of them. His younger face was a little softer than the one she remembered. His eyes looked sad and scared rather than cold like the ones Rachel had seen.

Frank nodded toward Austin. "You and another agent came here several months ago to tell us Alex disappeared into Mexico after his building blew up. You also said his company was suspected of illegal activities. We never knew anything about that."

"Yeah, but if he ran off to Mexico, he must have been in trouble. Do you have any current information?" Justine asked.

"We do," Rachel said. "We have confirmation that he's in the country again."

Justine looked surprised.

"It's especially important that we find him. Has he contacted you recently?" Rachel asked.

"No, we haven't heard from him at all. Are you sure?" Justine asked.

"We're as sure as we can be. If he tries to contact you, will you call us? I know this is difficult, but it's important that we get a hold of him." Austin took a business card from his wallet.

Frank took it. "We'll keep your card, but he won't contact us because he knows we would turn him in if we knew he was in trouble."

Tears streamed down Justine's face. "I'm sorry, talking about our son is hard for me. We knew he would be a tough case before we took him in. We tried so hard, we worked with him and thought our love would overcome his history. It didn't. Then when he was seventeen, I was tired of trying. Alex and I had a terrible fight, and I told my husband that night that our lives would have been easier without him. I didn't know he was standing right there until I looked up and saw the hurt in his eyes. The next morning, he was gone."

Rachel took hold of the other woman's hand. "Mrs. Hargrove, please don't blame yourself. You two are the only people who stuck with him. Who knows how he would have turned out if you hadn't taken him in? You did a good thing, don't regret it just because it didn't turn out the way you hoped."

"That's what he said. Several years after he ran away, we got a long letter. He thanked us for everything we did for him. He wrote that he understood why I had said what I said that night and not to feel guilty about it. From that point on, he sent us a check every month so we could retire comfortably. We saw him a few times and even took a tour of his building once."

She got up from her place on the sofa. "I guess I'm rambling. I'll walk you two out."

The agents said goodbye to the Hargroves. They were even more sure that the couple, though willing, would not be able to help them find Alexander.

*   *   *

When they got back in the car, Austin was silent until they were out of the neighborhood.

"That was very big of you to say that," he said once they were on the main road.

"I meant it. The damage was done before they ever got a hold of him. They're good people who tried to make a difference in the life of a sociopath."

"Why did you really want to come with me to this interview? It wasn't because of Charles' weekend plans."

"You're right. I do research to try to make sense of bad things that happen. I investigated his foster care records. One foster dad did time in jail for nearly killing him. Some foster families tried all kinds of disciplinary measures to try to get a handle on him. None of the foster parents kept him very long. I just wanted to learn about the people who stood by him for 11 years."

"Sounds like you almost feel sorry for him."

"I feel sorry for the boy these things happened to, not the man he grew into. Small children don't have choices, men do."

*   *   *

Alexander's cell phone rang. He picked it up on the second ring. This better be good. He had been in an Internet private chat and did not appreciate the interruption.

"It's me," Laura said in a serious tone.

"What is it?"

"You're high on the FBI's list of suspects for three murders and one attempted murder."

"Hang on a minute."

Alexander logged off the Internet and took a minute to calm himself.

"How the hell did that happen?!"

"I wish I knew. I waited a few days to call you in hopes of finding out, but they're being even more guarded than before."

"I can think of a few ways. Has there been talk of evidence at any of the scenes or of Shalayah Michaels waking up?"

"No, none at all. Shalayah's still in a coma. Rachel is incredibly good; she may have found something."

"Thank you, Laura. If you find out anything else, let me know right away."

"Will do."

Alexander sat at his desk looking around at the rich wood carvings that decorated his office. He thought and steamed for several minutes. He was thorough but not perfect. Could Rachel have found something? He always had Kevin double check for evidence. Was Kevin careless, or was he trying to get them caught?

He pressed the button on the intercom. "Kevin, get to my office, now!"

*   *   *

Within minutes, Kevin was in the office. When he entered the room and saw the look on Alexander's face, his stomach flip flopped, and the burning sensation of bile was strong in his throat.

"When I ask you to check the murder scenes, do you check them really well?"

"Yes, every time. You never leave anything behind."

"Is there a chance that when I ask you to help me clean up a scene you may have left something behind?"

"No, I swear, I'd never do that. I've never left anything. Really!"

Alexander got up from his desk.

Kevin was big enough to defend himself against Alexander but wouldn't dare try. Instead, he closed his eyes and braced himself for whatever would come. A hand grabbed the hair on the back of his head, and he felt himself being forced downward.

"Sit."

Kevin obeyed sitting in the leather office chair nearest to him. Alexander sat on the desk in front of him.

"The Feds now suspect me of killing Alan, his girl-friend, and Randy. Shalayah is still in a coma, so she hasn't told them anything. That leaves you. If I find out that you left evidence or if at any point you ever try to screw with me, it will be your last act as a living human being. Understand?"

Kevin only nodded.

"Good. Now go back to whatever you were doing."

Kevin ran from the office and out the back door into the tangerine orchard. The trees were a blur of green, brown, and orange in his peripheral vision. He stopped, gasping for breath, when he reached the far end of the orchard, his heart and mind racing. Alex knew. Maybe he didn't know the specifics, but he knew something. The FBI was supposed to find his evidence and do something with it. It seemed they found the evidence, and somehow, Alex found out about it and now suspected him. Images of Alan Solano and Randy Klausen flashed through his mind. He could hear Shalayah's screams as if she were being tortured right beside him.

"Damn it!" He threw a hardened tangerine against a tree.

One thing was sure: he wasn't going to leave any more evidence behind at any more crime scenes. Alex said that messing with him would be his last act as a living human being, and he had no reason to doubt it. The only real solution was to do everything Alex told him to do and do it perfectly, so he had no reason to suspect him of anything.

CHAPTER FIFTEEN

The opulent dining room at the Hotel Del Coronado was filling up fast with hotel guests and others who came to enjoy their Sunday champagne brunch. Mark and his wife of 35 years came here often after their church services let out.

While squeezing a lemon slice into his hot tea, Mark's hand slipped, and the lemon dropped into the cup, splashing tea onto his tie.

"Damn it!" He dipped a napkin into his water glass and dabbed at the tea spots to keep them from setting.

"Honey, you've been very distracted for the last few days. I know you can't tell me a lot, but please tell me what you can."

Allison had stood by him through his career as a Navy pilot, putting up with the many relocations. She was there for him in his early FBI career as a hostage negotiator and could always tell when he walked in the door whether the job was a success or failure. They pulled together through the death of their only child. She knew him better than anyone on earth and yet sometimes he still tried to act like everything was fine when it wasn't.

"I respected the wishes of two of my agents, and now I'm second guessing myself. A very dangerous man is likely after them, and they would rather help apprehend him than go into hiding."

"So why don't you order them into hiding?" she asked, cutting into her eggs benedict. "Because I trust their judgment as well as their ability to handle themselves should a situation occur."

"Then trust your own decision making. You got to where you are because of your great mind."

The smile returned to his blue eyes as he looked into the face of the officer's daughter who stole his heart a lifetime ago.

*   *   *

The top of the computer screen read http://www.moneychat.com. Hopefully, # 'sman would be there as he usually was at this time of the evening. As luck would have it, he was logged on to the chat room. Alexander, with the handle shortfuze, invited #'sman to a private chat.

shortfuze: I took your advice on those long shot stocks. They're doing great, thank you.
#'sman: No problem, always glad to help.
shortfuze: I was wondering what part of the country you're in. I'm in California, but I do a bit of traveling. If I'm ever out your way, I would love to meet with you.
#'sman: For reasons I do not wish to divulge, I won't tell you much, only that I'm in the Pacific Northwest. I'm probably not too far from you.
shortfuze: Whatever your reasons are, I understand. Your secrets would be safe with me, but we've only been chatting for a month so maybe later you can find me trustworthy.
#'sman: I hope I haven't offended you.

shortfuze: Not at all. In fact, I would like to switch sub-
    jects for a moment. I've been invited to go deep sea
    fishing this weekend, I've never been. Any advice
    you can give for that?
#'sman: Sorry, fly fishing is my thing. Fly fishing and bow
    hunting. I've never gone deep sea fishing either.
shortfuze: Oh well, we'll see how it goes. I'd better log
    off for now. Look forward to chatting again.
#'sman: Goodbye for now.

Valuable information was exchanged in that conversation. Harry Matteson was always saying "For reasons I do not wish to divulge." It was one of his favorite
lines. He also was an avid fly fisher and bow hunter.
Alexander looked up #'sman in the web site's directory.
#'sman was listed as Jonathan Thomas, age 52, no
city or state given. He searched his memory. No one
gives their real name on the Internet. Then it hit him,
Harry has two sons, Jonathan and Thomas. Of course!
Through the years, he would talk about them. How old
they would be, what they might be doing. He had to
get Harry to trust him and tell him exactly where he
was. He would search the yellow pages for Oregon and
Washington but knowing Harry, he wouldn't be listed
even with his assumed identity. Still, it was more than
he had before.

*　　*　　*

The cool evening air flowed through the wind-
screens into Rachel's apartment. She and Leo were in
the kitchen preparing dinner. On the nights they ate in,
Leo did most of the actual cooking. Rachel had returned

a few days ago from the assignment in Reno, Nevada, and the interview in San Luis Obispo.

Each assignment she successfully completed, whether a pickup, delivery, or detective work, made her feel stronger and helped her heal just a little bit more. This evening, she was feeling great. She had found a good lead to Zack Williams.

Over roast chicken, fresh green beans, and scalloped potatoes, she told him about the assignments, and he talked of their upcoming trip to meet his family in Walnut Creek.

Rachel wished she could take Leo to meet her mother in Wisconsin, but getting the time off during a big case was difficult. When she lost her father seven years ago, her mother decided to return to her old neighborhood in Milwaukee, Wisconsin and moved out of Ramona, California where Rachel had grown up.

Rachel and Leo sat on the futon in the darkening living room. Leo pulled Rachel to him and kissed her with the passion built up over her brief absence. She felt his heart beat fast against her chest. Like all other times, he told her he would have to go home. She could see the desire in his dark eyes and felt her own excitement flowing through her body like electricity.

"Wait. You don't have to go just yet. I missed you. I'm also ready to take things up one small step," she said as she began unbuttoning his blue 501 jeans.

*   *   *

He could feel himself growing hard as her hands worked at the buttons on his jeans. He laid back on the futon and looked at her beautiful face. All of a sudden, he was seeing that face at a time in recent history. He wasn't seeing Rachel smiling at him. Instead, he saw her anguished expression as Alexander raped her. Then the look of horror as Jason sodomized her. Finally, her face as she was forced to her knees in front of him flashed across his mind.

Before he realized what was happening, he pushed Rachel's hands away from him and buttoned up his pants. "Rachel. I can't have you do this; I have to go."

In seconds, he was out her front door. Through the window he caught a glimpse of Rachel staring after him in disbelief.

*   *   *

The next morning, Rachel met with Mark, Leo, Austin, and Charles about updates on the HARTECH case.

"Rachel, why don't you start the meeting," Mark said.

Rachel stood up, trying to avoid looking at Leo. Every time she glanced in his direction, her vision clouded with anger. She would lead this meeting like the professional that she was. She took a slow, deep breath.

"While I was in Reno I acted on a whim and looked up the wife of Zack Williams." Rachel motioned to Austin and Charles. "The two of you said you couldn't get a hold of her no matter how many messages you left. I remembered that Leo said she Zack told her men might come around and hurt her to find out where he is. Because of this, I thought she might talk to a woman. Fortunately, I was able to meet with her." She noticed Leo's drifting stare.

"Leo?" Mark tapped him on the shoulder.

"I'm sorry, what was that?" Leo said, looking in Rachel's direction.

Rachel looked into her briefcase and rifled through some papers for a minute. "I said that I acted on your tip and met with Zack Williams' wife. Kaye says he is definitely in Bullhead City, Arizona and works across the river in Laughlin, Nevada."

"That's all the time we have right now, I think we'll adjourn these meetings until three this afternoon," Mark said, interrupting the exchange.

Rachel was out of the room in seconds. She had to get to where she could be alone, and fast. What in the hell was Leo's problem? First, he didn't want her to touch him, now he can't even listen to her in a meeting.

*   *   *

Leo started to get up and leave the room with the others.

"Not you Leo, you stay here," Mark said. "What in the hell is going on today?"

"I'm not exactly sure."

"Well, you need to get sure." Mark took some files out of his briefcase for the next meeting. "Have you made any appointments with the counselor I recommended? I'm telling you, he's excellent at helping agents to transition from deep cover to real life."

"I'm not sure this has anything to do with that."

"I'm quite sure it does. You've been very distracted lately since we tied Hargrove to the murders. Making that appointment is not a sign of weakness; it's good sense."

"I'll be going up to that floor anyway. I'll see if he has an opening."

*   *   *

Ever since their friendship started, Rachel had been a tremendous help to Leo by listening to his feelings surrounding his eight-year undercover assignment. However, since finding out Alexander was on a killing spree, he would wake up in the middle of the night with a lot of guilt, anger, and frustration. He would see about an appointment, but first, he had to talk to Chantelle. Rachel raved about how good she was and how much she was helping her.

When he arrived at her office, Chantelle was just finishing an appointment.

"Do you have a few minutes?" Leo asked.

"Yes, come on in," she said, smoothing her sweater over her now flat stomach.

"You know Rachel and I are in a relationship, right?" Leo sat down on the couch.

"Yes, but I still can't discuss her sessions with you."

"No, no, I'm not here for that. I did something really stupid last night, and I need to make sense of it."

Chantelle listened while he relayed the story.

"I don't know what happened, I just couldn't let her touch me."

"That makes perfect sense. Last time she got you off, it wasn't her choice or yours, for that matter. Her giving you sexual pleasure reminds you of your own assault, and the guilt you still feel for taking part in her assault."

Leo looked out at the bay in the distance. With his emotions so close to the surface, it all became clear to him.

"Rachel always said what happened was an attack on me as well as her. While I never argued the point with her, I downplayed it."

"It's probably time for you to stop downplaying and start dealing. Alexander instigated the whole thing. You didn't go into that room intending to force yourself on Rachel."

Leo shook his head.

"I have a question for you. How do you feel about everything else that went on during your undercover work? You watched as he murdered people, probably helped in small ways such as securing the victim to the table. You helped him set up and execute deals where his explosives hurt and killed people. How do you feel about that?"

"Like I should have done more to stop him, more than just gathering information and stopping a few deals."

"Why didn't you do more?"

"Because if you were in deep with Alexander like I was, you didn't tell him no or question him. If he wanted you to do something, you did it."

"I can tell you this Leo; If you can't see the work you did as extremely valuable to the Weapons Task Force and forgive yourself for what you couldn't do, you're going to jeopardize your own mental health and risk your relationship with Rachel. I wouldn't be surprised if she took your actions last night as personal rejection."

"No, I wasn't rejecting her, I would never do that."

"I'm sure that's not what she's feeling right now."

After thanking Chantelle for seeing him and making an appointment with the man Mark recommended, he made a beeline for Rachel's squad room hoping she would be there.

*　　*　　*

Rachel tried to type the report of her Nevada assignment, but her mind would always drift to the night before.

She aggressively tapped the keys.

She had come to grips with the fact that the attack was not her fault and now blamed Alexander alone for what happened. That didn't change the fact that she felt like no man would want her now that she had to have blood tests every six months and was at risk for HIV and hepatitis. Leo's behavior the previous night confirmed her feelings. She was always so glad he respected her desire to save sex for marriage and didn't even try to get her in bed with him. Somewhere in the back of her mind, she wondered if some of the respect really meant he didn't want to be where Alexander had once been. Now she knew.

The knock at the door was not a welcome sound. For once, she had the squad room to herself when she really needed it. She remained silent, hoping whoever it was would go away.

Leo stuck his head in the door.

"Are you talking to me? If you're not, I understand, but I hope you'll let me stay."

"That depends on what you have to say," she said, still typing.

"I went to see Chantelle, and you're right about how good she is. She knocked me upside the head a few times."

"Then yes, I am talking to you. Let's go where we can be alone."

They went to Leo's BMW in the parking garage.

"Chantelle made me realize that I'm having more trouble than I realized dealing with my time at Hargrove and what he did to you. . . and what he did to me."

Rachel relaxed against him as relief flooded her being.

"The truth is, Rachel, so much happened right in front of me, and I did nothing about it, just like I did nothing to help you. When you touched me last night, it was the most wonderful feeling. Then somewhere during the wonderfulness, massive guilt washed through me, and I couldn't take it. I never meant to hurt you in trying to deal with my own emotions."

Fresh tears streamed down her face. "I hate the risks I face because of what they did to me. I know Alexander and Jason weren't selective in partners and I understand-"

"Is that what you think my actions were about?" He held her closer.

"Well, you kiss me, hug me, and touch me in other ways, but never in a sexual way."

"The risks you face now are not your fault. I'd be a lying fool if I said I didn't want to make love to you, but I'm also trying to respect your wishes, and I never knew if touching you sexually would be good or bad, so I erred on the side of caution."

Rachel drank in the security and affection she always felt against his broad chest with his strong arms around her. She wanted nothing more than to be with him for the rest of her life.

"I made an appointment with Stephen Barrenworth. I'm going to start seeing him next week to try to get a handle on all of this."

"Great, I've heard he's excellent."

He pulled her close again, and she just rested against him. Neither were sure how much time had gone by when they got out of his car. Both agents returned to work feeling resolved.

*   *   *

Later that afternoon, when Rachel and Leo met with Mark, Austin, and Charles, they were given the assignment to scour the Laughlin casinos to find Zack Williams. His wife Kaye knew he tended bar but couldn't remember which casino. They would leave the next afternoon. As Austin and Charles got up to leave, Mark told Rachel and Leo to stay behind.

"Su Lee booked four rooms at the Edgewater, like I said. Leo, I fully expect you to use your room, not Rachel's."

"Mark!" Rachel said, heat rising to her face.

It was then that she noticed the twinkle in his eyes.

"I didn't get to be the Special Agent in Charge by wearing blinders. You two have done an excellent job keeping things professional; I just noticed a few subtleties. I'm glad you two worked out the problems from this morning. The truth is, I knew you would be a good team. I was planning to put you on the wrap up case originally, Rachel. Then I was going to give you the transfer you requested and make you and Leo partners. When everything happened the way it did, my plans changed. It looks like the two of you hit it off despite the rocky start."

*   *   *

That night, after going out for dinner, Rachel and Leo returned to Rachel's apartment. When she put her purse down, he kissed her. This time he didn't hold back. His tongue brushed her lips and entered the warmth of her mouth as she opened it. Their eyes glowed with the unresolved passion of the night before. Leo pulled her closer, and she drew in her breath as his chest pressed against hers, causing her nipples to tingle. It wasn't long before she could feel his erection pressed against her abdomen.

"Can we pick up where we left off last night?" he whispered.

"Lie back on the couch," she answered.

He stretched out on her futon and closed his eyes as she ran her hands under his sweatshirt. Then he guided her hands to the front of his jeans. She held his gaze as she unbuttoned his 501s. She began to run her hands along his thighs until she could see that his desire had reached a very high level. It was then that she took him in her hands and caressed him until his body tensed then relaxed.

Rachel lay next to him with her head on his chest until he recovered.

His coming to a climax under her touch made her feel strong and very wanted. What happened next further confirmed those feelings.

He slipped his hand under her soft, yellow sweater tracing her bra line before gently working his way inside. Light caresses gave way to a firm touch as her desire intensified. Her breath caught when his hand descended her belly to the hem of her short, black, knit skirt. Anticipation built up inside her as he ran his hand from her knee up the length of her thigh several times before reaching the place where her legs joined. The pleasure seemed to radiate through her whole body until suddenly, it all converged in the place where his hand connected with her most intimate part.

"I love you. You're the best thing that's ever happened to me," he whispered as her desire reached its peak and subsided.

CHAPTER SIXTEEN

Rachel's cell phone rang while she was on her way to the airport.

"Agent Keaney, this is Larnell Michaels."

She could tell by his tone that the news wasn't good.

"We took my sister off life support yesterday. She is currently breathing on her own, but the doctors said she would probably be gone in a day or two. I told them to keep her on nutrients just in case. That's what she would have wanted."

"I'm sorry to hear that, I know that was difficult for you and your family. How is Carla handling it?"

"She's very down right now. She hasn't touched alcohol or drugs since the night she found Shalayah. She's focusing on her schoolwork and doesn't hang around her old friends anymore."

"That's good."

"Yeah. I have to tell you, Agent Keaney, I'm thrilled to have my baby girl back, but the price is high."

"Keep focusing on the changes in your daughter to get you through. The guard will stay at her door until she's gone. I'm continuing to look for Shalayah's attacker or attackers."

"Thank you," he choked out through tears.

When Rachel disconnected the call, a sense of sadness came over her. Alexander may have won again.

*   *   *

The Learjet touched down in Bullhead City, Arizona. Across the river, Laughlin's flamboyant buildings towered above the water. Other than the river and the casinos, there was little else to see. Bullhead City and Laughlin were surrounded by desert mountains. The wind had picked, up making the landing a little rough. After a shuttle took them across the river to the Edgewater Hotel and Casino, they checked in and made a game plan for finding Zack Williams.

They would have to conduct their search inconspicuously because Zack tended to be skittish. Announcing that they were federal agents would most likely result in a chase. For his own safety, they would have to be covert.

Leo stayed out of sight as much as possible, doing his part by phone or computer from his hotel room. Rachel, Austin, and Charles walked the long line of casinos browsing in the gift shops and ordering sodas at the bars. When a conversation could be struck up with a bartender, they would ask roundabout questions to find out if Zack worked for that casino. That evening, they all met at the Edgewater's buffet for dinner to compare notes. They discovered that Zack worked for the Riverside Casino under the name Christopher Larson. But as luck would have it, he had taken three days' vacation and would not return to work until Saturday.

*   *   *

Saturday evening, Rachel was ready to walk over to the main bar at the Riverside. She hoped her burgundy velvet dress would get Zack Williams' attention. From what Leo said, the short, clingy dress with its spaghetti straps would be just the thing to attract Zack. Her skin crawled at the thought of picking up slime like him. Had she been the type to pick up men in bars, she wouldn't have gone for someone like Zack, knowing what she knew.

She walked out of the teal green and gold of the Edgewater onto the riverwalk. When she passed the pink and navy blue of the Flamingo Hilton, she noticed the hotel's lights reflected in the gentle waves of the dark river. Music from a concert at the amphitheater drowned out the conversations of the people standing nearby. At last, she walked into the masculine burgundy and wood tones of the Riverside.

The town's namesake, Don Laughlin, who built the town on the Colorado River out of nothing, owned the place.

Rachel hoped Zack would be working tonight. It was nice to have a few days to catch up on paperwork, but now, she was ready to get back to her apartment and squad room. It seemed the noise of the slot machines as well as the colorful signs advertising food deals and entertainment were a little nerve-racking.

On her way to the bar, it seemed she could see herself everywhere she looked in the mirrors and polished brass that accented the wood tones. Before she took her place on the barstool, she saw him. Zack looked just like the five-year-old photo she had seen in the file, only more of his blonde hair had receded. His tall, thin frame and glasses made him look like an accountant or a librarian, not a bartender with a record. The charges against him ranged from theft to domestic violence.

Rachel sat down, took off her bolero jacket, and ordered a glass of wine.

She was uncomfortable ordering alcohol on the job but wanted to fit in with the other customers. It was busy on a Saturday evening, so she hoped she could engage him in conversation.

"Having any luck tonight?" Zack eyed her neckline as he sat the wineglass on a napkin in front of her.

"None. In fact, I'm down $100."

"Is that all? That's good compared to most people around here."

"I'm a conservative gambler. $100 is a lot for me."

"So, are you here by yourself?"

"Yeah. The people I came with left yesterday. I thought I would stay an extra day and see if I could get lucky. I guess not."

"Well, I get off at ten if you want any company."

"A little company would be nice." She wrote her room number on a napkin and gave him a nice tip. "10:30 then?"

"Looking forward to it," he said, leering.

*   *   *

By 10:30 that night, everything was set up. Rachel and Austin waited for Zack in Rachel's room while Leo and Charles waited in the adjoining room. Rachel and Austin heard a knock at the door. She took off her jacket. Austin's eyes widened when she walked past him to answer the door. She led Zack by the hand into the room while Austin, who had been hiding in the bathroom, crept out and blocked the door. Zack pulled her to him and ran his hand from her hip to her buttocks but suddenly did a double take when he saw Austin.

"What the hell's going on here?" he demanded.

"Zack, you're in danger. I'm Agent Keaney of the FBI and this Agent Davis," Rachel said while she put her jacket back on.

Leo and Charles entered the room through the adjoining doors.

"Hi Zack. It's been a while," Leo said.

"Andre, did you lead the Feds to me as part of a deal?"

"Andre is my alias, I'm Agent Acratelli, FBI."

Zack paled and sank into a chair. "Whatever it is, I have nothing to say to you guys."

"Alexander murdered Alan and Randy. Shalayah was just taken off life support and will probably die," Charles said.

"Well, if they talked and got on his bad side, that's their problem. I don't plan to make that same mistake. Like I said, I have nothing to say."

"Randy didn't talk to us, but he's still dead," Leo said.

"That's fine if he won't talk. We'll just take him to Reno and book him," Rachel said with a shrug.

"I talked to your wife. I assured her we could protect her from you. She'll testify to what you did to her and produce evidence for some of your theft charges. Or you could give us your testimony about Alexander's business, and we'll drop the charges and send you to a safe house until we can arrest him."

"What choice do I have?" He lowered his forehead into a hand. "Where do you want me to start?"

"Start with how you connected with Alexander in the first Place," Leo said.

Zack sighed. "I did a six-year tour of duty in the Navy. While in the service, I got into drinking heavily and gambling. When my tour was up, I arranged to have my wife come over from the Philippines, and we settled in Reno. Things were great for a while until I racked up some gambling debts with the wrong people. I guess the stress and drinking got to me because I sent my wife to the hospital a few times. If all that wasn't bad enough, I stole a few things to try and chip away at the debt. Some of the people I ran with knew of Alexander and how to get a hold of him. After our meeting he agreed to pay off my debt in exchange for my loyalty and service. I told Kaye I would have to leave and that she was not to talk to anyone about me. I made up something about men coming after me and trying to hurt her too."

"That explains why she wouldn't answer our phone calls," Charles said.

Zack continued, "Once Alex knew he could trust me, I began doing a lot of deliveries for him. I practically went all over the world exchanging bombs for money."

He gave dates, locations, and customer names for the many deals he was involved in. When he finished, Zack looked directly at Rachel.

"You said you talked to Kaye? Did she tell you I was here?"

"It doesn't matter what she told me. I turned her onto a few American ways of thinking and some ways she can pull herself out of the condition she was living in."

He glared. "I ought to-"

"You ought to do what?" Rachel stood up. "She's moved to where you'll never find her."

"But you know where she went."

"Yes, I do, but you won't."

He took a few menacing steps toward Rachel.

She stood still and glared. "What, you're surprised I'm not backing away and cowering like your wife probably did?"

"No, I'm not. You have three men in the room to protect you," he said with a sneer.

Leo stood between Zack and Rachel. "Rachel, can I talk to you outside?"

*　　*　　*

The cool February air blew across the Colorado River. Rachel and Leo walked down to a circular patch of cement and sat down on one of the wooden benches. Leo said nothing, just put his arm around Rachel while she watched people stroll along the river walk for a few minutes.

"I know, I got a little involved," said Rachel. "You just didn't see the way that poor woman was living. There was almost no furniture in the apartment, and no heating or cooling. She was terrified her husband would come back but didn't know how to stop him from doing so."

"So, who did you set her up with?"

"A high school friend from Ramona who's now a social worker."

"Then you've done what you can for her. I've never respected Zack or men like him. I was taught growing up that you don't ever take a hand to a woman. As many times as my ex-wife ticked me off, I never hit her. However, tearing Zack from limb to limb won't really solve anything."

"I know, it would just feel good."

Leo laughed and gave her a lingering kiss.

After they returned, Zack apologized for his behavior.

Rachel suspected that Austin and Charles had something to do with his apology.

The group of five went to Zack's rented home in Bullhead City to collect a few belongings. He stayed with the agents for the next two nights.

First thing Monday morning, Rachel called Mark's direct line.

"We have Zack Williams and his testimony. We just need a safe place for him."

"Good job. I'll call you back in two hours when everything is set up."

*   *   *

After he hung up the phone, Mark left his office for a meeting.

He dictated instructions to Laura in the outer office. "We need a safe house in the Nevada area for one of Hargrove's people."

"Will do." She picked up the phone and began the process.

*   *   *

That evening, the agents were back in San Diego.

Rachel was tired but relieved that at least one fugitive was safe. When she unlocked her door, she noticed a Federal Express package on her doorstep from Amazon. She didn't remember ordering any books, but since her mother discovered the Internet, she often sent her things through the computer bookstore.

After opening the package, she dropped the book on the table as if it were on fire. The book titled *The Perfect Victim* by Christine McGuire and Carla Norton was sent to her as a gift from someone who wished to remain anonymous.

The meaning of the book and its sender were clear. *The Perfect Victim* was the true story of the girl in a box, the much-publicized sex slave case. Alexander's words came back to her as if they were being spoken right then.

"...refuse, and you become my unpaid whore. Think about it. Your body would be available to me whenever I wanted it for whatever I wanted to do with it."

A chill ran through her. Just as Leo had said, he knew where they lived. While she thought this over, her phone rang.

"Rachel, it's me," Leo said when she picked up. "Did you get anything from FedEx when you arrived home?'

"Yes, a true crime book about the girl kept as a sex slave for seven years."

"And the sender did not wish to reveal himself."

"That's right. What did he send you?"

"A book of stupid criminal stories. A lot of times in between shifts, Alexander, Jason, and I used to read stupid criminal articles when they were in the newspaper. Do you want me to come and stay with you tonight?"

"No, I'll be fine. Just because he sent me a book doesn't mean he has the guts to come here."

"I'm not so sure of that. I know you can handle yourself if he tries anything. But why take chances?"

"He mailed us books through the Internet, which means he could be anywhere. Really, I'll be fine. I won't let him scare me like that."

"I see your point. I'm just on edge over this."

*   *   *

Rachel awoke to the shrill ring of her cell phone. In a sleep induced fog, she answered.

"Did you get the book, Rachel?"

She sat bolt upright and grabbed the pen and notebook she kept by her phone. "Yeah, I got it."

"You know, I really wish you would have told me what you knew back at my plant. Life with me would not have been as bad as all that. I wasn't planning to keep you in a box under my bed. I was actually setting up an apartment for you down the hall from mine. Eventually, I was going to give you a position in my company. You have a terrific mind, and I wasn't going to let it go to waste. Who knows, you might have even learned to enjoy being with me. I'm not totally selfish. I do know how to please a woman. Even if you couldn't get into the sex, you would have been well taken care of. I would have given you anything you wanted."

"Anything but my freedom and my right to say no. Why are you calling?"

Alexander chuckled. "I called and sent you the gift to let you know I haven't forgotten you. You and your lover are on my mind quite a lot. When I started this whole thing, it was purely for revenge. Now, I'm enjoying the game. I'm having more fun than I've had in years staying just out of your reach."

"You won't stay out of our reach, you son of a bitch. You're too damn arrogant, and you will make a mistake."

"Oh Rachel, it's almost cute the way you underestimate me. I suppose it would be cute if you hadn't destroyed everything I built. There's so much you don't know. First of all, you don't know where I am calling from. You can't trace this call because my digital phone is calling your digital phone. So, I could be outside your apartment on Mission Boulevard. Hell, I could be calling from Wisconsin for all you know." Alexander disconnected the call.

Rachel shook and broke out into a cold sweat. Did his comment about Wisconsin have any meaning, or was it just a state he picked out of the air?

She picked up the phone on her night table and dialed her mother's number. Relief washed through her when she heard her mother's sleepy voice on the line.

"Hi mom. It's good to hear your voice."

"I can hear in your voice something's wrong. What's this all about?"

"It's probably nothing. A guy I helped bring down is making threats. As a precaution, I'm going to call the field office in Milwaukee to have someone come check up on you."

"If you're in trouble, I want you to hide until it blows over."

"I'm taking care of myself, just let me make sure you're safe, okay?"

After hanging up from her mother she calculated the time difference and called the Milwaukee Field Office as soon as she knew someone was there. She would have to use her great people skills to get some security for her mom.

When the call was complete, the Milwaukee Special Agent in Charge agreed to send agents on some drive bys and a few home visits since all of Alexander's victims were in the western half of the country. It would have to be enough.

Later that morning, when she arrived at work, Rachel headed straight for Mark's office and found Leo there.

"I'm glad you're both here," she said, then told the two men about the phone call and showed them the notes she took.

"Well, we know he has both of your addresses and at least your cell phone number. There's still no telling where he is. Tracing a cell phone is difficult at best. Do you have caller ID on your phone?" Mark asked.

"Yes, but it came through as unavailable. He must have used a credit card to send us the books. I know Amazon is tight on confidentiality, but we could probably find out about the credit card from them."

Mark made a phone call to get someone from the New York Field Office to go to the bookstore's headquarters in person and get the card number.

"All the Milwaukee Field Office will do is drive bys and home visits," Rachel said, shaking her head.

"I think that will be enough," Leo said, putting a comforting hand on her shoulder. "I know him better than anyone, and even if he knows your mom lives in Wisconsin, he's not big on revenge by proxy. He prefers to go straight for the source. He's trying to get to you."

"Well, it's working."

She was comforted by Leo's words, knowing he wouldn't lie to her and give her a false sense of security.

*   *   *

Two hours later, the New York Field Office called.

Mark looked somber when Rachel and Leo came back into his office.

"We hit a dead end," Mark said. "The card turned out to be bogus, and I'm more concerned than I was before. What's going to happen if you meet up with him again? You two may freeze up and then he'll kill you, or you may be angry enough to kill him outside of protocol."

"We won't meet up any time soon. He's not ready to make his move yet," Rachel said. "As my notes say, he's enjoying the game. We just have to find him before he's ready to end it. If I were to kill him, it would only be in self-defense. I'd hate for him to miss the opportunity to sit in prison and realize that he couldn't elude us forever."

"I agree with Rachel. I've held my own with Alexander for eight years. Helping to put that bastard behind bars would give me a lot of satisfaction."

"I'm glad to hear that. What if he calls again?"

"I hope he does," Rachel said. "Believe me, having conversations with him is the last thing I want to do, but if he'll talk to me, he might slip and reveal something."

CHAPTER SEVENTEEN

At about 6:30 in the morning, Kevin unloaded luggage while Alexander checked them into a small hotel off the Las Vegas strip.

When they walked into the rundown room, Alexander shook his head. "Look at this worn shag carpeting."

Kevin wrinkled his nose at the strong odor of cigarette smoke that permeated the carpet, linens, and curtains in the room.

Alexander cracked open the window. "I hate staying in cheap places. The Luxor is more my style. Unfortunately, these places are the only ones run by crooks who won't cooperate with police. They have so much to hide that they avoid interviews at all costs." Alexander put his suitcase on a rickety luggage rack. He pulled off his shirt and unfastened his jeans to prepare for bed.

Kevin studied the muscular back and shoulders without a word. Alexander worked at keeping his body as well as his mind in shape. Kevin was always careful to be discreet when he looked him over for fear of provoking an angry reaction. Today, however, Kevin spoke up.

"Where did you get that scar?"

"This one?' Alexander said, running his finger along a now small, white line on his lower back. "When I was four years old, I was in one of several foster homes. I told the foster mom that I didn't feel good, but she made me eat anyway. As it turns out, I had the stomach flu and made the thoughtless mistake of throwing up on the carpet. The foster dad was drunk as usual and beat the crap out of me for it. The scar is from his ring."

"Oh man! Were you hurt really bad?"

"Yeah, I wound up in the emergency room. Most of the injuries didn't last except that I'm a little hard of hearing in my left ear and I'll never father a child."

"That's terrible!" Kevin said.

"Well for me, it's probably a good thing. I'm not exactly the fatherly type. Still, I would never hurt a kid like he did, or an animal for that matter."

Kevin realized his face betrayed his surprise when Alexander continued.

"I know, people like me usually start on children and animals. Everyone I've ever hurt or killed has been over eighteen and has done something to cross me in some way. Believe it or not, I do what I do for a reason. The fact that I enjoy it is secondary," he said, climbing into his bed.

Alexander fell asleep right away that morning. Kevin lay awake for the next two hours.

To Kevin, Alexander always seemed like an arrogant, self-assured man who could handle anything. Even though he made reference to his mother who abandoned him through drugs and the adoptive parents who tried to work with him, he never revealed much about his past. For the first time, Kevin saw him as a vulnerable little boy. Even though Alexander talked matter of fact about the events, Kevin saw hurt in the brown eyes that were always so cold. It was people like those foster parents who made Alex what he is. Who knew what other kinds of abuse he may have suffered as a ward of the state? Because of these people, Kevin lay here in a cheap motel room with Alex, forced to take part in his revenge killings or risk being killed himself.

He tossed and turned before he finally drifted off to sleep.

*   *   *

It was early on a Friday afternoon when Leo picked Rachel up at her apartment in his Red BMW M3 and headed for Lindbergh Field. They were flying to Walnut Creek to introduce her to his family. Both were relaxed. They had both promised themselves not to worry about finding the last accomplice, Harry Matteson, until the weekend was over. A few minutes after they were in the air, Rachel spoke up.

"I'm looking forward to meeting your family."

"They're looking forward to meeting you too. I know they're going to like you. First, you're not a thing like my ex. Second, you're wonderful the way you are."

"Where is your ex-wife now? Have you ever heard about her?"

"She's still in L.A. She's on her third marriage from what I understand."

"That's unfortunate."

"It really is. She had a lot of potential and really could have made something of her life had she made different choices and gotten the help she needed. I fell in love with her because I believed she needed me. I met her when I was a rookie cop responding to a domestic violence call. Her parents were high and at each other again, so she called 9-1-1. I wanted to protect her and make her life good."

"That's pretty typical of most of us in law enforcement," Rachel said.

"I suppose that's true. When I saw her, all I saw was her need. When I see you, it's very different."

"How so?"

"Most of the time, I see your strength and independence. I'm in awe of how you see people for who they are. Then sometimes I see your vulnerable side and I feel that same protectiveness of you."

"Why do you think that is?"

"I think it's because you're an emotionally healthy woman and not a needy girl, and our relationship is more like it should be."

"I agree. I have always believed that people make choices to determine the direction of their lives. I remember arriving home after everything happened. When I was finally safe at home, the emotions overwhelmed me. I'm not sure how long I cried, but the sun was well up by the time I finished. My stomach muscles felt like jelly.

When I finally sat up, I told myself that something horrible had happened to me. I couldn't go back and change it, so I now had two choices. I could stay down and let the anger, grief, and sadness destroy me and my relationship with everyone I knew. Let the anger loose on anyone remotely at fault."

"Like me."

"Yes, like you. Or I could get up and start working through the emotions and become whole again. I knew that would be the most difficult choice."

"I'm so glad you decided the way you did," Leo said, taking her hand and holding it.

"Me too. It's been a long, hard road, and it's not over yet. In fact, for me it will never truly be over. I'm just going to overcome all I can."

*   *   *

Rachel and Leo arrived in Walnut Creek just in time for dinner. Over the meal, Leo's family had many questions for Rachel about her life and background. At first, she felt a little on the spot, but their warmth and friendliness made it clear that they were thrilled Leo had brought her to meet them. Their questions were curiosity rather than an investigation. They were also more than willing to talk about themselves. She learned a lot about the architecture business Leo's younger brother Sal managed while his wife Marcia stayed home with their three children. Michael, Leo's older brother and best friend, talked about the salon he and his wife Sarah owned. Leo's parents, now retired, traveled extensively both in and out of the U.S. The stories they told were fascinating. The children at the table ranged in age from four months to 14 years. The older children had a million FBI questions for both Rachel and Leo.

After many hours of conversation, Leo's parents led the couple to a room furnished and decorated with antiques. Once Leo's mother closed the door, Rachel gave Leo a quizzical look.

Leo shrugged. "They're my parents. I assumed they'd give us separate rooms."

"It's okay. We've shared a bed a few times back home."

At this, he walked over and kissed her. "You just don't know all of the thoughts that have been going on in my head today. All day, I've been imagining what you may look like under these clothes." He rubbed her shirt sleeve between his two fingers. "So, I'm not sure sharing a bed is a good idea tonight. Not if I'm going to get any sleep anyway."

Rachel thought this over for a moment. Every time he touched her, it was either through or under her clothes. She hadn't felt ready to let him look at her.

She gave him an impish smile and put her hand on his chest in a stopping motion, then took two steps backward. Without a word, she slowly unbuttoned her light pink blouse and let it fall to the floor. His breathing quickened as she removed her bra and stood before him.

Rachel watched his eyes as they moved from her face to her chest. Last time she was looked over, she felt exposed and degraded. This time, she felt the warmth of a lover's gaze. The look of desire on his face was not mixed with the twisted need for power. His eyes only held genuine adoration.

He pulled her to him and gave her a deep, lingering kiss. His lips found her shoulder and moved over an ivory breast to the dusty pink nipple that crowned it.

Her passion spun out of control as his tongue and lips caressed her.

"I want you to make love to me," she whispered.

*　　*　　*

Leo willed himself to think, to override the pulsing in his groin. More than anything, he wanted to comply with her wishes and know her on the deepest level possible.

He couldn't, knowing that she may regret it when the passion subsided.

"If we break your commitment, I want us to decide with clear heads to break it. I won't take you this way, but I won't leave you hanging either."

Leo dimmed the lights, led her to the king-sized bed, and turned down the heavy quilt.

While they lay together, he kissed and caressed her a little longer before gently removing her denim skirt and satin panties. He kissed her thighs and abdomen, listening to her desire build again. Then his tongue found her most tender spot and he gently explored and savored her until she shuddered, drew in her breath, and relaxed.

When he looked into her face in the dim light and saw that Rachel had tears on her cheeks. He stroked her hair and held her close.

"If I did anything I shouldn't have, I'm sorry," he whispered.

"You didn't do anything wrong. You've done everything right including refusing to fully make love to me. Every time we have a good talk, or we're physically intimate, I feel like another piece has fallen back in place."

*   *   *

In a small house in the suburbs outside of Las Vegas, Alexander watched as Zack Williams slept peacefully until Kevin jolted him awake by throwing his full weight on top of him. Kevin's hand clapped hard on Zack's mouth. When he stopped struggling, Kevin took his hand away and let him up. Zack scrambled to his feet, then noticed Alexander.

"Alex! Shit! You scared the hell out of me."

"Nice safe house," was Alexander's calm reply.

"Oh man. Alex, they didn't leave me any choice. I was going to do time for my theft charges. You have to understand."

"With everything I've done for you, I'm supposed to understand why you would give the Feds information about my former business instead of doing a few years in minimum security? I'm afraid I don't," Alexander said.

"Alex, please, we can work this out. Whatever it is you're doing, I'll help you," Zack said with a pleading look.

"We are going to work this out. My car is just outside, and we're going for a drive in the desert."

"Yeah, I'm sure the policeman outside the door won't mind," Zack said with a smirk.

"You don't have to worry about him. He's dead."

At this point, Zack ran for the window and tried to jump through it. Kevin grabbed him and threw him against the wall, knocking down the two pictures that hung there. Alexander wrestled him to the ground and hit him twice in the face to subdue him again.

Alexander and Zack got into the Dodge Intrepid while Kevin followed in a dark gray cargo van.

Alexander bought the van with cash earlier that afternoon through connections he had in the area. He knew it had changed hands so many times without a paper trail that if the Feds found it, there would be no way to connect it to him. Of course, the victim would be connected to him, and the FBI had already linked him to the other killings. He mainly took precautions now just to keep himself from getting lax, not to hide the fact that he was the murderer.

They drove for several miles outside the city and into the desert. Alexander steered the car onto a dirt road and drove for many more miles into the darkness before parking.

Zack tried everything during the drive from begging to reasoning even threatening, to get Alexander to spare his life. When the car stopped far off the main road, he went limp, causing the two other men to carry him to the back of the van.

Once inside, Alexander lit two lanterns while Kevin handcuffed Zack's wrists to the two large eye bolts he had drilled into the vehicle's frame earlier that day. As he prepared to gag Zack, Alexander stopped him.

"We don't need that out here. No one can hear him."

Kevin got out of the van and shut the rear doors behind him.

With the calm of a surgeon about to do a routine operation, Alexander opened his briefcase and slipped on a pair of latex gloves. Zack began to whimper as Alexander took a long-bladed knife and held it with the flat side inches from his face.

"Why did you take off without me the night of the explosion? You could have at least seen that I got out of the building okay. Then maybe you wouldn't be here right now. Where should I start? Deciding that is always the hard part."

Zack froze.

Alexander began making superficial cuts. "This is how I treat people when they backstab me. You're wishing right now that you hadn't done it. Aren't you?"

Zack only continued whimpering.

Alexander held up a pair of pliers and examined them in the victim's line of sight.

"You know, I once used these to pull out teeth one by one to get information from a guy. Of course, I didn't get all his teeth. He told all after only a few were extracted."

"Please. No!" cried Zack.

"Teeth are a lot of work. I don't think I want to mess with that tonight. These pliers have another purpose with fingers and toes."

Zack was crying uncontrollably, begging Alexander to stop while Alexander worked his fingers with the pliers.

Zack's legs began to flail wildly when Alexander moved to his feet. He pushed open the back door of the van.

"Kevin, come and hold this sorry bastard's legs."

Zack's arms convulsed and strained against the handcuffs that held them. The screams were deafening as they echoed through the vehicle's interior.

"You know, Zack, you're very fortunate," Alexander said as he wiped the sweat from his forehead and face. "Rumors about what I do for revenge have flown around everywhere. You actually get to find out that the rumors are true."

The screaming turned to gibberish when Alexander took a scalpel and made deep cuts all over Zack's body.

The desert was cold, but due to the heat inside the lantern lit van, Alexander removed his black T-shirt.

His eyes gleamed as he made puncture wounds with an ice pick. The ice pick was soon replaced by the first long, sharp knife.

"I'm not sure what you told the Feds, but I'm sure it was enough to get you off the hook. Your testimony causes real problems for me if I'm caught. They can build a better case because of you. It's too bad I didn't find you first." Alexander paused for a moment. "Maybe I should fix it so talking isn't a problem."

He forced the weakened man's mouth open. Zack gagged on the blood that flowed down his throat and coughed, spraying blood over Alexander's chest and jeans.

Alexander stopped and drank from a bottle of water before making a series of long, deep cuts causing Zack to pass out. He continued cutting with the scalpel and knife until he felt justice had been served. It was then that he delivered the fatal cut to the jugular vein, not wanting to make the mistake he made with Shalayah. He watched as the last bit of life drained out of his once trusted employee.

* * *

The next morning was busy. Leo took Rachel into San Francisco to his old precinct and introduced her to some of his former colleagues, then later they toured the city.

Rachel was fascinated by the street entertainers and vendor stalls along Fisherman's Wharf.

They returned to Leo's childhood home for lunch and to visit with his family.

At a picnic table in the backyard, Rachel talked to Michael and Sarah. She was struck by how much alike Michael and Leo were, though their lives were vastly different. They had similar mannerisms, as well as the same dry sense of humor. The way Michael and Sarah interacted was very much like how she and Leo related to each other. She couldn't help but feel she was looking into her future. Rachel noticed Leo coming toward them, before stopping to answer his cell phone.

* * *

Leo watched Rachel visit with his brother and sister-in-law. They got along great. In fact, she seemed comfortable with all the family members she met. He knew it would turn out that way. *This is it,* he thought.

He drank some bottled water to ease the dryness in his mouth and throat.

What was he so nervous about? Everything was set, the ring was in his jacket pocket, he would invite her to walk with him among the tall redwoods behind his parent's house. When they reached the creek that flowed near the property, he would tell her that life without her didn't occur to him. Then he would drop to one knee and propose. He had brought up the subject of marriage a few times, and she always responded positively. Still, he was very anxious.

He set down the bottle of water, realizing that it wasn't helping, and walked toward the group at the picnic table. He had taken two steps when his cell phone rang. The caller I.D. indicated Mark's home number.

*   *   *

When he pressed the "End" button, the dry mouth was gone, but he noticed he had a death grip on the phone.

He now walked with purpose to the picnic table where Rachel sat.

When he reached the table, Michael was the first to speak. "I was just telling Rachel that Sarah and I would like to take the two of you to dinner tonight."

"We're gonna have to take a rain check Mike," Leo put a hand on his brother's shoulder and turned to Rachel. "We have to leave immediately."

"Why?!" asked Rachel.

"Zack Williams disappeared from the safe house, and there's evidence of foul play," Leo whispered as they made their way to the house to pack their things.

"I thought we saved at least one," was all she could say.

Leo jammed his clothes back into the suitcase. This was supposed to be one of the most romantic moments of his life. He was about to ask the woman he loved to spend her life with him. He had thought about this weekend so many times in the last few weeks. When he had bought the ring, he could barely contain his excitement as he imagined her answer to his proposal and his family's reaction when they announced their engagement. He continued stuffing clothes into the suitcase as he thought over the lost moment and Zack's disappearance.

*   *   *

The FBI field office in San Diego was deserted on Saturday evening except for some workaholic agents and the weekend security crew. The somber face of the Special Agent in Charge greeted the four agents called to the emergency meeting.

"As you have all heard, Zack Williams has disappeared from the safe house. I got a call this afternoon from the Las Vegas P.D. who were responsible for guarding him. At first, I thought he got tired of being confined and escaped because, like you said, Leo, he was a little unpredictable. The police officer on duty was found in the bushes on the side of the house with a single gunshot wound through his head. In addition, there were definite signs of forced entry and a struggle." Mark passed photos of the scene to the agents. "I don't want to think this way, but I'm wondering if someone here is on Hargrove's payroll."

"I've been suspicious of a leak ever since Rachel was abducted," said Leo as he looked over the photos of the safe house.

Suddenly Rachel, who was slumped in the chair, sat bolt upright. "Damn it, why didn't I think of this before! The day you gave me the delivery assignment for Alexander's company, Laura Galloway was filling in for Su Lee. When did she leave that day?"

"Before I did," said Mark. "No, wait. I left, then had to come back. She stayed to get things ready for Su Lee. When I came back, she offered to help me find the phone number I was looking for, but I sent her home."

"Ever since I returned to work after everything went down, she has been nervous around me," Rachel said, "I've always been friendly towards her, but she avoids any contact with me. That wasn't the case before the abduction. Who set up the safe house for Zack?"

Mark ran a hand through his silver hair then rested his forehead in his hands. "Su Lee was on vacation that week. Laura was filling in for her. I had her set up the safe house. I'm going to contact the Office of Professional Responsibility and order a full investigation. The evidence now is purely circumstantial; there's little probative value in it. In the meantime, you are all on a full-time search for Harry Matteson."

CHAPTER EIGHTEEN

Rachel startled awake when Leo opened the door to her squad room. The long night looking for Harry had proved fruitless.

"Looks like you're as tired as I am."

"Yeah, I needed to rest a few minutes," she said, stretching.

"I just talked to Austin and Charles. We all agree that we need a break. They're going to keep working and give us two hours. Then we'll come back and reciprocate. We're also taking tonight off so we can all sleep in our own beds."

"Sounds great. Maybe we'll find Harry by then."

"I hope so, I just wish our NCIC database had more information on him." Leo kissed her before they left together.

*　　*　　*

Seaport village was crowded on the cool but sunny Sunday afternoon. Rachel and Leo bought lunch at the bakery deli and took it to the grassy area near the ocean. They nibbled their sandwiches and took in the jumble of activity that was all around them. People of all ages rode bikes and rollerblades on the cement between the grass and the stone wall that bordered the water. Others flew kites trying to avoid the trees in the area. While Rachel watched the people, she saw a familiar family. Her ex-boyfriend Brad, his wife Brandi, and their daughter walked by.

Rachel called them over and introduced them to Leo.

"I can't believe how much your daughter has grown since I last saw her," Rachel said. The little girl had the carrot red hair of her mother but judging from her long legs, she would have her father's height.

Rachel smiled at the two-year old. "You were just a baby last time I saw you."

The toddler buried her face in her mother's legs.

"Uh oh, we're shy," said Rachel.

"Yeah, she is," Brandi said. "Don't know where she got that from with us as parents."

Brandi was not at all meek or timid. In fact, she was typical of the kind of woman Brad liked; he liked strong women. In Rachel's opinion, any woman who could make a marriage to a cop work had to be strong.

"Well, we've had some good news recently on a couple of counts," Brad said, beaming. "I'm up for a promotion to Lieutenant, and we're having another baby."

"That's terrific!" Rachel said and hugged the other woman.

After some catching up, the family went on their way and Rachel looked wistfully after them.

"Nickel for your thoughts," Leo said.

"I was just thinking that someday, I might make a decent mother."

"I'm sure you would. We make a good team. I bet we would make good parents."

"I don't know. I know I deal well with children on the job, but as far as the day to day, I can't even cook a real meal."

"I'd cook the meals."

She looked into his smiling face and saw by the look in his eyes that he was serious.

Being his partner in life had crossed her mind many times. Every time he mentioned marriage, she saw that same serious look. When would he make his move?

*   *   *

The phone rang only once before Rachel was awake enough to answer it. Over the last few months, she had received late night calls where the caller was silent on the other end. The calls were coming more frequently. Since Alexander's initial contact, they began to be unnerving. Tonight, she decided to talk to the anonymous caller.

"Listen, I'm tired of these calls; if you have a problem with me, why don't we just meet somewhere and talk it over?"

"Do you really think I'm that stupid, Rachel? You'd meet me all right; with twenty other agents coming out of the woodwork when I arrived."

She jumped and drew in her breath when she heard Alexander's voice on the other end of the line. She suspected it was him but didn't really expect him to reply.

"No, I don't think you're stupid." She took a deep breath. "I just want my life back, and I'm willing to deal with you to get it."

He continued talking as if she hadn't said anything.

"By the way, I've seen you twice with Detective Walsh from the San Diego P.D. What is he to you? Were you coworkers, lovers, what?'

"He's nothing to me. We worked a case together a few years ago, that's all."

"You're lying to me, Rachel. The way he put his arms around you at the hospital a while ago, that's more than working a case together. It was quite touching how he let you cry on his shoulder in his car that night. He has a beautiful family; it would be a shame for that little girl to grow up without a father, wouldn't it?"

"Damn it! It's Leo and I you want. Why don't we work something out and you can just leave all these other people alone?"

"Let's talk about that for a second. What could you possibly offer me?"

His calm manner on the phone made Rachel shiver.

"The most logical thing would be money, but you work for the federal government. If you gave me everything you have, it wouldn't be near the money I have. You're not high enough in the FBI to get me out of the country safely. Of course, you could talk to the Special Agent in Charge and convince him to give me safe passage. He could probably use a good blow job. Leo and I both know you're talented in that department."

There was silence on the other end of the phone. Rachel wasn't sure if the silence meant he was thinking or waiting for her reply. The pencil in her hand snapped in half. She grabbed a pen to continue writing if he said anything else.

"Why didn't I think of it before?" Alexander finally said. "You could offer me yourself for 24 hours. I'd pick somewhere nice, and we would spend the day together with you at my beck and call. I mean it wouldn't be rape if you agreed to it now, would it?"

She was silent for a moment before replying. "Obtaining sex through emotional coercion is considered rape. What makes you think I would agree to something like that anyway?"

"That's just it. You would never willingly spend 24 hours with me any more than I would meet you any-where. You and I both know it's more than your body I want unless I've overestimated your intelligence."

"I know full well what you want, you sick bastard, and you're not going to get it!"

"I will. The next time we meet, it will be on my terms, not yours."

Alexander disconnected the call, leaving Rachel alone in the quiet of 2:30 in the morning.

*   *   *

First thing the next morning, Rachel notified Leo and Mark of the second call and the threat to Brad and his family.

"This doesn't make any sense," Leo said, shaking his head. "When he has a score to settle, he goes right for the source unless there isn't an alternative."

"I'm not willing to take that chance," Rachel said. "Things didn't work out for Brad and I, but I care about him. He's an excellent detective with a family that loves him."

"I agree," Mark said. "After losing everything, he may have degenerated to a new low. We'll get them into hiding right away, and I'm calling Milwaukee and beefing up security on your mother's place."

"Thank you." Rachel turned to Leo. "If he's mad at both of us, why is he only calling me?"

"I know him too well. He's probably afraid that I'll catch something in the conversation that you wouldn't.

There's also a power play going on. He knows he can't get to me as easily as he can you. Because of what he did to you, he can upset you easier. I learned to control my emotions around him. I'm sure he's well aware of that. Problem is, the more I fall in love with you, the more I find myself hating him. I don't know if my control will be as strong as it once was."

"Either way, you two get to Detective Walsh and get him and his family into hiding," Mark said.

*   *   *

After reaching police headquarters and finding out that Brad was off that day, Rachel and Leo drove to his home. Brandi answered the door.

"Is Brad home?" Rachel asked. "We really need to talk to both of you."

"Yes, come in."

"Is everything okay?" Brad asked while coming down the stairs.

"I'm afraid not," Rachel said. "The man who instigated my attack is responsible for some recent murders. He's called me twice and made threats. Last night, he threatened you."

"Why would he do that? We've seen each other twice in the last several months," Brad said.

"The only thing I can think of is that he saw us both times we ran into each other and figured out you're more than a mere acquaintance. We are making arrangements right now to get all three of you into a safe house. There may be nothing to the threat, but we aren't taking chances."

"What does this bastard look like anyway? I wonder if I've seen him around," Brad said.

Leo handed Alexander's picture to Brad.

"Damn it!" Brandi said when she saw the picture.

"What is it?" her husband asked.

"I saw him this morning, in the parking lot at Vons. Ashley has a cold, so she was clingy and insisting on being held, and I was nauseous. There I was struggling with a kid and groceries when he came up and started loading bags into the trunk. When he finished, I thanked him, and he just waved and said, 'We reds have to look out for each other.'"

Rachel could see Brad's face take on a reddish hue. She had seen this angry reaction many times before.

"Brandi, you go pack for Ashley, and I'll pack for you. You'll go with Rachel and Leo."

"Brad, the threat was made toward you. You are going with them, aren't you?" Rachel asked.

"No, but I'll be on the lookout for him. That sorry bastard had better pray to any god he believes in that I don't see him first. First, he hurt you. Now, he's been near my wife and daughter."

"I don't advise that," Leo said. "I was undercover in his business for years. He's smart and dangerous. In fact, he's constantly just out of our grasp. You need to go with your family."

"You must be the agent that took care of Rachel after she was assaulted."

"Yes."

"Take care of my family the way you took care of Rachel, and I'll look out for myself."

Rachel knew too well that there was no convincing him, so they took Brandi and Ashley to safety.

*   *   *

Kevin sat against a tangerine tree and stared out over the hilly terrain below the orchard. The cool breeze was heavy with the scent of citrus. He was surprised to hear footsteps coming toward him through the trees. He looked up in time to see Alex sit down against a tree opposite him. Alex never came into the orchard.

"You like it out here, don't you?"

"Yeah, it's quiet, and I like the view."

Alex looked out over the hills. "It is nice." Then he turned to Kevin. "I've been thinking about our lives after Rachel and Leo are gone. We'll lay low in Mexico for a while, then go to Canada with new identities and become citizens. Of course, you could stay in Mexico if you wanted to. I'm planning to start another business. Nothing big like Hargrove Technologies was, but something that will make a good living. If you want, you could be my right-hand man in the business." Alexander shrugged. "Then again, maybe you'd want to start your own life apart from me. With everything you've been through with me, I would understand that. The point is, I take care of those who are loyal to me. When this is over, I'll give you enough money to get settled. What you do from there is up to you. What do you think?"

Kevin smiled. "It's a lot to think about."

Alexander got up and dusted the dirt from his pants. "You've got time to figure it out. At least now you know where I stand."

Kevin watched him go. Three more killings, two of which would happen on the same night, then he would be free. Unless the FBI found them first.

*   *   *

Alexander watched as Brad Walsh stood over his workbench in his garage/workshop.

When Brad turned around and saw him, he startled and dropped the piece of wood he was working on. Alexander's laser-sighted Baretta was on him. Brad raised his hands to the level of his shoulders.

Alexander looked up at him. "I bet your height intimidates a lot of people. . .However, I'm not easily intimidated."

"That surprises me. Men who prey on women are usually pussies."

"That's where you have me figured out all wrong. Rape isn't normally my thing. Mostly, I deal with men, I just thought rape was the best way to break Rachel down. Of course, I was wrong. . . maybe she enjoyed it too much." Alexander smiled at Brad. "So, you two are ex-lovers like I thought. I can see it in the anger flashing across your face. I could hear it in her voice the night I threatened you. It's very sweet that you two still care about each other."

"What's your point, you son of a bitch!?"

"My point is," Alexander continued, "though I have no real problem with you, I have a big problem with Rachel and her boyfriend, and I have a message for them."

With the last sentence, Alexander fired the gun.

*   *   *

Leo tried to keep up as Rachel ran through the emergency room doors of Scripps Mercy Hospital and nearly crashed into a row of empty wheelchairs. He caught up with her when she reached the admit desk.

The two agents were led to a room on the surgical recovery floor. Brad's left leg was already in a cast and rigged up with wires and pulleys. The bullet, aimed at his shin, shattered the tibia and lodged in the muscle. A few hours went by before he was cognizant enough to talk.

He stared at the ceiling. "The bastard could have taken me from my family permanently. He said he had a message for you, then he shot me in the leg. When I was down, I thought he was going to shoot again, but he told me to tell you that he can get to anyone, and he would get to the two of you. I called out an APB and dispatch sent an ambulance. As soon as I get out of here, I want to go where my family is. I'll hide with them."

"Good," Rachel said gently. "In the meantime, someone will guard your room."

Brad took one of Rachel's hands in both of his. "He's after the two of you. I thought he couldn't get to me because I was too careful and too good a cop. Go into hiding like I am, Rachel, don't let him get to you again."

Leo held his breath while Rachel thought over Brad's statement. He had tried everything to get her to hide, but she always refused. Maybe the turn of events will make her change her mind.

"No, I will be there when he's brought down," she said.

Leo let out his breath in a sigh.

"If I thought it would do any good, I'd argue the point with you. I wish you'd listen to reason." Brad released her hand.

"You need to rest now. We'll be in touch when you're released," Rachel replied.

CHAPTER NINETEEN

Two weeks later, on a Saturday morning, Rachel returned from a jog along Mission Beach near her apartment. She relied on her exercise routine to work off the stress of her job. The past few weeks had been hell. First came Alexander's phone call. He hadn't called back since, and Rachel didn't know how she felt about that. She was glad she didn't have to listen to his arrogant tone, but she wanted to talk to him to get him to make a mistake and reveal something. Then Zack's decomposing and scavenger-eaten corpse was found miles from the main highway in an abandoned van. According to Nevada Highway Patrol, there wasn't much body left due to the desert animals that had gotten to it. Brad finally came to his senses and hid with his family, but only after a run in with Alexander. She and Leo worked around the clock trying to find Harry Matteson, the search was going nowhere, and they were all taking a much-needed weekend off. Finding Harry meant protecting at least one accomplice. They all kept the search for him and the concurrent search for Alexander quiet to avoid any leaks. Once Harry was safe, a trap could be set to snare Alexander. She was almost to her place when she noticed Leo sitting on the steps waiting for her.

"How long have you been here?" she asked.

"Not long. How about we drive to La Jolla and have breakfast at The Cottage?"

After Rachel showered, she changed into a burgundy, blue, and tan broomstick skirt and a dusty blue sweater with a matching cardigan. They drove to The Cottage, a former Victorian house converted to a restaurant. The yellow house with white trim attracted a crowd on Saturday and Sunday mornings. After a 30 minute wait, Rachel and Leo were seated at a table on the patio, the cool ocean breeze and warm sun making the location perfect.

Over a shared slice of coffee cake, Leo began talking. "I've been doing a lot of thinking lately about the directions my life could take. Every time I think about it, several things come to mind, but one thing remains the same." He took Rachel's hand. "Every time I look at my future, I see you. I guess what I'm really trying to say before I lose my nerve is, Rachel, will you marry me?"

He held both of her hands in his and looked directly into her eyes.

"Yes!" she said, beaming.

When he slipped the engagement ring on her finger and they kissed, people at the nearby tables cheered.

Over the rest of their breakfast, Leo told her his other thoughts about the future. "I'm considering starting my own private detective company after I retire in seven years."

"Really?"

"Yeah, I feel ready to call my own shots after spending so many years following orders from two different sources. I got paid a lot for my undercover work. I was paid very well at Hargrove, the FBI accountant and the attorney agreed I could keep some of that money. I used my computer and wisely invested it, so I have what I need to start and build the business."

"That's great."

"I would love it if you would be my partner in the business, if that's what you wanted to do after your retirement."

"Years ago, when I joined the police force, I dreamed of being a private eye someday. I think that would be great."

After paying the bill, Leo suggested they go to Horton Plaza before going to Rachel's apartment to make phone calls.

Rachel loved the multi-story shopping mall with its multicolored buildings in red, purple, yellow, and terra-cotta. The sculptures, fountains, banners, and street musicians made the place seem a world unto itself.

When they arrived, he led her straight to Versailles Fine Jewelry where he bought her engagement ring.

Leo approached a salesgirl and handed her a receipt. "You have something on hold under the name Acratelli."

"Yes, just a minute," she said, flashing a beautiful smile at them.

Rachel looked at him questioningly.

He smiled at her. "A little engagement gift I picked out."

The salesgirl returned with a white box. Rachel carefully set it on the counter and opened it. Inside, wrapped in tissue paper was the Lladro sculpture titled "Classic Water Carrier." She took a minute to study the porcelain figure of the dark-skinned girl in a peasant dress sitting next to a water pitcher.

"Leo, this is beautiful." She threw her arms around him and kissed him.

"I knew you liked these because you have one in your bedroom, and every time you see these figurines on display you stop to look at them."

She had loved the collectable series of statues for a long time but always felt they were an expensive indulgence, so the only one she owned was a birthday gift from her mother.

She kissed Leo again while the salesgirl carefully packed the sculpture for the trip home.

"I love it," she whispered as they walked out of the store.

When they got to Rachel's apartment, she unpacked her new statue and placed it on the light oak coffee table. She then picked up the phone and dialed her mother. She wanted to call her anyway to check up on her.

"Hi, Mom."

"Hi, those FBI men have been visiting and driving by, but no one else."

"That's great to hear. You know how you always say I'm too wrapped up in my career to get married?"

"Yes, if Leo didn't already work with you, you probably wouldn't have time to see him."

"Well, I'm going to be seeing a lot more of him soon. I'm going to marry him."

"Oh, honey that's wonderful!"

She could hear her mother starting to choke up.

"I didn't want you to miss out on a loving marriage like your father and I had together."

"Looks like I won't. He proposed today, and I didn't even have to think about it. I just said yes."

"I couldn't be more thrilled!"

Rachel smiled into the phone. "Me either."

"Well, although I haven't gotten to meet him yet, I would at least like to talk to him."

Leo and his future mother-in-law talked for 30 minutes before Rachel got back on the line. "Well, honey, he sounds like the gem you say he is. I was just thinking, do you want me to ask your Uncle Patrick to walk you down the aisle?"

"Actually, I have someone in mind to join you in walking me down."

After more wedding talk, Leo went home late in the night and Rachel went to bed with visions of her dream wedding. For one day, it was as if Alexander Hargrove never existed.

*   *   *

First thing Monday, morning Rachel walked into her squad room ready to tackle the search for Harry Matteson. She now had additional motivation to find him. The sooner this case went down, the sooner she could concentrate on her wedding. She noticed the message light on her voicemail and checked the messages. The last one had come just 15 minutes before she had arrived. She listened carefully as Larnell Michaels gave an account of his sister Shalayah's recovery. She returned his call right away.

"I can't believe it, Agent Keaney." Larnell began. "The head nurse and the guard heard her stir and went in to check on her. She was wide-awake and talked to them. No one expected this. We hoped for it but didn't expect it. As I was saying on the message, when my sister first woke up a few days ago, she didn't have any memory of what happened to her. Now, she remembers, but she won't talk to anyone about it except you and some other agent she worked with. That doesn't make any sense."

"I know exactly who she's talking about. How is she?"

"She'll have to build up her motor skills again, but everything else seems fine."

"That's encouraging. Let me run this by the special agent in charge. I'll see how soon we can come out there."

*   *   *

When Mark was able to see Rachel and Leo, they told him of Shalayah's progress.

"You two need to get out there right away and take her statement," Mark said after they relayed the story. "When we apprehend Hargrove, we want as much evidence as we can get to secure a conviction."

"We can leave right away," Leo said.

"We can leave in a minute. First, we have something to tell Mark." Rachel smiled up at Leo. "Leo proposed to me on Saturday, and I accepted. We're talking about a July sunset wedding."

"More good news. Maybe our luck is turning after all. I'll be there to celebrate with you, you can be sure of that."

"Actually, I was hoping you would do more than just be there," Rachel said. "As you know, my father passed on several years ago. I wondered if you would walk me down the aisle along with my mother."

His face fell for a second, and mixed emotions flashed in his eyes. "Rachel, I would be more than honored. Thank you."

At this point, Rachel and Leo hurried out of the room. Rachel knew he needed to be alone.

*   *   *

As they approached the hospital room, Rachel and Leo showed their badges to the guard at the door. The two agents walked quietly to Shalayah's bedside.

The minute she saw Leo, she began to cry. "I would have done anything for that man!" Rachel held her hand, and Leo put an arm around her while she cried bitter tears.

After a while, she composed herself and told the story of Alexander's visit to her home. In horrific detail, she described his attempt to take her life.

"You're very lucky, Shalayah," Leo said in his calming voice. "Everyone else we found wound up with their throats cut in addition to what you described. You lost a lot of blood, but you're still alive."

"How many of us did he find, Andre? I guess that's not your name, is it?"

"My name is Leo, but you can call me whatever you're comfortable with. Alan, Randy, and Zack are dead; we haven't found Harry Matteson yet."

"Harry," she said as though she were thinking aloud. "I've talked to him. I found him through a chat room. We talked a lot over the Net before I was attacked. He lives in Eugene, Oregon, last I heard. He asked me not to tell anyone since he can still be arrested. He figured it was so far away from North Carolina, where he had all that trouble, that no one would find him there. When we started chatting and emailing, I told him what you all had done for me, but he was too scared to contact you."

Leo looked at Rachel, and their eyes met.

She nodded, addressing Shalayah, "Excuse me for a moment, please." She quickly left the room to call Mark.

When Rachel returned, the interview had just come to a close, and Shalayah's niece, Carla, walked into the room.

"Hey, girl," Shalayah said, reaching out to hug the young woman. "This is my niece, Carla. She's been coming to see me every day after she gets off school."

"We've met." Rachel smiled at Carla.

The young girl looked so much healthier than the last time Rachel saw her. Today, there was a sparkle in her dark eyes. Her hair, held back in butterfly clips, had a healthy sheen. A Fallbrook Warriors T-shirt replaced the tight spandex halter top.

"We'll leave you two alone. You have our number if anything else comes to mind," said Leo.

Before they reached the door, Carla called out to them. "Agent Keaney, I have something to ask you, but if you're too busy, it's okay. I have a school project due in a month. I'm supposed to interview someone in a career field that I am interested in. Because of everything that has happened to my aunt, I've become interested in law enforcement. Can I interview you sometime? My parents said they would drive me to San Diego."

Rachel opened her organizer, and the two set up a time and place to meet.

Carla looked down for a moment then back at Rachel. "I've admired you since you came to investigate the attack on my aunt. I'm glad you can do the interview."

Rachel felt warmth rush to her cheeks. "We need smart young women in law enforcement. I'll be glad to answer any of your questions."

*   *   *

Mark stood up and shook hands with Special Agent Russell Sims of the Office of Professional Responsibility. The two men served in the Navy at the same time and spent a few minutes talking about ships they were stationed on before getting down to business.

Agent Sims' large hands deftly unlatched his briefcase and pulled out a file folder. "Well, we've been studying her work record and it's nothing but exemplary. Of course, we've had her under surveillance here at the field office, and she's done nothing to arouse suspicion. When we investigated her background, we did find something interesting. She and Alexander Hargrove were students at UC Berkeley at the same time. However, they didn't have any classes together nor did they attend any extracurricular clubs together."

"So, we're still dealing with coincidence, just like the fact that she was filling in for my secretary the day I gave Agent Keaney the Hargrove assignment and the fact that she set up the safe house for Zack Williams. What's our next move?"

"I think we're going to surveil her outside of work for a while to see if we can pick up any suspicious behavior. I would suggest we tap her home phone, but the judge I'm working with won't give me a warrant based on coincidence."

"I can't say I don't understand. What we have is incomplete at best. On the one hand, I hope you don't find anything, and we can clear her name. On the other hand, I want to know how Hargrove gets his information."

"We'll just keep after it. If she's guilty, we'll know soon enough."

When Agent Sims left, Mark took a moment to think before tackling the next project on his desk. Visions of two good agents cut down in their prime by Alexander Hargrove flashed through his mind's eye. Then the words of Rachel's statement in the HARTECH file came to mind. Whoever caused all of this should be fully prosecuted.

CHAPTER TWENTY

The Borders bookstore in Mission Valley was busy as usual on a Saturday afternoon. Rachel stood just inside the entrance waiting for Carla and her parents. While she waited, an average sized man with dark sunglasses and a straw beach hat walked by. When he passed her, she caught the scent of Drakkar causing her to shudder.

For nearly a year now, she couldn't take the scent of that cologne. It was Alexander's cologne of choice. The scent of it was on his body when he violated her that first night. The cologne lingered in his bedroom when she was brought there for the second assault. The build of the man only added to the uneasiness she felt. In her detective work, she developed an eye for things like height, weight, and build. This man was like Alexander in all those respects. She didn't think Alexander would be crazy enough to come into the store even if he happened to be following her.

She took a deep breath to calm herself just as Carla and her parents walked in. Her parents gave Carla a cell phone and told her to page them when the interview was over, then they left for some shopping in the area. Rachel and Carla took a seat on one of the couches near the entrance.

Carla turned on a tape recorder and asked her first question. "How did you get to your current job?"

"Well, I started as a uniformed police officer, then became a detective, and then became interested in the FBI and applied. When I was accepted, I had to go through the FBI Academy in Quantico, Virginia. Luckily, there was an opening in the San Diego Field Office, so I didn't have to relocate."

"Who influenced you to go into law enforcement?"

"I was always interested in that line of work. I used to watch cop shows when I was young. Shows like Kojak, and Baretta, even Charlie's Angels," she said with a laugh. "I was always policing the school playground and my classrooms. That drove my teachers nuts. My father always told me that I could do anything I set my mind to. So I did."

"I understand the police and the FBI are both male-dominated. Is it hard to be a woman working with so many men?"

"From the very beginning, there is a lot of pressure on a woman to prove herself. Female officers are often thought of as secretaries with guns. I worked hard to be seen as a fellow officer. I earned the respect of detectives by volunteering every time a case required the help of uniforms and by protecting crime scenes well. Many detectives were glad when they knew I was the first officer on the scene. However, when I was promoted to Homicide, I got the cold shoulder from men I had joked around with as a uniform. It was one thing for me to help them, and another thing altogether for me to be one of them. Instead of whining that they weren't being nice, I used my energy putting down cases, and again, earning the respect I deserve. Since I worked for the San Diego P.D., my reputation preceded me when I joined the FBI, so it was a little easier."

"What about sexual harassment? Is that an issue for female officers and agents?"

"It goes on, but I've seen it handled very well in both organizations. It's not tolerated. The only reason it goes on is because it isn't always reported. The thing to realize is that if you're a woman working in a male dominated field, you're going to hear guy jokes and guy talk and you have to be able to deal with that."

After a few more questions Carla excused herself and walked toward the ladies' room. On her way, she bumped into a large built young man causing him to drop his book.

"Sorry," Carla said and helped him retrieve his book.

When Carla handed him the fallen book, he looked right at Rachel. The baseball cap he wore pulled low did not hide his face when he looked at her. She immediately recognized him as Kevin McCray. When she stood up and began to walk toward him, he panicked, knocked Carla out of the way and ran to the front door.

"Go to the ladies' room and stay there," Rachel told Carla.

She obeyed without question.

*   *   *

Alexander, in a straw beach hat, sat in a chair near the couch where the interview took place, his face concealed by a copy of Rolling Stone magazine. He waited for Rachel to run after Kevin who had stupidly let himself be recognized. When she didn't, he peered over the magazine to find himself looking at the barrel of Rachel's ten millimeter.

"Get up slowly and keep your hands where I can see them," she ordered. "Get the manager and security," she said to someone out of his line of sight.

He let the magazine fall and did as she instructed.

"Alexander Hargrove, you're under arrest…"

For months now, Alexander had been following Rachel and Leo. He always stayed a safe distance away and never let himself be seen. Today, he was feeling gutsy and decided to enter the crowded bookstore telling Kevin to wait a good 15 minutes before going in after him. Walking past her gave him a rush just like sending her the book. The game was a lot of fun, but he had taken one risk too many. Rachel looked pleased to have him in the position of do or die.

"Put your hands on the back of the chair."

He made a move to obey, but as he was about to turn around his foot shot out, connecting enough with Rachel's abdomen to knock her down. Alexander shoved through the crowd that had gathered and ran to the car Kevin had running and waiting for him. He would have to stay out of sight for a while.

*　*　*

Inside the bookstore, employees and onlookers had gathered around Rachel. The store's security officer reached her just as Alexander ran out the door.

She jerked her pistol off the floor and pointed to her badge that she had clipped to her belt. "FBI, it's okay."

Mark would chew her out for this mistake. She should have gotten the security guard's cooperation first. If she had succeeded, any amount of chewing out would have been worth it.

Rachel retrieved Carla from the restroom and waited with her until she was safely with her parents.

The young girl had a lot to tell them and many questions Rachel couldn't answer for her.

*   *   *

As the dark green Dodge sped down Friars Road, Kevin noticed that Alexander kept a watchful eye in every direction, looking for police cars or any signs that someone was tailing them. He figured they would avoid the freeways at all costs since Rachel would have called an APB out with a description of them and their car. This car, an average-looking, midsize sedan, had served them well. They always kept it not too clean and not too dirty so it wouldn't attract any attention. Unfortunately, Rachel had seen it, so it no longer served its purpose. When Friars Road turned into Mission Gorge Road, Alexander must have been confident that they were not being followed because he turned onto Highway 67, then onto Highway 78, doubling back through the San Pasqual Valley and Escondido to reach his home.

Sensing Alexander's anger and concentration on getting home without being seen, Kevin remained silent through the whole trip. He was relieved that Alexander had not spoken to him except to demand that they switch places so he could drive.

When they arrived at home, Kevin swallowed hard. "What are we going to do now?" he asked.

Instead of an answer, Alexander hit him in the face and shoved him into the wall.

"Sometimes I wonder if you're an asset or a liability."

"I'm sorry," Kevin said, bracing himself for another hit that didn't come.

"Why did you have to look at her? I told you that since the Feds know I'm involved in the murders, they may also know I'm not working alone. You could have thanked that girl for picking up your book and never looked in Rachel's direction. I don't know how she figured out it was you I was working with, but she figures out things. As much as I hate her, I respect her detective skills."

"I'm sorry, it won't happen again."

"Sorry isn't enough. Don't screw up like that again." Alexander unlocked the door and shoved it open.

Kevin took a deep breath. There was a lot of warning behind those last few words, and their meaning chilled him to the bone.

The two men packed some belongings, and Alexander made a few phone calls. Within minutes, he had arranged for a five-year old burgundy Toyota Camry with an untraceable paper trail. Alexander and Kevin took the cars, drove to Highway 5, and abandoned the Dodge at Oceanside.

*　　*　　*

Late that same evening, Rachel got a phone call from the San Diego Police telling her that Oceanside authorities found the car near Highway 5 indicating that Alexander and Kevin headed out of town. They canceled the APB on the car but kept the one for Alexander and Kevin open. They had alerted the Highway Patrol as well as Border Patrol. Rachel thanked the police department for all their help and disconnected the call.

"I almost had him, Leo. I was this close to bringing him in." She held her thumb and finger a centimeter apart. "Mark called just before you got here. I am officially off the case. Damn it, I feel like Alexander's winning."

"Hey." Leo got up off the futon and pulled her close. "His luck can't hold out forever. He's going to make a mistake."

"I'm going to live to see that son of a bitch behind bars or dead."

"We both will. Remember how you said that the day we got engaged it felt like Alexander didn't exist?"

"Yeah, I remember," she said smiling.

"Let's spend this evening as if he doesn't exist," he said, leading her to the futon and kissing her, gently at first then more passionately.

CHAPTER TWENTY-ONE

Alexander and Kevin saw the sun rise a brilliant golden orange as they drove north on Highway 5. They were going to Oregon because Alexander suspected that Harry Matteson lived in Eugene. He had gone into financial themed chat rooms where he met a person with the handle #'sman. He asked the person questions that seemed innocent but provided him with valuable information. He knew Harry well and probed into some of his interests outside of money such as archery and fly fishing. During many private chats, he got the man to trust him and reveal more. When his new online friend revealed that he had gotten into trouble years ago stealing from the customers whose money he managed, Alexander knew he hit pay dirt. #'sman never revealed his city, just his state, however, Alexander knew Harry's best friend in high school was named Eugene, so on a hunch, he was going there to look for him. Not only that, after the incident at the bookstore, he wanted to get out of state for a while.

* * *

A few hours after sunup, the two men stopped at a small hotel to sleep for the day. The hotel was the same as the others they stayed in during their visits to "old friends," located in seedy parts of town, small, and privately run. Alexander knew either from experience or word of mouth which hotels to stay in.

When Alexander walked into the lobby, a college-aged blonde woman was managing the front desk. She didn't try to hide the fact that she found him attractive. She smiled brightly when he approached the desk. Her smile faded when Kevin walked in and stood beside him. She obviously thought the two men might be an item.

After he requested one room with two queen beds and check-in was complete, Alexander sent Kevin to the room with their luggage and lingered in the lobby while the girl helped another customer.

What struck him about her was her blue eyes, the same color as Rachel's eyes. They sparkled as he imagined hers must have under normal circumstances. Other than that, she was different from Rachel in every way. She had long, blonde hair styled into many curls and large breasts that stretched her collared pullover. She wore a lot of makeup and had four earrings in each ear.

When she was free, he approached the desk. "What time do you get off work tonight?"

He leaned his elbows on the desk.

"About 5:30, why?" she said with a teasing look in her eyes.

"Because my business partner will be off on an errand around then and I could use a little company."

"Room 10, right?"

"Yes."

"I'll be there at quarter 'till six."

*   *   *

Alexander nudging him awakened Kevin from a sound sleep.

"Get up. You need to be out of here in half an hour."

"Where am I going?" Kevin said.

"Out wherever for about an hour. Then we'll check out and get on our way."

When he left, he saw the front desk girl headed toward their room and knew why he was rushed out in such a hurry.

*   *   *

Alexander had changed into a pair of tan casual slacks and a navy-blue shirt with gold and cream-colored designs throughout the material. Since the destruction of his business, he opted for a more casual look than the $500 suits he wore at the office. Nowadays he wore either jeans or slacks with casual button up shirts or sweaters.

A knock at the door signaled his visitor's arrival. When she entered the room and set her purse down, he noticed she carried a plastic bag.

"What's in the bag?"

"I brought us a couple of beers and some protection. I insist on condoms."

"That's great. So do I. I'll pass on the beer though, I don't drink."

"Really? Well, do you care if I have one?"

"Suit yourself."

She cracked open a beer and took a long sip. Alexander watched her, looking her up and down, then walked slowly over to her and put his hand on the back of her neck, running his fingers upward through her hair.

She put down her beer and traced the outline of his arm with her fingers, then ran her hands down his chest, unbuttoning most of the buttons on his shirt.

When she looked into his eyes, his desire magnified.

Alexander kissed her hard on the mouth before moving to her ear. "I love the way your eyes sparkle," he whispered.

He sat down on the bed leaving her standing between his parted thighs. Slowly, he untucked her shirt and helped her pull it over her head. He kept his eyes on her sensuously opened mouth as he stroked the large, firm globes of her breasts through her satin bra. His hands moved to her shoulders, and he exerted a light downward pressure. Without hesitation, she dropped to her knees and freed his erection from his pants.

While her lips and tongue worked his swollen organ, he closed his eyes and thought back to the last time a woman had performed this act on him, the time he had forced Rachel to do it. The memory was almost too much.

"Stop," he said. "You do that much longer, and it will all be over."

She smiled with a twinkle in her eye and stood in front of him to remove her bra.

Alexander pulled her to the bed, took off his shirt, and lay down beside her. His tongue traced the line of her neck to her breasts. He sucked hard on one nipple, then the other causing her breathing to come in short gasps. She fumbled with her jeans, tossing them aside, leaving only tiny black lace panties. He nibbled along her inner thigh, causing her to moan and caress him.

The pressure in his erection became unbearable, and he forcefully removed her panties and entered her. He could feel her body tense in climax as she tightened around him. The burning trails of her fingernails down his back pushed him further toward the edge. He pumped in and out of her faster and harder as she thrust her hips to pull him further inside her.

At the edge of a climax, he spoke in a whisper. "Open your eyes."

Her eyes didn't have the fear Rachel's had a year ago but looking into them brought an explosion of pleasure.

*　　*　　*

Kevin walked the city streets that were not a lot different than the streets of L.A. He came to an area of run-down buildings where people, mostly women, were working the streets.

It occurred to him that he should make a little money on the side. Alexander had complete control of the money whether they were at his home north of San Diego or on the road. Now that he had been clean for many months, Kevin had turned into an attractive young man. His large frame now looked strong. The shine had returned to his sandy-brown hair, and his skin once again looked healthy. Picking up a few johns would be easier now.

Standing beside a building, he waited for a car to slow to a stop and signal him. In his heart he hoped it was an undercover cop who would arrest him out of this mess.

"Are you dating?" the driver said.

"Yes, what can I do for you?"

The two men made a deal and drove off.

25 minutes later, he was back on the same corner ready for another customer. It didn't take long for

another man out for a good time to stop for him. This time, the trick took a little longer. When the second john deposited him on the corner, he was $50 richer and late meeting Alexander back at the hotel.

*   *   *

While he waited for Kevin, Alexander booted up his laptop and logged onto the Internet.

His buddy list indicated that #'sman was online so he invited him to a private chat.

Shortfuze: I am currently traveling through Oregon in route to Washington. If you have time, I'd like to meet with you.

#'sman: I don't know. Let me check my schedule. I'm pretty busy nowadays so I don't know.

Shortfuze: I'm sensing some apprehension about meeting me. Let me put your mind at ease. I am a straight male, so I'm not hitting on you. Secondly, I don't care what you did in your former company. We all make mistakes. I've had a few brushes with the law myself in the past.

#'sman: Both of those things are comforting. I would like to meet with you, when will you be passing through Eugene? I assume you're taking Highway 5.

Shortfuze: You assumed right. If it works for you, why don't you pick a nice restaurant, and we can meet tomorrow at 6:00 p.m. I would like to take you to dinner to thank you for all your investment advice.

#'sman: That would be nice. 6:00 p.m. tomorrow night at Kowloon Restaurant. See you then.

Alexander had just shut down his laptop when Kevin walked in the door.

"You're late. We have a long way to go tonight." Alexander put his laptop in its case.

"By the way, what did you do with the body?" Kevin asked.

"I walked the body to her car, and she drove home or wherever. Where were you?"

"I thought if you were getting some, I would too," was Kevin's terse reply as they walked out to the car.

*   *   *

The alarm clock on Rachel's night table rang at 6:30 a.m.

More than anything, she wanted to pull the covers over her head and forget about today altogether.

Instead, she climbed out of bed. She ran a brush through her hair and looked at the Lladro "A Basket of Fun" figurine on her dresser. The girl looked so peaceful with her basket of kittens. Rachel wished she felt that peaceful, but she knew that was going to be difficult today. It was one year from the day she was abducted from Pacific Beach then used and degraded in a basement room.

She turned away from the statue and went into the bathroom to shower and begin her quick, simple makeup routine. Over the blow dryer, she barely heard the doorbell. Wrapped in a robe, she looked out the peephole to see a woman nearly hidden behind a spray of roses and baby's breath.

She wasn't sure what to make of this. Would Leo send her flowers today to cheer her up?

After tipping the girl who gave her the bouquet with an envious look, she opened the card with her heart pounding. When she read the card, she threw it and the flowers on the floor as if they were contaminated.

The card read:

> <u>My dearest Rachel,</u>
> <u>You didn't think I would forget you on the anniversary of our meeting. I'll never forget those two nights we shared and I'm suspecting neither will you.</u>

She sat down on the couch and tried to calm herself. Tears stung her eyes as the anger welled up inside her. She knew then that she'd be late to work.

*   *   *

Agent Sims lowered his broad frame into a chair across from Mark to give him an update on Laura's Investigation.

"So far, we haven't found much in the week we've had her under surveillance. She spends most evenings at home. She did a lot of shopping over the weekend, bought herself some nice clothes and jewelry."

"Too nice for a secretary's salary?"

"Maybe."

"I don't know much about women's clothes, but she does wear a lot of good quality jewelry. I complimented her once on a necklace she wore. She said her boyfriend gave it to her."

"Well, if she has a boyfriend, he must be out of town because she hasn't seen anyone. Not only that, but she also paid for the stuff in cash."

Mark's eyes widened. "That is unusual. Let's keep the surveillance going."

"I think we should use a scanner to monitor her cell phone."

"Good thinking. I'll be curious to see what turns up."

CHAPTER TWENTY-TWO

Charles and Austin had been looking for Harry Matteson in Eugene, Oregon, for over a week now. One thing was clear to the two men: the guy knew how to hide. When two days turned into seven, Charles decided they should make a desperate attempt to get his attention. He made arrangements to appear on KEZI News This Morning. While Austin waited near a phone off stage, Charles explained to the anchors that a man named Harry Matteson was important to a case they were working on. He reiterated twice that Mr. Matteson was in no danger of arrest, and that his help would benefit them and him. It was a Monday morning, and if Harry himself wasn't watching someone who knew him might be. The show was the most watched morning show in Eugene and within minutes, the station's phone lines lit up. Both men took calls from people who had met with a man named Jonathan Thomas who advertised in the want ads as a financial consultant. The man they contacted fit the description of the man the agents sought. None of the people could give an address because his business card listed a mail drop box number and a cellular phone number.

The calls eventually died away, then stopped altogether.

Charles sighed. "Well, we've tried his cell number with no answer. We still haven't made contact with him.

We can get a warrant so the Mailboxes Etc. will cough up the address, but since everyone knows we're looking for him, he's probably halfway to who-knows-where by now.

"If that's the case, then it means Alexander will have trouble finding him and give us more time to find Alexander and arrest him," Austin said.

"I hope you're right. Let's get out of here. We'll get his address just in case."

The agents were nearly to the door when the station's receptionist ran to catch them.

"There's one more call. I really think you should take it," she said out of breath. Austin, being younger and faster, ran with the woman to take the call. When Charles caught up to them, he heard Austin talk excitedly into the phone.

"Harry, you did the right thing by calling. I swear you won't regret it. 20 minutes? We'll be there."

*   *   *

20 minutes later Charles, Austin, and Harry were at a small art deco themed coffeehouse. The breakfast rush was over, and they had the place to themselves. The agents told Harry of Alexander's mission and Shalayah waking from her coma.

After hearing the story, he stared into his coffee. "Thank heaven I contacted you guys before he found me. I can't believe he's killing people that were so loyal to him."

They drove to Harry's secluded home outside the city. Like Alexander, he liked living away from other people. There, he spilled out the story of his role with Hargrove Technologies.

"For years, I was a respected CPA in Raleigh, North Carolina. Having a lot of money got to me, and I started taking illegal cuts of my customers' investments. I did it for ten years before anyone ever suspected a thing. They were making money, I was making money, everyone was happy. As was bound to happen, everything came crashing down. My wife left me and took our two boys with her. I knew the police would come knocking on my door, so I just got in the car and drove. I was keeping a low profile and planning to escape to Mexico when I met another fugitive in a bar one night. He was going to California to seek refuge from a man who hid people in exchange for their services. Well, I knew I had something to offer the guy, so I came along. I figured what the hell? I could hide and still stay in the U.S. As it turns, out I spent nine years doing Alexander's books and keeping them above suspicion. I also turned him onto some investments that worked out well for him. On the night of the explosion, I woke up with a bad feeling. I wanted to go for a drive. A few hours later, I heard about the explosion on the car's radio, so I just kept driving. Nowadays, I just make money advising other people and investing on the Internet. Through the Internet chat rooms, I came in contact with Shalayah. All of a sudden, I lost contact; I had no idea she was in a coma all that time."

Charles and Austin decided that they would stay with Harry until a safe house could be arranged.

When the three men settled in, Harry turned on his computer to check his investments. "It's a shame I'm going to have to e-mail my online friend and cancel for tonight. He was going to take me to dinner, and I was looking forward to meeting him."

"Tell us about this online friend," Austin said.

"Just a guy I met in the chat rooms I helped him with some investments, and he's coming through town on business."

"Keep the appointment," Charles said. "I have a feeling."

"What kind of feeling?" Austin took the tape of Harry's testimony and put it in his briefcase.

"I don't know, just a hunch. It could be Hargrove trying to meet up with you. If I'm wrong, then you get to meet a new friend."

"I don't think Alexander would show up after you were on television this morning looking for Harry. If he's in the area, he probably saw the segment on the morning show," Austin said.

"Maybe, maybe not, but we're going to be there to find out," Charles replied.

When they arrived at Kowloon Restaurant, the hostess took Harry to his table near the picture window with a view of the Willamette River. She then led Austin to a seat in a corner with an unobstructed view of the dining room. Two other agents from the Portland Field Office were seated at a nearby table. Since Charles had been on T.V., he didn't want to risk being recognized if his hunch was correct, so he found a place in the kitchen. All the agents had carefully hidden microphones and earpieces so they could communicate if necessary. They instructed Harry to receive Alexander as if he were glad to see him.

*   *   *

In a motel room in Creswell, Oregon, south of Eugene, Kevin flipped channels on the television while Alexander put on a periwinkle blue shirt and gray sport coat to go out for the evening. Kevin stopped channel surfing when he found the evening news.

"A local mystery. A Eugene man named Harry Matteson is being sought by the FBI. Special Agent Charles Longview appeared on KEZI News This Morning and asked for any information on a man in his early 50's. He is described as 5'8", salt and pepper hair, and blue eyes."

When the description was given, a picture of Harry appeared on the television. "There is no word on why he is being sought or if the federal agents have found him."

Alexander took the tie off his neck and threw it on a bed. "Well, there's no way I'm going to that meeting. If the Feds are here, they've either found him and will be with him or they're going to be crawling all over the city looking for him. It's too dangerous, I may be recognized. I'll have to let Harry go. It's just not worth it."

Kevin could see Alexander's anger and frustration mounting. His own fear about the situation was building as well. He decided to take the risk of further angering Alexander and spoke up.

"Alex, I've been thinking. It's getting more dangerous every day for us to carry out your plan. I know you want to screw over Leo and Rachel for what they did to you, but the way I see it, you raped her. Even if you don't get to kill her, you still fucked up her life real good. Man, you took something from her she'll never get back. She'll never be the same after what you did to her. Since Leo fell in love with her, then you got revenge against him because you messed up the woman he loves. You'll always be a part of their relationship."

"What have you been reading, Cosmopolitan? Where are you getting this stuff?" Alexander asked.

"I just knew some people it happened to. I think you got your revenge even though it's different from the way you wanted it. The Feds are close, but so is Canada. We could drive out of the country from here. We could lay low and leave in a day or two."

Alexander looked deep in thought. A few minutes later, he told Kevin to order a pizza for their dinner and continued thinking.

*   *   *

After three hours, no one had arrived to meet Harry at Kowloon Restaurant. The trio decided to return to Harry's house. Charles called the Eugene police to comb the area for a man fitting Alexander's description. Early the next morning, the three men would leave for a safe house on Coronado Island close to where Mark lived. Harry would be guarded round the clock by the FBI's own people. Tonight, Austin and Charles would stay up and keep watch. Austin made sandwiches in the kitchen while Charles looked out a window scanning the dark woods outside.

"What do you think of Rachel and Leo getting engaged?" Austin asked, handing Charles a sandwich. "I mean after the way they met; how can she even be near him?"

"It actually doesn't surprise me. As you know, I was in Nam, so I know what it's like to hold someone's life in my hands then have my life held in theirs. A strong, unbreakable bond is formed. It's not that different for

Rachel and Leo. They saved each other's lives. Since they are both single and opposite sexes, it's natural that the bond they formed grew into love."

"I just think they may have problems because of what they went through."

Charles shrugged. "All marriages have problems. I believe they would walk through fire for each other, so I have no doubt that they'll make it work."

CHAPTER TWENTY-THREE

One evening, as Rachel came up the walk to reach her apartment, her downstairs neighbor, a woman also in her mid-thirties, met her.

Immediately, Rachel noticed that she didn't look happy.

"Karen, is everything okay?'

"I'm not sure. Can we talk for a second in my apartment?" Karen replied.

"Sure," Rachel said, following Karen inside.

"Were you expecting a visitor today?"

"No. In fact, I knew I'd be late tonight. I'm surprised I'm here this early. Why?"

"I stayed home sick today and heard someone on your deck, so I went upstairs to see if it was you. There was a man looking around on the deck and in the windows. He looked like he was scoping out the place. When I confronted him, he acted like he knew you, but I'd never seen him around here before. Something about him made me nervous. He scared me enough that I called the police, but when they arrived, he was gone."

The two women went upstairs to see that no one had disturbed Rachel's alarm system. During her stress leave, she bought the best security system she could find. In the system, she had a special code to see if any part of the alarm had been tampered with or had gone off while she was away. Every time she returned home, she checked the system with that code before going very far in her front door.

"Tell me everything you remember about him," Rachel said as they sat down on her futon.

"That's the problem, I couldn't tell you much of what he looked like. I would say he was about 5' 10"or 5' 11", 170 pounds roughly. He wore sunglasses, and I couldn't tell his hair color because he wore a hat."

"If you ever see him around here again, don't approach him, just call this number," she said, handing her Mark's card. "If you ever see me with him, call the number as fast as you can. That's all I want you to do."

"Can you tell me what this is about?"

"I would like to, but I really can't."

*   *   *

That night, sleep did not come easy. Alexander seemed to be just out of reach all the time. She wanted to get up right then and drive to Leo's apartment and tell him that they should go into hiding as Mark suggested. She didn't; too many things kept her rooted to her spot. All the bad female cop jokes and stories rang through her head. The jokes hurt even though she laughed them off in an attempt to lighten the situation. Then her ex-boyfriend Brad came to mind. He respected her as a detective but wanted her to give up everything she worked for and dreamed of to stay home and have his babies. She was successful despite these men. Then there was Alexander who delivered the worst insult of all. Since the incident at the bookstore, Mark told her supervisor to keep her in the building as much as possible as if to protect her from herself. There was no way she was going to hide like some scared little girl. She was going to live her life, and Alexander was not going to stop her. Leo was right; his luck couldn't hold out forever.

* * *

Alexander looked over Rachel's body, naked and handcuffed to his bed. While Leo looked on, helplessly handcuffed to a chair, Alexander had violated and degraded her in every way he could think of.

Now, he could feel her life slipping away. He looked at the blood-soaked sheets; it wouldn't be long now. The bitch had stopped begging for her life about an hour ago, and the pleading gave way to the incoherent talk of those in severe pain. She was now too weak from torture and blood loss even to moan. Leo begged for her life until he knew it was too late. Now, he sat waiting his turn, his face a mask of pain and fear.

He walked toward Leo....

Alexander sat up in bed and rubbed his eyes. The dream was always the same. As the day came closer, it reoccurred more often. Again, he rehearsed in his mind what he would do when he got Rachel and Leo to his place. After he forced himself on her, he would give her time to contemplate the fact that she was raped again by the same man, then the torture would begin. He knew he could violate her at least twice since cutting on people always made him hard. He thought again about what he would do to them. When the bodies were found, the authorities would describe the murders as "overkill."

* * *

The next evening, Laura's cell phone rang.

Alexander's gruff tone came over the line.

"Laura, I need to know exactly what type of information goes on FBI credentials."

"Okay," she said, her hand tightening on the receiver.

She gave him all the information and the exact layout of the FBI identification.

"Thanks, Laura. You can expect your FedEx package within a week."

She hung up the phone and poured a drink.

*   *   *

At 3:30 a.m. Rachel's cell phone rang. When she picked it up, there was silence on the other end.

Her anger and fear boiled over. "Alexander, if that's you, I swear I'll cut it off if you come near me again!"

Then she pressed the End button and threw the phone across the room, just missing the wall.

*   *   *

When Mark stood up to greet Agent Sims, he noticed a smile on the man's full-moon face.

"You have news for me?"

"We definitely have something we can work with." Russell Sims took a miniature tape recorder out of his pocket and played the recording of Laura's suspicious cell phone call.

Mark tapped a pen on his desk. "We can't say for sure that she was talking to Alexander Hargrove, but Agents Keaney and Acratelli can identify his voice. Either way, she was giving FBI information to someone in exchange for a package from FedEx."

"Yes, and fortunately that was enough for the judge to issue some warrants. We will be intercepting the package, photographing, and documenting its contents; then we'll send it on to her, so all appears normal. Of course, we'll photograph her receiving the package."

"Good thinking. If she misses her package, she may get suspicious and run or worse yet, tip off Hargrove."

Sims opened his briefcase. "Here are her phone records for the past eleven years." He handed Mark the phone records.

Mark pressed the intercom button. "Su Lee, please get me the entire Hargrove file."

After hours of comparing the phone records to key events in the Hargrove Technologies case, the two men looked at each other.

Mark took off his glasses and sighed. "How could this have been going on for years without my knowledge? She called Hargrove Technologies almost every time they were going to be investigated. She called them right before Agents Lin and Kamden were killed, and the day before Agent Keaney was abducted. Damn it, she was right under my nose!"

"Hey, no one's going to blame you for this. She and Hargrove worked as a team, an incredibly good team."

"I'm afraid I'm going to blame myself for this whether anyone else does or not."

CHAPTER TWENTY-FOUR

Alexander walked toward the receptionist for Fortress Security Systems and flashed FBI credentials.

"Can I help you?" she said, smiling.

"Yes, I need all the information you have on a system you sold one of our agents."

"If there's a problem with the system, he or she can call customer service."

"No, there's no problem, but I need to see the person in charge."

The young woman went to get the manager.

"How can I help you sir?" the manager said once they were in his office.

"One of our agents bought your system several months ago. Her name is Rachel Keaney. A man she pissed off about a year ago is stalking her. I need the codes to her alarm."

"She could give you the codes if she wanted you to have them."

"You know these women who work around men a lot. They won't admit they need help. She's being stubborn, and I'm trying to protect her from herself. It's important."

"Wait right here."

The manager got up and retrieved Rachel's file. "I won't allow you to take the file, but you can look at it here in my office."

"Thank you." He began to study the file.

"I don't mean to get personal, but you must care about this lady a lot."

"Let's just say I'd be with her if another agent hadn't been quicker on the draw."

"I'm sorry to hear that."

"It's okay, things are working out for them. Thanks for the information. You've helped us protect one of our own. I really appreciate it."

The two shook hands and Alexander left.

*   *   *

The dinner dishes were in the dishwasher, and Laura lit a pine scented candle and stepped into a hot, foaming bath. She leaned her head against the tub taking in the candle's spicy scent and the steam from the water. The doorbell interrupted her relaxation. She had a few friends, but none who would come by unannounced at this hour. Laura threw on a robe and ran downstairs. When she opened the door and saw Alexander, she didn't know if she was happy, frightened, or a little of both.

"Laura, it's been a long time."

She invited him in.

"Last time I left your life, I didn't even leave a note. This time, I've come to say goodbye in person."

"Goodbye?"

"Yes, I have some old friends to catch up with. A few loose ends to tie up you could say, then I 'm off to Mexico and I'll fly to Canada from there."

"How much trouble are you in? I haven't seen any papers related to your case."

He set a large envelope on the coffee table. "The U.S. will be very dangerous for me in a few days. Let's just say the less you know, the better."

He sat next to her on the couch, moved the hair out of her face and kissed her. The look in his eyes was one she had seen many times.

"It really has been a long time. There's a lot I miss about what we used to have," he said.

When he kissed her again, he ran his hand up her arm and brushed the side of her breast before reaching down for the tie that held her red satin robe closed.

Her heart began to beat faster than it did when she opened the door to him. She remembered his touch from long ago and wanted to feel it again. However, the man who now slid the robe off her shoulders was a world more dangerous than the one she knew back in college. The warmth of desire that radiated through her body was in sharp contrast to the cold chill of fear that ran down her spine. The way he looked at her, Laura knew he could read the mixed signals in her eyes as she sat nude in front of him.

He said nothing but continued running his hands through her short, dark hair.

"You're every bit as beautiful as you were back at Berkeley," he whispered while kissing her ear and nuzzling her neck.

She didn't try to stop him. He kissed her from her neck to her inner thighs while both her desire and conflicting emotions intensified. She watched him undress and allowed him to ease her back on the couch. When he entered her, she cried out and savored every moment. Making love with him was as wonderful as it was so many years ago. However, all the risks she took for him coupled with the fact that he was leaving for good gave the whole event a bittersweet tone. When they finished and were dressed, he pulled her to him. "You've been the only one I could truly count on," he whispered. "I wish I could take you to Canada, but you'd never have a normal life with me. You're paid in full and then some." He patted the envelope on the coffee table. "I'm more grateful to you than you know."

When he kissed her and left, she wasn't sure how she felt. A few tears crept down her cheeks as she thought about a future that could have been.

At one time, she dreamed of marrying Alexander and building a life with him. She knew he couldn't give her children of her own, but she always used to think they would adopt as his parents had done for him. Somewhere in the back of her mind, she thought that if he ever did leave the country, he would take her with him. Now, she knew he was going to Canada leaving her with an envelope full of money.

At this realization, she dissolved in tears on the couch where they had just made love.

*   *   *

Leo pushed the Mute button on his television remote when he heard his phone ring.

"Agent Acratelli? My name's Enrique Vasquez. I've been assigned surveillance at Laura Galloway's place, and I've been following Alexander Hargrove for the past 20 minutes since he left her. He's driving a burgundy Toyota Camry. I saw him go north on the fifteen before a semi cut me off and I lost him."

"Good thinking following him like that. I'll get the information to the right people."

When Leo hung up the phone, he was relieved that at least for one night, Alexander was headed away from his and Rachel's apartments. He wanted to call her and tell her the news he had just heard but knew she wasn't sleeping well and didn't want to risk waking her if she was asleep. Over the past week or so, she seemed insistent on going to her apartment alone after work. At first, he thought she was mad at him for something, or that she needed time to adjust to the fact that they were making a permanent commitment. Neither possibility seemed right. If she were mad at him, she would tell him, and she seemed thrilled to be planning the wedding with him.

He went to the freezer and dished up vanilla ice cream, and drizzled it with raspberries and chocolate sauce. While he ate, he thought through their conversations over the past two weeks.

Her going home alone every night had nothing to do with him; it had everything to do with proving something. He wasn't sure what she was trying to prove to whom. He knew she was upset about being mostly confined to the building. Then again, she could be trying to show Alexander that she isn't afraid of him. It could be that she wanted to prove that she was capable of handling a situation as well as any man. He, for one, never doubted her abilities and couldn't understand why she wouldn't think of the dangers involved in her behavior.

CHAPTER TWENTY-FIVE

Austin Davis searched the computer for homes sold or rented around the time they destroyed Hargrove Technologies. He found out through Leo that Alexander liked to live in secluded areas. The latest information from Agent Vasquez gave him a focus for his search. After getting a good list of realtors who handled out-of-the-way properties, he began making phone calls. Finally, he dialed the number of a real estate agent who sold homes in the Pala and Bonsall areas north of San Diego.

"Jeanne Hallington," a voice answered.

"Ms. Hallington, I'm Special Agent Austin Davis of the FBI in San Diego. I have some questions about properties you sold around March and April of last year. What can you tell me about the people you dealt with during that time?"

"Not to sound uncooperative, Agent Davis, but we're on the phone, so I don't know if you're really from the FBI."

"I understand. I'll come by with a warrant to look over your files."

*　　*　　*

Austin and Charles drove to Jeanne's Escondido office. After she saw their badges and looked over the warrant, they began talking.

"Anything unusual about the people you dealt with during March and April?' Austin asked.

"Not really. Some families and young couples wanting farmland. There was a man who wanted a home but was not too interested in farming. He paid for a huge out-of-the-way property with a check from a foreign bank. A couple getting a divorce just wanted out from under it. He bought the property for just a little over what they owed on it. I wondered if he wasn't a drug dealer having all that money up front." She shrugged. "Then again, just because somebody has money doesn't mean they got it illegally."

"What can you tell me about him?' Austin looked up from his notes.

"Mid-thirties, thin but built, nice looking, really. Auburn hair, brown eyes. Really seemed to want a place where he wouldn't be bothered. He kind of made me uncomfortable, like I wondered if I should have been showing him the property alone."

"Was it this guy right here?" Charles handed Jeanne Alexander's picture.

"Yeah! That's him. Look, I'm not in trouble for selling him the place, am I? Because I didn't know you were looking for him."

"No, relax, you've helped us a lot. Let's look at the file on that sale," Austin said.

"We've got you now, you bastard!" Charles said once they were in the car. They drove back to San Diego to get a search warrant for the property.

*   *   *

Later that same day, Laura sat at her desk looking through the papers she was about to file when three agents from the Office of Professional Responsibility surrounded her desk.

"Special Agent in Charge would like a word with you. We're to escort you to his office," stated a large, moon-faced man with a gray crew cut.

"I-I don't understand."

"You will soon enough."

She was always careful not to contact Alexander from anywhere in the FBI building and never took any papers or copies home with her. She wrote down information in a notebook then destroyed the sheets of paper once she relayed the information.

Once in Mark's office, she was asked to sit down.

"Laura, do you know why you're here?"

"I'm sorry; I don't." She felt hot all of a sudden.

"Okay, we believe someone in this building is giving inside information to Alexander Hargrove. Do you know anything about that?"

"No! I don't know what you're talking about. I've worked as everything from a file clerk to a secretary for you for 11 years. I can't believe I'm a suspect."

"Well, we looked into a few things, and we have evidence to say otherwise. First, we obtained a warrant for your phone records for the last 11 years. It seems that every failed attempt to nab Mr. Hargrove was preceded by a phone call from your phone to Hargrove Technologies. Then we picked up a recent call you received on your cell phone where you gave someone information about FBI credentials. Two agents identified Alexander Hargrove's voice on that call. After that, we intercepted a package sent to you that was full of cash. By the way, who is the man you invited into your house last night?" Mark slid photos of her and Alexander toward her.

A chill ran through her body.

Mark looked into her eyes. "Do you have any idea what you're responsible for? We had the chance to stop illegal explosives from getting into the hands of dangerous people. Because of your information, he changed the time and place of the deals, and they went down anyway. Two of our finest men were horribly killed because you revealed their identities. He kidnapped and raped one of our best female agents, and you called him the night before she was abducted."

Laura broke down.

"I'd suggest you tell us everything because if we get Hargrove, I'm sure he'll be willing to talk as part of a deal. We almost had him last night, except the agent who tried to tail him lost him near Highway 15."

When she finished crying, she told of all the information she could remember that she related to Alexander.

"What did he tell you about his plans?"

"He said something about catching up with old friends, then he's going to Mexico then to Canada. That's all I know, I swear. He just came to say goodbye. He didn't tell me much."

*　　*　　*

Leo burst into Rachel's squad room just as she was locking her desk and shutting down her computer.

"Hey." Rachel smiled and kissed him.

"Did you hear they busted Laura this afternoon?" Leo asked as they walked toward the parking garage.

"I heard, but I haven't gotten any details."

"I tried to be part of Mark's meeting with her, but he wouldn't let me in. I did find out that she's been slipping information to Alexander for close to ten years now."

"That long?" Rachel's eyes widened.

"Apparently, they were college sweethearts, and she never stopped loving him."

Rachel shuddered momentarily.

"I didn't know a thing about her, and thank heaven she didn't know about me while I was there," Leo said.

"Does she know where he is now?"

"He never told her about his whereabouts after the explosion. But Austin and Charles found out he's been living north of Escondido under an assumed name. In fact, we're going to make the arrest tomorrow night." He beamed at her. "I convinced Mark to let you be part of it."

Rachel threw her arms around him. "Really?"

"Yes, you get to read him his rights, and I get to drive him to Metropolitan Correctional."

"I can't believe this will finally be over." She pulled Leo to her and gave him a lingering kiss.

He held her a moment longer, taking in the scent of her skin and raspberry body spray.

"Laura said Alex was only going to be in the country for a few more days, which means he's going to make his move on us soon if he's going to at all. Come and stay with me tonight. I think we're safer together."

"I think so too."

Leo relaxed, and she smiled at him.

"You thought I'd fight you on that, didn't you?"

"Yeah."

"I finally got a good night's sleep and woke up realizing that I've been making some poor choices due to a chip on my shoulder. Staying together is safer."

"Why don't you follow me to my place, then we'll cook dinner."

"We need to go to my apartment first. I got to go out in the field yesterday and checked out a Handy Talk radio. Wouldn't you know I left it at home this morning."

"That is important, let's go."

Leo's pager sounded.

"Mark wants to see me. Probably wants to know what I know about Laura which is nothing."

"I should just go get my Handy Talk and check it back in then meet you at your place. I'll be careful. My alarm system will tell me if anyone's messed with anything."

"Okay, keep your eye out for a bugundy Toyota Camry. The body style just before the new ones."

CHAPTER TWENTY-SIX

The sky was dark when Rachel pulled up behind her apartment. Normally, when she arrived home, there was some light left since it was April and the sky was staying lighter longer. Tonight, however, an accident caused a major traffic jam.

When she got out of her car and walked to her stairs, Rachel carefully watched her surroundings. Her hand was on her Glock, ready to draw it if necessary.

She scanned the mist covered cars looking for the Camry Alexander was driving the night before. No sign of it, everything looked normal.

She unlocked the door of her apartment, walked in, and drew her Glock. The entryway light she kept on was out and the apartment was completely dark.

First, she checked her alarm using the light in the security system's box. Nothing was unusual; the light must have burnt out. She locked her door, put her pistol back in its holster, and walked toward the end table to turn on a lamp. Before she could reach the lamp, she felt herself being forced against the wall, the muzzle of a gun pressed firmly against the back of her head. Rachel froze. Her assailant jerked her gun out of her holster and pulled her purse off her shoulder which hit the ground with a thud.

"We're going on a little trip, Rachel," said a voice that rattled her nerves.

Her stomach turned at the scent of Drakkar.

"If you're going to kill me anyway, why don't you just shoot me here?" she said.

"I'll kill you on my terms. If I have to shoot you, it will only be to subdue you. Besides, my new assistant is probably at Leo's apartment by now. Any trouble you give me will make things worse for him and vice versa."

He reached for her left wrist to handcuff her when he eyed the beautiful ½ carat engagement ring on her finger.

"Nice," he said, taking a closer look in the dark. "Leo always did have impeccable taste. After all, he wants to marry the woman I wanted for myself. I wouldn't be so crazy to marry him if I were you. His loyalty is in question."

"No, it isn't. His loyalty never was with you."

The minute that statement left her lips, Alexander slapped her hard, knocking her to the ground. She landed inches from her coffee table.

He then sprang on her and held her to the floor with his body, hissing as he talked. "You think I raped you at my building. That was a romantic encounter compared to what I'm going to do to you tonight. This time, I'm going to do what I should have done then!"

The weight of his body on hers was something she hoped never to feel again, but instead of struggling, she held still and tried to grab hold of the Lladro figurine Leo gave her as an engagement gift. While he talked, she found the statue and raised it to strike him until he grabbed it and wrenched it out her hands. He threw the expensive decoration across the room causing it to shatter against the wall. Then he handcuffed her, held her wrists above her head with the chain in one hand, and continued talking as if nothing had happened.

"You said something on the phone about castrating me if I came near you again. Well, it looks like I'm the one with the knife, bitch!" he said, drawing a knife from his belt and nicking her throat so a trickle of blood oozed out of the cut.

There was a knock at the door.

"Rachel, are you okay?" a woman's voice said. "Sounded like you fell."

"Get rid of her or I will," Alexander whispered.

"Relax, I'll send her away."

Alexander covered the handcuffs with a sweater he found hanging over a chair. Rachel answered the door while Alexander stood to the side out of sight.

"I'm fine Karen, I just tripped in the dark. My entry-way light burnt out. Thank you for checking. You got that card I gave you, right?"

"Yeah, I got it. I'm glad you're okay," she said, turning toward the stairs to return to her own apartment.

The minute Rachel shut the door; Alexander grabbed her with lightning speed, pulling her to him.

"We'll wait a few minutes, then leave and get into my car as if we have a date tonight."

Rachel nodded.

Minutes later, Alexander opened the apartment door and smiled as he held it for her.

She could feel the saliva collecting in her mouth as the urge to spit in his face became almost unbearable. It was clear she was letting him get to her. If she was going to survive, she had to keep her emotions in check and above all, not piss him off.

Alexander led her toward a champagne-colored Mercedes 500 SEL.

"Beautiful, isn't it? I got it yesterday. I wanted a nice car for tonight. Get in," he ordered.

She noticed right away that the passenger-side door had no door handles.

*   *   *

Mark was driving across the Coronado Bay Bridge when his cell phone rang.

"Special Agent in Charge, Mark Sergan."

"Yes, my name is Karen Miles. I live below Rachel Keaney, and she told me to call you if I thought she was in trouble. I heard her fall in her apartment and went up to check on her. When she answered the door, she looked scared. She asked me if I had the card she gave me, the card with your number on it. Then I saw her get into a car with a man who I'm sure I saw on her deck one day when she wasn't home."

Mark listened intently as Karen described Alexander and the car he and Rachel got into.

"Thank you, Ms. Miles, we'll get right on it."

First, he called a team to meet him at the field office then dialed Charles Longview's number.

"Charles, it's Mark. Hargrove has Agent Keaney in his car."

"Do we know if she's okay?"

"As far as we know. I need you and Austin to get to Leo's place and bring him to the field office for his own safety. Tell him that I've got a team going after Alexander and Rachel and that he's under my orders to stay put at the field office."

"Yes sir, we'll do everything we can."

*   *   *

Leo began slicing mushrooms and chopping green onions for a salad. He was running behind due to the same accident that delayed Rachel. She called him to warn him about the traffic jam and tell him she would be late. Unfortunately, he was a few miles behind her in the jam when she called. She should be here any time now. He'd give her a few more minutes then call.

*   *   *

With a trembling hand Kevin knocked at the door of Leo's apartment.

The orders were to flash the gun Alex recently gave him and tell Leo that Alexander had Rachel and he was to come along quietly, or things would be a lot worse for her. He was going to tell Leo that Alexander had Rachel, but he had come to make a deal, protection in exchange for help capturing Alexander. They had nearly been caught twice. First, Rachel almost arrested Alex in the bookstore. Then if he hadn't been flipping channels in the Oregon hotel room, Alex never would have heard the news story and would have gone to meet Harry. The Feds may have arrested him then. They had their chance to get away while they were in Oregon, but Alex wouldn't listen to reason. Now, he was going to go through with his crazy plan of abducting and killing two FBI agents. Alex was playing with fire, and Kevin was not going to burn with him on this one.

When Leo answered the door, Kevin knew he recognized him because Leo grabbed him, shoved him against the wall, and began searching for weapons. When he found the gun, he jerked it out of Kevin's waistband.

"Rachel's on her way to Alexander's house. I'm supposed to take you there. I'll help you get him if you'll protect me from him."

Leo's eyes narrowed on Kevin. "We'll protect you from Alex, but you'll get a better deal if Rachel gets out of this unharmed. An even better deal if we both do. Let's go."

The two men rushed to the burgundy Toyota.

*   *   *

Mark briefed the ten-member team on the assignment ahead.

"First, we'll try to intercept Alexander Hargrove and Agent Keaney on the road. If we can't, we'll surround the house and I'll negotiate."

Mark unrolled the map and aerial photographs of Alexander's property and assigned positions to everyone.

"Let's move!" he said.

Five cars bolted out of the parking garage and headed for Highway 15.

Mark sat in the passenger seat of a bureau car and thought over his negotiation strategy. At first, he thought of offering to get Alexander out of the country safely, but he knew Alexander was too smart to trust him. He figured the best way to reach Alexander was to shift blame. He would explain that Rachel was acting under his orders. Mark would then offer to trade places with her saying that it was his fault Alexander's business was destroyed not Rachel's. While the trade was being made, he would signal his people to storm the place. He now set to work on forming a plan B.

*   *   *

While the burgundy car sped up Highway 15, Leo dialed Mark's number on his cell phone. After explaining the situation, Mark told him they were already on the way. Leo asked for their position and noted that they were ahead of the team.

"I sent Longview and Davis to your place to take you to the field office. Agent Longview called me a few minutes ago to tell me you weren't home but your door was unlocked and your car was in its parking place. I was worried. Get McCray to the field office and let us take care of it. Alexander's trying to lure you to his place to kill you."

"I don't care. I failed to protect Rachel once before, and I won't do it again."

"Your attitude is extremely dangerous! If you don't get yourself and Kevin to the field office and let us handle it, I'll have you suspended for insubordination."

"Fine. Do it." Leo disconnected the call, then handed Kevin his phone. "Dial, Alexander's cell, now!"

*   *   *

Rachel did everything possible to keep calm as highway lights and dark hills whipped past them. Despite her efforts, she continued to feel alternately hot and cold. Her stomach muscles contracted, threatening to expel the digestive acid. Her thoughts frantically searched for an escape plan, but all she could seem to think about was the phone call her mother would receive telling her that her daughter had been murdered. Then she heard Leo's words the day they got engaged telling her that his thoughts of the future always included her. Her anger built up inside her, and she vowed that the evening would not go as Alexander planned.

His words interrupted her thoughts,

"You know I was never really planning to go after your mother or Detective Walsh and his family. I threatened them to get you and the FBI to use safe houses and man hours unnecessarily. It was a lot of fun getting you guys to run around."

Hearing this, Rachel dug her nails into her palm. When she thought of her mom and Brad, she knew taking a risk with them would have been foolish. This wasn't the first time they had protected someone unnecessarily.

"I think I told you before that I was eventually going to give you a position in my company. As I've said, you have a terrific mind, and I wasn't going to let it go to waste. You and Leo ruined everything I worked for. You will both pay for what you did to me. I just have one question. Did you know who Leo was when he was shoving his cock into your mouth?"

When Alexander's cell phone rang, Rachel jumped.

"Hello," he sharply answered the phone. "Leo, old friend! . . . Yes, she's right here beside me. I'm looking forward to our evening together. You both have seen the bodies, so you have a preview of coming attractions. . .Yes, she's fine. I had to rough her up a little, but that's it so far... Romantic as that sounds, there's no way I'm going to let her off on the roadside. . . You stabbed me in the back. Why would I trust you to give yourself up quietly? I'm afraid that won't work, my vengeance is toward her as well as you. Besides, there are things I can only do to her, and I would hate to miss out. . . He wants to talk to you." Alexander handed Rachel the phone.

"Hello."

"Is it true he hasn't hurt you yet?"

"Yes, it's true."

"I want you to listen to me very carefully. I'm on my way and Mark and a team are behind me. If you see any chance to get away, you grab it with both hands. I love you. Promise me."

"Okay-"

Alexander jerked the phone from her. "Enough talk! You can see her when you get to my place. Goodbye!"

*   *   *

When he disconnected the call, Alexander couldn't help but notice that Rachel didn't look as scared as she had a few minutes ago. This change in her manner infuriated him.

"You look calm for someone who's about to be raped and killed in front of her boyfriend. You're about to die a slow and painful death. I would think you'd be a little more upset."

"I was just thinking about all the hell you put me through. After it all happened, I thought you had destroyed my whole life. Now I'm thinking about all that you didn't take from me. I'm still an excellent detective, I'm still a fighter and over-comer, and I still fell in love with Leo. You couldn't touch those parts of me no matter what."

"Those things won't serve you after you die."

*   *   *

Rachel noticed his tension mounting to a dangerous level. The set of his jaw and the grip he had on the steering wheel made it clear that she had to calm him so her rescue and his apprehension wouldn't be hindered.

"When was the first time you killed someone?" she asked.

"Why?"

"I'm just curious,"

"Answer my question and I'll answer yours."

"No, I didn't know who Leo was at the time."

"I was 21 years old and in college at U.C. Berkeley. Some guy at a party tried to get a little too close to my girlfriend. I took her home and went back and waited for him to leave the party. When I saw the asshole, I approached him and offered him a ride home. He was too drunk to remember what happened earlier. My plan was to take him to a remote location and pound on him a little. I didn't realize what had happened until it was over. During the fight, I hit him in the throat and collapsed his windpipe. Instead of feeling bad and regretting what happened, I felt exhilarated. I was on a natural high for a week after that. Of course, when they found the body, my girlfriend lied for me saying I had spent the night with her. How about you, Rachel? In your line of work, I'm sure you've killed before. Tell me about your first time."

"I was working for the San Diego P.D. A convenience store hold-up turned into a hostage situation. We had the place surrounded, and I was one of the officers covering the back while we were waiting on the S.W.A.T. team. Without warning, the perp. and the cashier walked out the back door together. He moved into a position where I had an unobstructed view of his side, and he was almost completely blocking her. I took the shot. He was dead before he hit the ground. My sergeant didn't know whether to yell at me or commend me."

As soon as she finished her story, they arrived at Alexander's house.

The house looked expensive with beveled glass windows and a large front deck. Rachel's plan was to fight every inch of the way into the house to buy some time for Leo and the others to arrive. She didn't know who would get there first but allowing him to get her inside would complicate matters.

When he came around and opened the passenger side of the car, she waited for just the right moment and elbowed him hard in the diaphragm. Then with her wrists still in cuffs she ran for the driveway leading to the road. She almost made the end of the driveway when she felt herself being forced to the ground by his weight.

"Don't try that again!" he said while raining down blows over her body wherever he could make contact.

Rachel curled into a ball protecting her face and stomach.

Pain shot through her as his fist crashed into her left shoulder blade. She felt her ribs flex as another blow landed on her side. She held on, hoping the team would arrive while he was still beating her.

When he finished, Alexander began to lift her off the ground. She flailed out of his arms. When she hit the ground, the impact knocked the wind out of her. She was finally able to force air into her lungs about the time Alexander threw her on the bed and secured her handcuffs to a padlock held by a ring attached to the headboard. The room had been set up in advance. The bed was turned down. A chair was located near the head on the left side of the bed. On the other side was a small table, which held a metal tray containing pliers, a scalpel, an ice pick, and knives of assorted sizes, all laid out.

He set her gun on the table with his instruments. He climbed onto the bed and knelt, straddling her. Both hands ran up her thighs and under her skirt. Slowly, as if he were a gentle lover, he removed her nylons and panties.

She prayed Leo and the team would arrive before Alexander got too far. They had to get there soon.

Alexander unfastened his belt and jerked it out of his belt loops with a snap.

*   *   *

The burgundy Toyota raced down Highway 76. Leo could feel adrenaline coursing through his entire body. He knew Rachel would stall him as best she could, but he also knew that Alexander was difficult to sway when he had his mind set on something. He desperately prayed that Rachel would not be raped again. He had to get there on time.

"Tell me when to turn," Leo said. "If you mess with me, I'll bury you."

"I won't. Turn right about a mile up the highway. The road is just past the gas station and the burger place."

The Toyota pulled into the driveway of the house, and a moment later, they were in the living room.

"We're here, Alex, I'm bringing Leo to your room," Kevin said.

"Good, I haven't started yet, so you're just in time."

Leo sighed with relief at those words.

"You stay here," he whispered to Kevin.

*   *   *

Hope welled up inside Rachel when she knew Leo was coming, but she couldn't let it show. The way Alexander smirked at her, she knew he fully believed that Leo would be led subdued and handcuffed into the room.

Instead, he entered the room alone with his gun drawn.

Alexander raised his hands and froze. He said nothing; his face reflected his anger and realization of betrayal.

"He's armed," Rachel said.

"Put your hands on the wall." Leo glared at Alexander.

Alexander obeyed. Leo took Alexander's gun and tucked it behind his back in the waistband of his pants.

Rachel relaxed for the first time in what felt like hours, knowing the situation was under control.

For a second Leo's eyes met hers.

While his attention was turned, Alexander grabbed the tray containing his instruments and flung the sharp objects in Leo's direction. He whisked Rachel's gun off the table and fired. Leo fell, blood seeping into his white shirt on the left side.

Rachel strained against the handcuffs, trying in vain to pull the ring loose from the headboard. The cuffs dug into her wrists and her knuckles continually banged against the headboard, but she didn't feel any of it. Adrenaline fueled by fear coursed through her, deadening any pain.

The sound of cars screeching to a stop outside diverted her attention. She stopped struggling and looked up to find Alexander standing over her. He held her gun inches from her face.

"This isn't the way I wanted it, Rachel."

She closed her eyes and prepared for the inevitable.

Two shots were fired.

It took her a moment to realize that she had not been shot. When she opened her eyes again, Alexander was falling back against the wall. Leo was sitting up with his pistol in his hands, his arms braced on his knees. Leo's eyes met and held Rachel's just before they rolled back, and he fell again.

*   *   *

Mark heard shots. Tearing out of the car door when the vehicle had barely come to a skidding stop, he instantly changed his plans.

Drawing his gun and running for the house, he shouted. "Storm the place now!"

*   *   *

Inside, both men were unconscious on the floor. Rachel strained even harder against the handcuffs, driven by desperation and helplessness.

Kevin ran into the room. "Shit!"

"Get me out of these things!" Rachel said.

Kevin grabbed the keys from Alexander's pocket and released her. Rachel ran to Leo; he was pale, and his blood now stained the whole front of his shirt.

She heard the agents storm through the front door,

Mark was the first into the room. "Get paramedics in here now!" he said.

A female agent who was also an EMT began instructing Rachel and Kevin as to what to do for the two wounded men.

Rachel calmed herself and did everything the other woman told her to do.

*   *   *

Within five minutes, paramedics were on the scene. Rachel allowed Mark to escort her to the living room to wait.

She prayed while Mark talked quietly trying to comfort and encourage her.

Another agent took Kevin, now in handcuffs, through the living room toward the front door. He looked back at Rachel.

"Thank you," she mouthed.

He nodded before an agent led him out the door.

A cacophony of voices could be heard from the bedroom. A paramedic's voice rose above the roar of the helicopters outside.

"Come on guys, we're losing him!"

Rachel and Mark froze. The two minutes of silence that followed felt like two hours.

"Okay, this one's stable, let's get him to the hospital," were the next words that drifted down the hall.

Paramedics brought Leo down the hall on a stretcher. He still looked terribly pale.

Rachel followed the stretcher. "How is he?"

"Stable. We almost lost the other one though." The paramedic continued walking out the front door.

"Come on Rachel, we'll meet them at Palomar," Mark said.

On the way to Palomar Hospital, Mark's cell phone rang.

"This is Mark. . .Okay, thank you." He turned to Rachel. "Alexander is stabilized and on his way to the hospital."

That didn't matter as long as Leo pulled through.

"Rachel, he didn't . . . hurt you again, did he?"

"No. He knocked me around, but he didn't get that far."

"Good. When we get to the hospital, I want to have you checked out to make sure he didn't do any damage when he roughed you up."

Rachel nodded, knowing that Mark wouldn't take argument in the matter.

*   *   *

Rachel was getting dressed after her exam when she heard Mark's voice outside the exam room. "Rachel, let me know when I can come in and talk to you."

"Just a minute."

Her heart pounded wildly. What would he tell her? His voice didn't sound solemn as if Leo had died, but it didn't sound upbeat as if to tell her he was going to pull through either. Maybe he would live but had life changing injuries. Her fingers kept slipping as she hurried to button up her blouse.

Finally, she was able to open the door. "Did you find out something?"

Her breathing sounded ragged even to her own ears.

"I don't know anything about Leo yet, he's still in surgery."

He paused to take a breath. "Alexander Hargrove was pronounced dead a few minutes ago."

She sank into a chair feeling like all muscle tension had left her body. The relief that flooded her brought cleansing tears with it. It was over. Alexander would never hurt her, Leo, or anyone else again. It was really over.

* * *

Due to sheer exhaustion, Rachel fell asleep on a waiting room couch after her exam. Mark making phone calls was the last thing she remembered until a gentle hand shook her awake.

She heard Mark's soft voice through the fog. "The doctor's here to talk to us."

She got up slowly because of the aches from being beaten and thrown to the ground.

"Your fiancé is one hell of a fighter. He's going to make it," the doctor said with a smile.

"Can I see him?" Rachel asked, her eyes tearing up.

"He's not awake yet, but I bet he'd like you to be there when he comes to." The doctor led her to the recovery room.

* * *

Rachel held Leo's hand and thought about how grateful she was that they were both alive. Things could have turned out a lot differently. When she saw him get shot and fall, it seemed like the world had stopped.

Leo stirred and slowly opened his eyes, then made a choking sound.

"You have a tube down your throat. Don't try to talk, the doctor will take it out soon." He relaxed.

Rachel looked into his eyes. She hugged him as best she could around all the tubes and monitors. Relief washed over her, and she cried for the second time that night. He placed a hand on the back of her head and held it there until she finished. When she regained her composure, he motioned for a pen and paper. One word was written on the notepad: ALEXANDER?

"He's dead. They lost him on the operating table." She could see him fully relax. Then, changing the subject, she said, "Your parents and Michael are on their way. In fact, they ought to be here in a few minutes. Mark sent a Leer for them."

A few minutes later, the breathing tube was removed, and one family member was led in at a time. Rachel tried to stay with the conversations, but her exhaustion overcame her, and she fell asleep with her head on the bed next to Leo.

CHAPTER TWENTY-SEVEN

Rachel locked up her desk and took the elevator to the lobby. Tonight, instead of heading for the parking garage, she walked through the courtyard toward the San Diego Metropolitan Correctional Center.

On her way, she thought over the last three weeks. The first week after their ordeal, Rachel stayed with Leo and nursed him through the worst of his recovery. The following week, she was back at work and took Kevin's statement. Leo, still on disability leave, insisted on being part of that meeting. Rachel's heart filled with tenderness when she thought of how Leo changed his tone from agent to friend when he told Kevin not to be another casualty of Alexander. He encouraged him to work toward his dream of being an engineer when he got out of prison. Kevin called his mother, now divorced from his stepfather, and they had a tearful reunion. Then last week, Rachel and Charles took Harry Matteson to Lindbergh Field to fly home to North Carolina. He was nervous about seeing his 18- and 20-year-old sons again. He didn't know what he would tell them, he was only glad his ex-wife didn't try to poison them against him. Rachel recommended that he tell his sons the truth since they were young men now and could probably handle it.

When she arrived at the jail, the visitor's lobby was deserted since visiting hours were over. She chose to come at this time on purpose knowing she would have the place to herself. She was waiting to face one last demon. When the guard entered the room with Laura, the look on her face was clear.

"No! I don't have to see her. Take me back to my cell now."

"She just wants to talk to you."

"Don't leave me alone with her."

"I'll be right outside."

Rachel watched the scene unfold with no emotion on her face. She waited until Laura gained her composure and wilted into a chair.

"What more do you want from me? I gave you 10 years' worth of information and now face the maximum sentence. I don't know why you're even here."

"I think we need to talk."

"Talk? About what? I know what happened to you was my fault."

"Your fault that I was abducted. The rest was Alexander's fault alone."

Rachel sat down across from Laura. "I'm here to tell you that I'm going to speak at your sentencing."

"Why? They're locking me up for a damn long time."

"You deserve to serve time. But I'm going to tell the judge that you deserve leniency."

Her shocked brown eyes looked into Rachel's face. "I'm afraid I don't understand."

"I can't respect a woman like you, Laura, and I don't think you can either. Still, I feel he raped you too. Not in the physical sense, but mentally and emotionally. I've done some research on you, and I see how your life could have been had you not gotten involved with him. I don't need to explain any of that to you; I'm sure it keeps you awake plenty of nights. There's nothing I could do that would be worse than that."

"I'm sorry. I couldn't see any way out. I'm sorry for what he did to you."

Laura burst into tears, and it was clear to Rachel that she couldn't take much more. She quietly got up and left the room nodding at the guard outside the door.

CHAPTER TWENTY-EIGHT

Leo sat on the heavily pillowed couch in the bridal suite at the Wyndham Emerald Plaza waiting for Rachel to change and come out of the bedroom. Everything was laid out exactly as he requested. Champagne was cooling beside two crystal flutes. A plate piled high with fresh strawberries sat between the glasses. Soft classical music played low on the stereo. When Rachel was ready, he would open the champagne.

The day could not have been more perfect. They were married in the courtyard of the Hotel Del Coronado with the beach and the sunset behind them. His parents and all his brothers and sisters were in attendance. Everyone they knew from the FBI also witnessed the event. Leo had been to many weddings, but nothing prepared him for the sight of Rachel walking down the aisle. She was a vision in her white satin, beaded gown. He pictured her in his mind and the words of his brother Michael rang in his head.

After he and Rachel had shared their first dance, Michael took the microphone to begin the toast.

"A little over a year ago, my brother started telling me about a new friend he was spending time with. He told me she was the most amazing person he'd ever met. Last February, I finally got to meet Rachel, only this time Leo was referring to her in much more romantic terms. When I met her, I could see why he was so impressed with her. As I saw them together, I could see the bond between them and knew she was everything the family and I wanted for Leo. In the short time I've known you, Rachel, I can honestly say that if your father could be here now, he would be extremely proud of you and very happy with your choice in a husband."

Everyone raised their glasses as Rachel and Leo circled their arms and sipped the champagne.

The day was perfect, and he hoped the night would be too. This night was one he had looked forward to for months now. He knew he would have to go slow because his bride, although not a virgin, would need to be treated like one. He wanted their first time together to be a pleasant memory for her and a great beginning for their married life.

*   *   *

Rachel ran a brush through her hair; she looked at her wedding band that joined the diamond solitaire on her finger. The ring further emphasized that she was now Mrs. Leo Acratelli. Smiling, she thought about how long she had considered remaining single because finding a man who would truly treat her as an equal partner seemed impossible. He did. Committing to him was easy. Tonight, they would consummate that commitment. She felt the sensation of butterflies in her stomach at the thought. For months now, she had been waiting for this night, still, she couldn't help but be nervous. She had not completely given herself to a man since her break up with Brad six years ago. No one had entered her since Alexander's assault over a year ago. She wondered if her attack would have an effect on such a wonderful event. It wouldn't; Alexander would not be part of their first night together.

At this, she walked toward the bedroom door where she knew Leo was waiting for her in the living room of the suite.

*   *   *

Leo heard the handle to the bedroom door turn, now Rachel was walking toward him in a long ivory silk nightgown. Her thick brown hair tumbled over her shoulders covering the straps that held the gown.

He stood up. For a moment, he was unable to speak.

"You're the most beautiful woman I've ever seen," he said when he found his voice.

Then he kissed her just before pouring the champagne. They shared the bottle and talked about their life ahead. When Leo could tell she was relaxed, he stood up and led her by the hand into the candle lit bedroom. Rachel walked over to the bed and turned down the satin sheets. Leo stood behind her pulling her to him. Her back rested against his chest, and he kissed her neck down to her shoulder, taking in the scent of her skin and the vanilla body spray she wore.

"I love you. I'm honored to have you as my wife." he whispered.

Rachel turned to face him, he could feel the softness of her hands on his neck and chest as she opened his burgundy, satin robe. A small smile played on her lips while she took in the sight of his body. He guided the straps of her gown off her shoulders, letting the garment spill around her feet. She was so beautiful. He took off his robe and eased her onto the bed, sliding next to her, kissing her waiting mouth.

*   *   *

Her desire was so aroused before he touched her that now, as his hands and lips caressed her body, she found herself drinking in every touch. She ran her hands along his outer thigh, then began to gently caress his erect member.

I can't handle too much of that tonight," he said.

He moved her hand away and continued exploring her body. She closed her eyes and took in the gentleness of his fingertips mixed with the softness of his lips and the roughness of his mustache goatee. The sensations awakened the nerves all over her skin. Leo reached for the candle to blow it out and leave the room in darkness, but Rachel touched his hand.

"Leave it lit. I don't want to miss anything," she whispered.

He set the candle down then slowly and gently entered her. Tears of joy escaped her eyes as she savored the feeling of his body on and in hers. It was as if nothing existed but their oneness. Pleasure coursed through her until the moment it all converged on the place where they were joined. She knew his desire was not yet complete, so she caressed his back and enjoyed every sound and movement he made. When it was clear that he was on the edge, she looked into his eyes as he climaxed inside of her.

In each other's arms, they drifted off to sleep.

EPILOGUE

eo looked up from his cluttered desk when Rachel entered the room from her office next to his. His wife at 49 was as beautiful as the day he kissed her on the deck of her apartment years ago. The flecks of gray in her chestnut hair didn't change her beauty. His own hair had gone completely gray several years ago.

"I got your message that you wanted to see me in your office." She smiled playfully.

He got up from his chair and pulled her to him.

"Yes, in fact I wanted to see all of you in my office," he said, unbuttoning her top button and kissing her.

At that moment, Shalayah walked in from the outer office.

"Well excuse me for walking in without knocking. When you two can keep your hands off each other, I need to talk to you."

"It's okay, Shalayah, what do you need?" Rachel said, laughing and refastening the button.

"I got a call from Carla last night. The big guys in Quantico want her to do a deep cover assignment. She's thrilled. Leo, I was hoping you would call that child and talk her out of it."

"I'll do what I can, but she's 30 and she'll do whatever she decides."

"I know, I just hope you'll talk some sense into her. Not only that, but Kevin's also going to be in town next weekend for an engineering conference. Says he can get away for lunch if you're available."

"Great, we'd love to meet with him," Rachel said.

The phone rang in Shalayah's office, so she went to answer it. "Acratelli Intelligence and Investigations Shalayah speaking. How may I help you?"

While Shalayah took the call, Leo and Rachel went over some current information on the case they had been working on over the last month. Within minutes, Shalayah was at Leo's office door again.

"That was Palomar Junior High. You have a meeting there in a half hour."

*   *   *

12-year-old Danielle sat outside the principal's office. She put her dark hair into a scrunchie and pulled a mirror out of her purse. The soft brown eyes that matched her father's were fearful. She would try hard not to show that fear.

She couldn't believe she had been caught and now her parents had to find out. This had to be the worst day of her life.

When her parents entered the outer office, Danielle ran to them with the tears she fought so hard to control coursing down her cheeks. Rachel and Leo hugged their daughter while she talked a million miles a minute.

"I'm sorry. I didn't mean to cause trouble. I was just playing around. I didn't mean to do anything bad, honestly."

At this point, the principal called the three of them to the meeting. Once inside the office, the principal, a balding man with gray hair, explained the situation.

"Danielle hacked into our computer system and obtained the addresses, phone numbers, and background information on all of our teachers. That information is private."

Rachel coughed. "Danielle, go back to the outer office for a minute."

The strong will she inherited from her mother was weakened by the day's events, and she obeyed without a word. When she shut the door, she heard her mother burst out in laughter.

REQUEST FOR REVIEW

Dear Reader,

Thank you for reading Revenge Game. Writing it was a labor of love and a wonderful growth experience. I hope you enjoyed it. If you did, please take a moment to post a review on Amazon. Your review will help others choose to read Revenge Game as well. Again, thank you.

Lynn Campbell

ACKNOWLEDGEMENTS

I have been fortunate to have found supportive individuals to encourage me when authoring this novel. I want to thank Debbie Plogman, Edith Dunn, and Terrie Calderon along with my parents, Linda and Mike Thiel, for their honest feedback and giving me the confidence to pursue publication. I appreciate the good industry advice I received from Jenny Cary and Ruth Douthitt. Thank you to my editor Borbala Branch who guided me through the final drafts. Also, my husband David and son Michael. You two may not be readers of fiction, but you have been in my corner all the way.

ABOUT THE AUTHOR

Lynn Campbell is an elementary school teacher who lives in Phoenix, Arizona with her husband and son. Revenge Game is her first novel with more to come. In addition to writing, she spends time reading, doing jigsaw puzzles, and traveling with her husband in their Beech Debonair. San Diego, California remains one of her favorite destinations.

Also By Lynn Campbell

In addition to Revenge Game, Lynn wrote and publish aviation-themed romance Flight Plan in 2025.

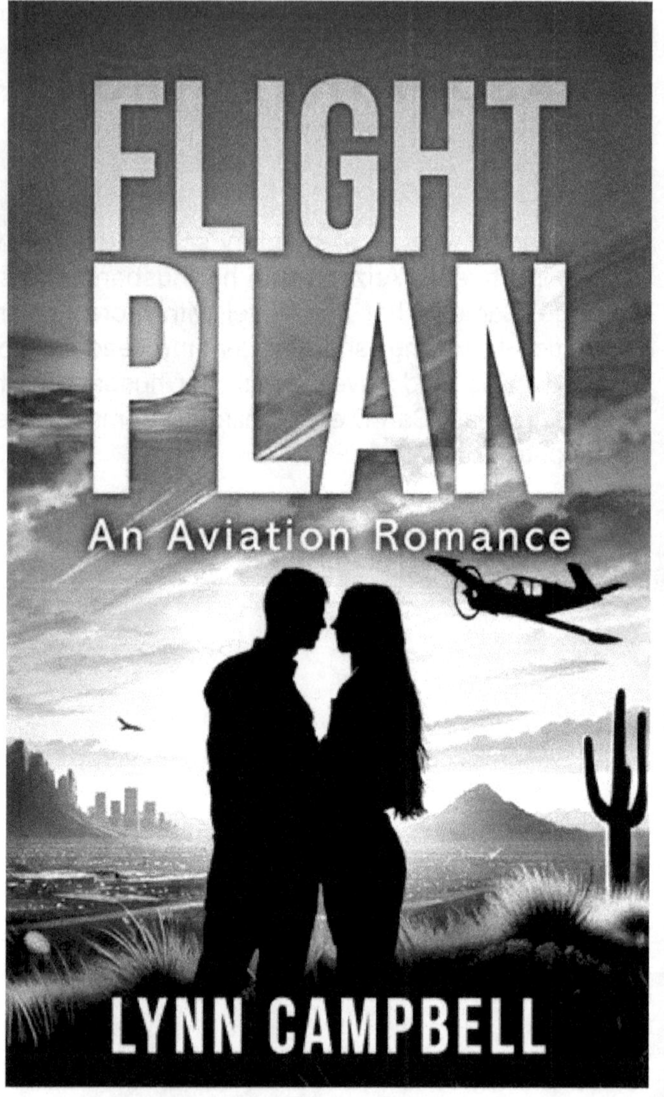

Sometimes the heart takes a detour.

9 781966 176008